DON'T
LET
HER
GO

BOOKS BY WILLOW ROSE

Detective Billie Ann Wilde series

Then She's Gone

DON'T LET HER GO

WILLOW ROSE

bookouture

Published by Bookouture in 2024

An imprint of Storyfire Ltd.
Carmelite House
50 Victoria Embankment
London EC4Y 0DZ

www.bookouture.com

ISBN: 978-1-83790-917-9
eBook ISBN: 978-1-83790-916-2

PROLOGUE

Cocoa Beach, Florida

Marissa Clemens smiled the way only a mother could when looking at her child. Her four-year-old daughter Emma was dancing in the backyard, while Marissa was cooking dinner inside the house, watching her through the kitchen window.

"Look at me, Mommy!"

Emma was wearing a tutu, and it spun in the air as she twirled. On her feet she was wearing pink Crocs, while her small legs were bare. On top she wore her favorite shirt, the one with glittery unicorns and rainbows on it. Marissa could tell that her daughter had worn it a lot, because most of the sparkles had fallen off. She wondered if she should get rid of it, but the girl loved it so much, she didn't dare to. Emma's strawberry blonde hair was tousled and curly and kept falling into her face. Her smile was the most beautiful on the planet and could melt any hardness in her mother.

"Look I'm dancing!"

The girl mimicked a video from YouTube that she had watched, featuring a group of young girls who were twerking, and it made her mother laugh, even if it was slightly inappropriate. Seeing a four-year-old do it was just too darn cute.

Marissa looked down at the potatoes she was peeling, allowing herself a brief moment of happiness. Could she finally relax? Were they safe?

What if things stayed good from now on?

She didn't dare believe it. Marissa shook her head. No, it was simply too dangerous to fill herself with that kind of hope.

"Mommy, Mommy, can I go down to the water?"

Marissa looked up with a drastic change in her expression. Her blissful smile became a frown, and she raised her finger and kept Emma's eye contact. She made sure her daughter looked at her and understood what she was saying.

"No. No going to the pond without Mommy."

"Please? I wanna see the fishies," Emma said, making those big begging eyes. It usually worked if Emma wanted snacks, but not when it came to this. The big pond behind their backyard was Marissa's nightmare. She had often dreamed of finding her floating in that water, and the very thought made her nauseated. She had sacrificed so much to get them to where they were. She wasn't taking any chances.

"No."

Emma made a sad face, but then spotted a squirrel as it darted across the lawn and decided to run after it, quickly forgetting everything about the pond. Marissa watched her as she talked to the small animal that had taken shelter on the top of the palm tree.

"Mommy, the squirrel is back," Emma yelled.

Marissa watched her for a few seconds, then finished peeling the potatoes. It was still scorching hot out even if it was October, and she had to make sure Emma drank enough water while playing outside. She put the potatoes in the buttered pan, then placed them in the oven after sprinkling cheese on top. She heard the washing machine play its annoying little song, letting her know it was done.

Marissa looked at her watch. She needed to put the clothes in the dryer, and, for that, she had to go to the garage. She hesitated. Should she ask Emma to come inside while she did it? No, that would be silly. She was having so much fun and getting fresh air.

Marissa walked to the garage and opened the lid of the washer. She started to pull out clothes and put them in the dryer. Emma would be fine. Besides, it would only take a few minutes to empty the washer and turn on the dryer. Five minutes at the most, she told herself. She emptied the washer and closed the dryer, while pushing back that intense nagging sense of urgency inside of her, telling her to go out and check on her daughter. She slammed the dryer shut and turned it on, then stared at the rest of the dirty laundry in the basket. She really needed to get another one going. There was time to put on another load, right? After all, it would only take another minute. Emma was fine. Of course, she was.

Marissa tossed the white wash into the washer, added detergent, and pushed the button to start. Happy that she was ahead of her own schedule for today, Marissa then rushed into the kitchen and peeked out the window.

But she couldn't see Emma.

There's no reason to panic. She's probably just playing somewhere I can't see. She's fine. Nothing can happen in a closed-in yard.

Heart throbbing in her throat, she grabbed a bottle of water from the fridge on the porch. She felt a humid blanket envelop her, as was usual in Florida when walking outside from the dry and cold air-conditioning inside. She took in a deep breath to calm herself down and felt sweat spring to her forehead immediately. That was Florida for you. You could get soaked in sweat from the brief minute it took to walk from your house to your car in the driveway.

"Emma?" she said. "I brought you some water, you need to remember to drink enough in order to stay..."

Marissa paused. She looked by the tree where she had last seen her daughter talk to the squirrel. But she wasn't there. She wasn't in the bushes behind it or on the porch. Then she turned to look toward the small grass area at the end of the yard, where Emma often liked to play, and where she had hosted a tea party earlier for her imaginary friends, but she wasn't there either.

"Emma?"

She could hear it in her own voice. The panic that was slowly spreading, eating her up from the inside, like a cancer.

"Emma?"

She rushed down the stairs, into the grass, and let her eyes frantically search for any sign of the little girl. Her voice was shrill as she yelled her name again and again, almost finding it hard to get the word across her lips because of the anxiety rushing through her slender body.

"Emma? Emma?"

Marissa ran to the end of the yard and stopped at the fence. She looked at the gate. It was still locked.

Marissa turned and looked at her small townhouse. Emma could perhaps be on the other side of the house. Marissa calmed down slightly. Of course, that's where she was.

Marissa ran up to the house, then went around it, and rushed into the front yard. She would have to get angry at Emma for doing this when she knew she wasn't allowed to. She might even have to put her in time-out. It wasn't that big a deal, but with the circumstances they lived under, Marissa couldn't be too careful. She couldn't risk a car driving by in the street and someone seeing the child.

Time-out it was. Just for ten minutes. Maybe she would serve ice cream for dessert after dinner, as compensation. To make her happy again. Yes, that would work. Marissa didn't like having to discipline her child.

"Emma? Emma, come here now. You know you're not allowed to..."

Marissa turned the corner of the house, then paused.

There was no sign of the girl in the front either.

Then where could she be?

Maybe she went back into the house? Maybe she ran inside just as you stormed outside?

It was getting harder for Marissa to calm herself down. She ran around the house and up the back patio, then hurried inside. Sweat was springing from her forehead and upper lip now, and not just because of the high humidity and heat. These were pearls of anxiety.

"Emma? Don't hide from me."

Her voice sounded angry, but it was hard to hide the fear.

"Please Emma? I don't have time for this, come here now."

She looked through the living room, then the kitchen and ran upstairs. She rushed into Emma's room, thinking she might be in there, playing, oblivious to her mother's panic attack. That she would be sitting on the floor and look up at her with those big, beautiful eyes, like she didn't understand what the urgency was about.

"Emma? Are you in here?"

She pushed the door open, but there were no eyes staring up at her. No cute smile or strawberry blonde hair falling into her daughter's eyes.

And there was no Emma.

"Emma?" she yelled. "EMMA?"

Could she have been...? Could it be...?

For a moment she dropped her face into her hands. *Don't think like that. I mustn't.*

She lifted her head, unable to stop her torso from shaking. She tried to calm her thoughts.

Think, Marissa. Think!

A small deep growl left her throat as she looked out the window and saw something in the grass. Something pink, left by the fence in the high grass that should have been mowed long ago. Marissa could barely breathe, and she held a hand to her mouth as the realization sank in of what it was she was looking at.

It was her shoes. Emma's pink shoes.

ONE

BILLIE ANN

"You're an impostor. A liar."

I whispered the words to the woman staring at me from inside the mirror. To be honest, then I had no idea who she was anymore.

I was in my bathroom, naked after the shower, a towel still wrapped around my hair that had finally grown back to its old length. I stared at my chest and touched the scar where my left breast used to be. It felt strange. My right breast looked the same as it had always been, but I didn't trust it anymore. Anything could be growing in there. I had learned that the hard way.

It was three years ago today that I had been declared in remission. My latest checkup had shown the cancer hadn't come back. Still, the feeling never left the body. The first time they had told me it was cancer, it had come as such a big shock and had been so aggressive there was nowhere I really felt safe. No part of my body felt secure. It had deceived me. I had thought I was healthy, but my treacherous body had other plans.

It could come back. It could always come back. There

would forever be that threat hanging over me. I was living with an expiration date. That's how it felt. And that had made me want to change things.

I needed to stop surviving and start living.

I reached into the drawer beneath the sink, then pulled out my husband's shaver. I took off the towel and threw it on the floor. Then I looked at the impostor with her long wet hair dangling from her head, sweeping across her shoulders.

It was time to get rid of her.

I turned on the shaver and placed it on the top of my head. I had done this once before, but for different reasons. Back then it had been because of the cancer, because I looked death in the eyes in the battlefield that was my body. Now it was because I had survived. I had won.

The shaver slid through the hairs like it was butter. It felt so satisfying, a smile grew on my face as I watched the big locks of curly blonde hair fall down into the sink. Last time I had seen that I had been so scared. Back then it had represented me losing control. Now I was taking it back.

And it felt great. No, it was more than that. It felt empowering.

I ran the shaver across my entire head, leaving just half an inch of hair all over. I wasn't going for bald, just a buzz cut.

When I was done, I stared at the woman in the mirror and smiled again. "There you are," I said to her, then cleaned the shaver and put it away. I studied my reflection once more and ran a hand across my head, feeling the short hair prickle the palm of it.

Then I got dressed. I found my black pants and button-down blue shirt, then put on my belt with my badge and my gun, that I retrieved from the safe. I looked at myself in the full body-sized mirror in my bedroom, and I felt good.

For once I looked like me.

I walked down the stairs, taking nervous but determined

steps. I could hear my husband, Joe, and the kids in the kitchen. My heart throbbed for a second as I walked in and all their chatter stopped.

"Whoa," my son, William, said. He had just taken a bite of his pancake and stared at me, mouth wide open. William was fourteen and as handsome as they get, but right then, he wasn't showing off his best side.

I smiled as casually as I could.

"What did you do?" he continued.

I touched my hair, or lack thereof. "This? You like it?"

"I think it looks badass," my sixteen-year-old daughter, Charlene, said, nodding her head acceptingly. "Buzz cuts are so in these days. You rock it, Mom. You look like Kristen Stewart in that movie we watched, where she's underwater."

"I think you look good too," my nine-year-old son, Zack, said without even looking up from his phone. He grabbed his cereal bowl and took it to the dishwasher. The two others stopped staring as well, as the news of my hair became uninteresting, and they left the kitchen to get ready for school. Now it was just me and Joe, and our golden retriever, Zelda, left in the kitchen. Joe stared at me, fighting his tears. His upper lip wobbled slightly.

I smiled compassionately at him.

He shook his head. "Why? Why would you do this?"

I shrugged. "I thought it was time for a change."

He nodded and looked down at the lunch boxes he was packing with peanut butter and jelly sandwiches. I bit my lip, feeling his sadness across the room. I approached him and touched his shoulder.

"It's gonna be okay."

He lifted his gaze, then touched my head gently, tears springing to his eyes. "You had just gotten all your hair back after..."

He paused.

"After the cancer. You can say it, you know?"

He nodded. "I know. But why would you cut it all off?"

"Listen, Joe. Change is going to come. For all of us."

He bit back his tears. My stomach began to hurt. I hated seeing him like this. I loathed myself for doing this to him.

"So... you're really going through with this?" he asked.

I exhaled. Tears were coming to my eyes too, but I fought them. "It's not gonna go away. These things don't go away."

He started to cry. It broke my heart, and I pulled him into a hug. He whispered between sobs.

"I don't want to lose you."

"Shh," I said, holding him. His six-feet-two and two hundred and twenty pounds were shaking in my arms. "You won't, sweetie. Things are going to change, yes, but I am still here. We have our kids together. We have been together for eighteen years. We'll figure things out, okay? It's a process. Both of us are in uncharted waters here. But there has to be a way."

He nodded and pulled away. "I'm sorry. This can't be easy for you either. I know it isn't. I'm just... I just don't understand. We've been married for this many years, we had a great life together, children, the works. I just keep thinking... how could you not have known that you were gay? Was everything we had just a lie?"

I sighed. This was all Joe had been able to focus on. "I guess I didn't want to know," I said, repeating the words he'd already heard me say. "Deep down I have always known. But I didn't want it to be true. It wasn't a lie, or maybe it was, sort of, but I was also lying to myself. That's why it is so hard. Because I can't ignore it anymore. I need to live out who I am. Be authentic. Life really is short. It's not just a cliché. We've learned this the hard way these past few years. I need this now."

He nodded again. I had told him all this the night before when I had sat him down over dinner for a talk. Just the two of us. It had taken me four years to get the courage to finally tell him this deep secret that I had kept from everyone my entire life. That I was gay. I was attracted to women and always had been. But growing up the way I did with my religious parents, it simply wasn't an option. I had to marry a guy and have children. That was just the way it was. And so I did. I married a wonderful man who gave me three beautiful children. But I wasn't happy. I had this deep feeling inside that I was in the wrong place. Something was missing. I knew I was breaking his heart. We had promised each other we'd stay together forever. But now I just wasn't sure I had forever to give anymore. Time was running out, or so it felt at least. And I wanted to be me. Fully me. Even if it meant risking everything I had.

I needed this.

I'm gay. I'm a lesbian.

The words were still so hard for me to say, even to myself.

Once you let that toothpaste out of the tube, you can't get it back in again. It's as simple as that.

Even if it meant destroying everything I had built. My marriage, my family, maybe even my career. Would it be harder to climb the ranks? How were my colleagues going to react? Would they be disgusted by me and who I was? Cocoa Beach was a small beach town on a barrier island where everyone knew one another, and the locals were on a first name basis with many of the officers. Would I still gain the same respect among them? Among my coworkers? Or would coming out ruin all that?

My therapist had told me not to use words like *ruin* and *destroy*, because of their negative connotations. What I was doing was positive; I was finally becoming who I was meant to be. But it felt like I was ruining things. I had everything, and now I was throwing it all away.

There it was again, one of the words. *Throwing*. According to my therapist I was gaining a new life. That's what I needed to focus on. But that was so hard. I felt selfish. I felt like I was doing something wrong.

Yet now that I had told my husband, there was no way back.

Joe leaned forward and kissed my forehead. I could tell he was holding back tears.

"I love you so much, and I just want you to be happy. I'm just still a little... I'm finding it a little hard to grasp."

I swallowed, trying to get rid of the huge lump in my throat. I wanted to scream or run away or both at the same time. We barely slept all night. He was tossing and turning and getting up every half an hour, pacing back and forth. I knew it was a bomb I had thrown the night before. I knew he was still in shock and needed time to process it. Heck, so did I. Even if I had been dealing with it for years. It was still new territory for me, and I kept wondering if it was worth it.

"I know," I said. "It's gonna take some time for all of us to adjust."

"I just... I don't get it," he continued, sipping his coffee. His skin was gray from the lack of sleep. It was torture to watch him like this. He kept staring into blank air, repeating the same thing over and over again.

"I just don't get it..."

I couldn't blame him. While it had taken years for me to get to this point, his whole life had blown up in his face overnight.

So far, we had agreed to continue our normal lives and not talk to the children about it yet. Not till we knew how to deal with this situation. Not till we made any decisions that would affect their lives. I had told Joe about the numerous times I had ended up kissing girls when I was younger and had too much to drink. And that it had happened more recently...

Joe handed me a cup of coffee without looking at me. He had been my partner and best friend for eighteen years. Was that about to end? We hadn't been intimate for a long time, but we were a team. We were best friends. I would do anything not to lose him completely.

The kids came storming down the stairs, backpacks in hands, grabbed their lunches and took off while fighting over something ridiculous. I watched them from the window as they got into Charlene's Toyota pickup truck, which we got her for her sweet sixteen, and took off. I spotted our neighbors, Trevor and Marge, walking their goldendoodle on the sidewalk outside my window. Their dog, Sonny, stopped to pee by the tall palm tree in front of my house. I lived at the end of the cul-de-sac, which had been a very safe environment for my kids to grow up in. They would bike and skateboard around, and I never had to worry about them. Sonny did a little more than just pee, and Trevor bent down to pick it up. They were an elderly couple who had lived in Cocoa Beach their entire lives and never wanted to leave. "This is paradise but don't tell anyone because then they'll all want to come here too," they always said.

I waved at them. They waved back with big smiles in tanned faces. They were both very fit for their age. Marge did beach yoga every morning with her friends, and Trevor was an avid surfer. Our street was only two blocks from the beach, so he would get up at the crack of dawn and sometimes I would see him rushing down the street, barefoot, wearing nothing but boardshorts with his surfboard under his arm. That's when I knew the waves were good and most of the town would probably be out there in the lineup. Most of the neighbors on my street with only eight houses surfed or stand-up paddled on the river, some kayaked in the canals behind our houses. We all had boats by our docks in the backyards that we would occasionally go out on. It had been a while, though, since Joe and I had last been out on the water with the kids. They used to love it and would fight over whose turn it was to go in the tube, being pulled behind it. Or to go wakeboarding. That was fun. I chuckled at the memories we had created, then felt awful for my children. They had no idea what was about to happen to them, how their world was about to crumble, once their parents separated.

The very thought made me want to throw up.

"Can you take Zelda out?" I asked Joe, and he nodded quickly as I looked at my watch. "I'm running late for the morning meeting."

TWO

OLIVIA

She was ahead of her target time. Olivia Thomson's Apple Watch told her so in her Air Pods. She had run the first kilometer in less than five minutes, and that was a good time for her. She was going for ten kilometers this morning, as she did three times a week, getting herself ready for the half-marathon she had signed up for in two months. Today she felt stronger than she had in a long time. She was almost flying as she ran through her neighborhood, her Salomon running shoes crunching on the pavement. In her ears she was listening to Pitbull, and the upbeat Latin rhythms made her go even faster. She wasn't usually a Pitbull fan, but she had found that when running, she was way faster while listening to his music.

When she reached two kilometers, her Apple Watch told her she had run the last kilometer at 04:45. It was a new record for her, and now she couldn't stop smiling.

Olivia had started running after her boyfriend of six years broke up with her. One day they had been on the couch, watching TV, when he paused the movie and simply told her he was leaving to be with her best friend of more than fifteen years.

She'd needed to get the anger out. It was piling up inside of her. Olivia wasn't good at showing emotions, especially not anger; instead, she would internalize it and that wasn't very healthy for her, her sister said.

"You need to yell at him. Get angry. Tell him how you really feel," she had told her over and over again.

But Olivia simply couldn't. She didn't feel like she was allowed to for some reason. She didn't like people seeing her being vulnerable. She needed people to think she was strong. After all she was an investment banker, one who had made it well for herself in a man's world. She couldn't lose her cool.

Besides, she wasn't going to give her ex the pleasure of seeing her angry or even sad. So instead, she had just watched him pack his stuff and leave, then decided never to talk to him or Katie again. It wasn't like she needed them or anything. She was very fine on her own.

Running had given her the outlet that she needed. When she pushed her body to its limits, that's when she was able to let it all out. The anger, the tears, the frustration. It would all come at once, and she could push through it, making her body ache so bad she was about to throw up.

Boy that made her feel good.

She ran the third kilometer in 04:35, her watch told her.

Olivia smiled widely. This was yet another record. She couldn't believe it. Usually, she would slow down on the third and fourth kilometer and struggle at the fifth, before picking up pace again on the sixth. But not today.

Today she was on fire.

Olivia turned a corner around the pink house, which she had always thought was so cute, then ran into another street and down toward the pond. There was such a nice little water fountain in the middle of it, making the entire neighborhood look expensive. It was beautiful. The houses with yards facing toward the pond were old and gorgeous. Olivia was always on the lookout for one of them coming up for sale, because she would love to buy one someday. Lord knows she had the money for it. But they rarely came up for sale.

"I'd really like that one," she mumbled to herself and pointed up at a small house with wraparound porches and the cutest little fenced-in yard. That one was her absolute favorite because it was so private. She had often tried to look into the yard when running past it on the trail surrounding the pond, but the tall bushes blocked her view. She liked that a lot.

"Privacy is king," she mumbled, then continued on her run. There was no slowing down now that she was doing so well. She would circle the pond, then go back. Once she made it halfway around it, she would hit five kilometers, and then she was halfway. Olivia took in a deep breath of fresh air. She could smell the ocean and the beach on the other side of A1A. She would occasionally run on the beach, but it was so darn hard on the knees when it wasn't low tide. She was scared of getting an injury and then where would that leave her? She needed to run. She was addicted to it, her sister had said. And maybe she was right.

It wasn't exactly the worst thing to be addicted to, was it?

Olivia shook her head with a scoff at the thought of her sister who couldn't get her own life together, and then she dared criticize Olivia's. Who did she think she was? Telling her she needed to grieve her loss and face her emotions.

It was all nonsense.

Olivia had her own way of dealing with things, and running was all she needed right now.

She ran the fifth kilometer in 04:40. Slower than the last one. She'd have to speed up, if she wanted to run her personal best, like she had been on track for. She wasn't going to slow down now.

Olivia accelerated, pushing her legs to the limit of what she was capable of, feeling her heart pound in her chest as she sprinted across the trail and around the pond. She turned for a second to look at the fountain in the middle, and how beautiful the rays of the sun hit it and created such a gorgeous light, when there was something else that caught her eye.

At first, she thought it was a gator. She had seen them occasionally in the pond, which wasn't a big deal, as they were in most ponds in Florida from time to time. But there was something about this floating mass that just struck her as odd.

It was sort of bobbing up and down below the surface.

Was it an animal?

Olivia stared at it as she came closer to where the lump was stuck in the mangrove bushes growing at the edge of the pond. She didn't even realize she had started to slow down till her watch suddenly said she was way behind her target pace.

But at this point, Olivia wasn't listening. She took out her Air Pods and stopped running. She stared at the small mass in the water, especially at the pink shirt bobbing on the surface.

Then she screamed.

THREE

BILLIE ANN

"Billie Ann Wilde, as I live and breathe. What the heck did you do to your hair? You joining the Army or somethin'?"

Big Tom stopped himself, and his expression became serious. "Wait a second, you're not telling me that it's back, are you? Is the cancer back—?"

I raised a hand to prevent my colleague from saying something he would be embarrassed about later.

"I'm gonna stop you right there. It's not back," I said. "I'm still in remission."

He stared at me with his brown eyes. His handsome face smiled with relief. Tom was a big guy, hence the nickname, not as much in height as in volume—and character. He took up a lot of space in any room. He was very muscular and went to the gym several times a week, working out with the other guy in our division, Scott. I had recently been promoted to be the head of homicide, which basically meant the Chief left me in charge of these two goofballs. They were good people, and hard workers, and I loved them dearly, but they were also young and untrained, whereas I came with experience from another homicide division, not far from my hometown.

I grew up in Central Florida, out in the wetlands, fishing and hunting hogs and gators in the Green Swamp with the boys of my town. If I saw a snake, I knew not to tread on it, because it was my friend. If it snuck into my house, I knew how to grab it by the neck so it couldn't bite me and take it outside and let it go. My dad had taught me how to shoot a rifle from the moment I could hold one, and I was a better shot than both of my brothers. I knew how to deal with boys like Tom and Scott and had done so my entire life.

"Ha. You got me there. You got me good."

"I wasn't trying to but thanks," I said.

I sat down at my desk, across from Tom's, in the newly built police station in the center of downtown Cocoa Beach. It was a tall, ugly, square, gray building, and kind of an eyesore to this small quaint town with all the many beach houses and bungalows from the sixties and seventies. The space program had flourished then, and the town had grown to house the many workers at Kennedy Space Center.

The old building before this one had a leak in the roof after a hurricane, and mold was growing on the walls and floors. If a big rainstorm came by, and they did for most of the rainy season in summer, at least once a day, it would literally rain inside too. The AC was old and barely working, and on hot summer days we would be sweating like pigs inside of it. It was really no wonder we enjoyed this new modern building, even if it was very ugly.

"So, what's with the hair then?" Tom asked, sipping his big YETI cup that I knew contained a protein shake, his first of at least four that he would devour in a workday.

"I mean not that you don't look dashing," he added with a wink. "You always do."

I shrugged and touched my hair. "I don't know. I kind of liked it short and missed it, I guess. Besides it's too hot to have long hair in Florida."

I smiled awkwardly while secretly scolding myself. This was an opportunity for me to tell him the truth. I mean I had to do it at some point, right? I had to tell them all. But I feared so badly I would lose their respect for me. It just didn't feel like the right time.

Was there ever going to be a right time to say something like that?

Just get it over with. Say it!

I took in a deep breath and looked at my two colleagues. Tom was staring at his computer screen, probably flipping through emails, before this morning's meeting. Scott was on the phone, his soft black curls bouncing on his forehead as he spoke.

"Tom?"

"Mm-hm?" he said without looking away from his screen.

"There's... there's kind of something I need to tell you."

He sipped his big protein drink, then looked at me. "What's up? You look so serious?"

"I'm... I wanted to tell you that Joe and I... I mean I am..."

I couldn't even look at him as I babbled on. I was making no sense, I knew that, but I couldn't figure out how to say it right.

"What's going on with you and Joe?" he asked with a frown.

I lifted my gaze and met his. My heart sank as I saw his concern. Tom loved Joe. Heck, so did Scott. We would often do cookouts at my house, and the boys would hang out by the grill, chatting. This was going to break his heart too. Maybe he would even resent me?

"I'm just... I have—"

I didn't get to finish the sentence before our boss, Chief Jake Doyle, came rushing out of his office and approached us. He looked at me and Tom.

"You two will miss the meeting this morning. They are dragging a body out of the retention pond on South Brevard Avenue at Tenth Street as we speak. Brace yourselves. First responders said it was a kid."

FOUR

Then

The first time she met him, she couldn't have been more than ten years old. All she remembered was how tall he was as he approached her. She was playing in the front yard of the mobile home where she lived with her mom and stepdad, Cole. She paid no attention to him till his shoes were right in front of her in the grass. His black shiny shoes that were as big as the length of her entire arm.

"Hey there, little girl," he said and squatted down in front of her.

She looked up and met his big blue eyes. In his hand he was holding a Barbie doll wearing a wedding dress. It was the new series, Bridal Barbie. She was gorgeous. Kitty had wanted one ever since she had seen it at the Toys "R" Us, but her mom said she couldn't afford it. Then her friend Patricia had one for her birthday, and Kitty felt such deep jealousy she almost considered stealing it from her.

The doll moved in his hand, and Kitty's eyes followed it closely.

"Might this be yours?" the man in the black shoes asked.

Kitty shook her head. She stared at the doll. She wanted it so bad, she wanted to say yes, but she couldn't. After all this guy was in uniform. He was a police officer, and you didn't lie to the police.

"N-no."

He smiled and looked at the doll. "Are you sure?"

"Y-yes, sir."

He narrowed his eyes and looked at her. "I find that hard to believe because she just told me that she got lost and that she belonged to the prettiest little girl in the neighborhood. Now that can only be you, the way I see it 'cause you are the prettiest little thing I have ever seen."

That made Kitty chuckle. She placed a hand over her mouth, feeling shy. She couldn't help blushing. No one had ever told her she was pretty before. Her stepdad always said she was like the ugly duckling, except she would never turn into a swan, not with that mother she had come from.

"Are you sure it's not your doll?" the man asked again.

"It's not... sir," she said.

"Well, I think it is. Here, you have it."

He reached out the doll toward her, and she looked up at him, eyes wide. He was the police, and you had to obey them, she had learned in school.

"I..."

"Take it."

She took it. Hands shaking, she grabbed the doll and pulled it toward her. She hugged the small Barbie doll and couldn't stop smiling. The officer chuckled. He tousled her hair.

"That's better. Now... what do you say?"

She swallowed, feeling so happy she could barely contain it. "Thank you! Thank you, officer."

He laughed. "Call me Damian, kiddo."

"Okay, thank you, Officer Damian. Thank you so much. I love it."

"I had a feeling you might," he said, then touched her cheek gently with his finger, before standing up straight.

"Well, I better get going," he said. "You take good care of that doll, you hear me?"

"I will, Officer Damian, I promise. I will sleep with her every night and never let her out of my sight."

He made an imaginary gun with his finger and winked at her, then turned around and walked to the cop car he had parked on the side of the road. He got in and waved at her once again, before he took off.

Kitty stared at the nice man in the nice car, then ran back to the house to show her mom her new doll.

FIVE

BILLIE ANN

Neither of us spoke in the car. Tom and I hadn't said anything to each other since the Chief had spoken. Just those four infamous words.

It was a kid.

Now as I drove the car down South Brevard Avenue toward the spot where it met Tenth Street, Tom finally made the first sound to break the silence.

A deep sigh.

It wasn't often we had cases involving children, but drowning accidents did happen from time to time in Florida. Usually, it was tourists coming down on vacation and running into trouble in pools or getting caught in a rip current in the ocean. Rarely, we had a shark bite, but that was usually not fatal.

Chief Doyle said the girl was already dead when she was pulled out of the water. Having children myself, it made me sick to my stomach. The coroner had declared her dead and something about her body was suspicious. Otherwise, we wouldn't have been called out there. We were needed because it was likely murder.

I killed the engine and looked at Tom. "You ready for this?"

He swallowed. Tom had a huge heart underneath all that joking and sarcasm. Often, I believed he tried to be funny just to hide how soft he really was. Calling him a gentle giant would be a cliché, but hey if the shoe fits, and it did.

"I guess I'm as ready as I will ever be." I wished for a second I had asked Scott to come along, but he had another case he was finishing up his report on. I could have used him here. He was good at keeping his head cool in these types of situations.

I exhaled. "We'll need a drink tonight."

We got out and walked toward the police blockade. The forensic tech department was there in their white vans, and the place was crawling with people in blue body suits. Someone handed us plastic shoes and gloves to wear as we showed him our badges.

I spotted my colleague from the coroner's office, Dr. Phillips. He was talking to someone, a young officer, when I approached him.

"Tom and Billie Ann. Just the duo I was hoping for."

"What have you got?" I asked. I threw a glance toward the body by the side of the pond. It was covered by a white mortuary sheet.

Dr. Phillips pushed his glasses back on his nose and started to walk. I followed him. Tom stayed back and told me he would have a chat with the responding officer. I knew he had a hard time seeing bodies, and I didn't mind him not coming. Even if I knew I was going to have nightmares for a very long time, there was no reason for us both to have them. Besides, I was the far more experienced one.

Dr. Phillips knelt down and pulled off the sheet so I could see the girl's face. I bit back my tears as I saw her eyes staring blankly into the air.

"Oh dear God," I said.

"As you can see, we're dealing with a female body here. She

has been in the water all night, probably longer, but no more than twenty-four hours I'd say."

I swallowed, trying to remain calm. I stared at the young girl, then thought of my own daughter Charlene.

"Anything to identify her?"

He shook his head. "She's barely wearing any clothes."

"Did she drown?" I asked.

"That's what I thought at first."

Uh-oh. I didn't like the sound of that.

"But...?"

He sighed, then pointed at the girl's neck. Seeing this made me close my eyes briefly to compose myself. I had seen bruises like these before.

"Death by asphyxiation," I said. "She was strangled."

He nodded. "That would be my initial judgment yes. But of course, I can't tell you with certainty until after the autopsy. I will have to open her up and see if she has water in her lungs, to determine if she was dead before she fell in."

"Someone hurt her," I said, "whether that's what killed her or not."

He exhaled. "Yes, and the bruises are very likely made by a rope or a cord of some sort that was wrapped around her throat from behind."

I rubbed the bridge between my eyes. It was always worse when it was children. "All right. I need that autopsy ASAP," I told Dr. Phillips. I stood up. In the meantime, it was my job to find out who this poor girl was.

SIX

MARISSA

Marissa could hear her own pulse. It was pounding in her ears, making it impossible for her to hear anything else. She tried to listen to the chatter among the spectators as she elbowed her way through the crowd. Words like *body* and *child* were among those she heard, and they terrified her. She wanted to get closer to the pond, so she could see.

"Excuse me," she said and pushed her way past a man. He grumbled something angrily at her, but moved aside.

"Excuse me. Excuse me. Excuse me."

She continued till she could see the police blockade and the officer guarding it. Then she stopped. She didn't want to get so close they might see her in the crowd. Instead, she stood on her tippy-toes, and soon she could see enough for her to realize that there were people in blue bodysuits crowding the area. She knew enough to realize that there had to be a body.

Her heart stopped.

Could it be her Emma?

She had been searching for her all over the house, and even in the attic. She had then taken her bike and ridden around the neighborhood, searching for her everywhere and also around the pond. But she had been nowhere to be found. All day and the entire night, she had looked for her everywhere. She had passed out when she returned home, before she was woken up by the sound of sirens and saw police car after police car arrive, along with an ambulance.

She had watched them from the house, heart throbbing, paralyzed, until she worked up the courage to approach the crowd.

"Excuse me, I was actually standing there," a voice said behind her. "And now you're blocking my view."

Marissa turned to look at the woman behind her. She was short and stubby and wearing a red T-shirt that read:

IF YOU THINK I'M SHORT, YOU SHOULD SEE MY PATIENCE.

Marissa stared at her, confused. "I'm... I'm sorry."

She moved to the side and found another spot where she could see. The area where she believed the body to be was covered by a screen, so she had to hunch down by the edge of it where there was a small crack. The crowd surrounding the pond was growing rapidly as news spread fast about the finding of a body. It wasn't every day that type of thing happened in their quaint little town. This would be something the neighbors would talk about for years to come. Mostly the chatter was about the sight of a coyote or the one time someone claimed to have seen a black panther on the beach. Most people believed it had just been a big black housecat, but it was still a topic they discussed from time to time. That and then the rocket launches.

Please tell me it's not my daughter.

Marissa could barely breathe as she watched a female police officer walk toward the body, and a man pull off the sheet. It was hard to see properly through the crack. She braced herself for it, told herself it probably was her daughter, and she prepared herself for the shock it would be to lose the biggest love of her life.

Marissa gasped lightly as she could see the color of the girl's hair. She tried to move, yet she still couldn't see much. She felt like someone was sitting on her chest, but as the sheet was removed completely, she slowly realized this wasn't her worst nightmare.

It wasn't Emma.

Baffled at this, Marissa rose back up, then backed out of the crowd and rushed back into her house, where she closed the door and fell onto her knees behind it, crying.

This might not have been her nightmare, but she had a feeling it was about to become something even worse.

SEVEN

BILLIE ANN

I searched for Tom and found him still talking to the responding officer. I approached him, wondering how we were going to identify our victim. Dr. Phillips had told me he believed her to be between fourteen and fifteen years old, but that was all we knew so far. Would we have to wait for forensics to get a look at her teeth? Would we be combing through missing person records? As far as I was aware there were no children missing— no one had reported anything yesterday or the day before.

"What have you got?" I asked.

"Officer Steele here was first on scene," Tom said. "Got the call at seven forty-one on his radio while on traffic patrol nearby. A runner found the body in the pond when she was out on her morning jog. I talked to her and got her statement, but she couldn't help us much. She was very shocked and could just tell me that she saw the body bobbing on the surface then called nine-one-one."

"Okay, we will keep her name on the notepad for now," I said, "and focus on finding out who the girl is. Has anyone reported a teenage girl missing in town? I haven't heard of it, and usually it's something we all know about from the second it happens. There have been no reports, have there? No search parties?"

Tom shook his head. "Nope. I called the Chief just to be certain, and he said they heard nothing."

"Does anyone know this girl?" I asked.

"I do."

I turned to look at who was coming up behind me.

"Officer Craig," I said.

He was one of the younger ones in our little police force, fresh out of school. He had only been with us for a few months. He and Officer Hansson served as school resource officers. Their job was to patrol at the high school, and the elementary school, during school hours. The job also required them to control traffic around the time when school was out in the afternoons and to make sure the traffic went smoothly. But they were also the ones who kept a close bond with the kids at the schools, and part of the job was to get to know that one kid who might try to bring a gun and to avoid the one catastrophe we all feared so deeply.

"She goes to the high school," he said. "Her name is Cassandra. I don't know her last name, but I have seen her around the school. She bikes back and forth so she can't live far. I'd say somewhere on Minutemen."

I nodded. Most of the school kids lived on the main street in town and biked or skateboarded every day. A lot of them used electrical bikes now, and it annoyed me greatly. My kids had all asked for one, before Charlene got her driver's license, and I had said no. Kids needed exercise.

I wrote Cassandra's name on my notepad, then grabbed my phone and called the school. There couldn't be that many girls with that name enrolled there. I was right. Only one Cassandra. She was a freshman and fifteen years old, according to Diana at the office. And she hadn't made it to school today. I didn't tell her what this was regarding, as I knew she spoke to each and every parent who came in, and I had to be careful. I couldn't have Cassandra's parents finding out about their daughter through anyone but me.

"Cassandra Perez," I said and looked at my notepad where I had written the name and address.

Tom came up next to me with a deep exhale.

"I guess we're about to ruin Mr. and Mrs. Perezes' day."

"Try their life," I said and tried to swallow the knot in my throat while we walked to the car.

Having teenagers myself, I knew this was going to be more than tough. It was going to be heartbreaking.

EIGHT

Then

He stopped by a few weeks later, on a Sunday, when he was off duty. The nice police officer with the shiny black shoes drove up in their driveway and walked to the door and knocked. The way he knocked was so particular, Kitty would always recognize it for many months to come.

And she would be so excited every time.

Police Officer Damian turned out to be a good friend of her stepdad's, and as he walked inside, after her stepdad had opened the door for him, Kitty stormed toward him, the anticipation bubbling inside of her.

"Hi, Officer Damian," she said.

"Hi there, Kitty," he responded. "How's that doll working out for ya?"

She blushed. She was holding the doll in her hand still. She had slept with it, brought it into her bath with her, and was playing with it every chance she got. She had taken it in her backpack for school, even if the children weren't allowed to bring toys anymore, because their third-grade teacher Miss

Taylor didn't allow it. Not since Barbara and that boy Aiden had gotten into a fight over a truck he had brought to school. Miss Taylor wasn't having it anymore.

"Y'all are way too old to bring toys to school anyway."

And that was it. But Kitty had kept her Barbie doll inside of her backpack and only taken it out to peek at it under the table every now and then, when no one was looking.

She loved it so much.

"Really good," she said with a smile as she looked down at the doll in her hand.

"Hmm," Officer Damian said and tilted his head. "I think she looks a little lonely. Don't you?"

She glanced up at him. What did he mean by that?

He smiled widely. He had a friendly smile.

"Let me take a look at her."

He grabbed the doll from her hand, and Kitty gasped, worried that he was going to take it away from her. After all, he was the one who had given it to her, so he could take it away too.

Officer Damian looked at the doll's face.

"I really think she does look a little lonely," he repeated. "Maybe she needs a friend."

"She has me," Kitty said, standing up straight. She reached out for the doll, ready to snatch it out of his hands if he let go of it. He wasn't taking her doll back. She wouldn't let him. "I'm her friend."

"Oh, I bet you are," he said and handed her the doll back.

Kitty hurried up and grabbed it, then held it tight to her body, swearing she would never let go of it again. No matter what.

That's when he pulled out something from behind his back. "Maybe she would like a boyfriend?"

Kitty stared at the package in his hands. She couldn't believe it. There it was. The Ken doll that everyone in school was talking about. Wedding Day Groom Ken. Not even Patricia had that one.

Kitty's jaw dropped.

"I think your doll would like to be with her boyfriend, don't you?" Damian asked.

Kitty nodded, mouth gaping. Was this really for her? Was he giving her another doll? If so, then she would be the most popular girl in her class.

She stared at the Ken doll as the man handed it to her.

"Here you go, pretty girl. Now she isn't lonely anymore."

Kitty took the doll, holding it like it was burning, barely touching it, to not make it dirty. Ken was so perfect and now she could play family with them. They could get married and live in a house that she could make out of a cardboard box and color with crayons. She could even make them a yard. They were going to be so happy.

Police Officer Damian bent down and touched her curls. "Everyone should have a special someone in their lives, don't you think?"

Her stepdad called for him to come out on the patio and have a beer. He told him to *stop playing with the girl*.

Officer Damian stroked Kitty's cheek gently with his finger, then winked at her before he disappeared.

NINE

BILLIE ANN

Mrs. Perez's hazel eyes stared up at me. She looked puzzled at first, then worried. She was a small woman, but with strong features. Her body looked tiny as she stood in the doorway of her home, but she wasn't skinny. Her muscles were bulging in the tank top she was wearing. Her brown hair was pulled up in a tight ponytail and her bangs needed to be trimmed. They fell into her eyes, and she swept them to the side.

"Yes?"

I showed her my badge. My heart was throbbing, and I still had a huge knot in my throat. I recognized her instantly, having seen her around the school at recitals and other events. I wondered for a second if Charlene or William knew Cassandra. They had to. It was a small high school. And a small town. This was going to hit hard everywhere.

Her worried eyes became terrified as she looked at my badge, and I could tell she was going through all the scenarios in her mind. Imagining all kinds of things.

"Can we come in?" I asked.

"Yes, yes, of course," she said and stepped aside. Tom

followed me, and he nodded politely at her as he passed her with a quiet *ma'am*.

She closed the door behind us.

"We can go in the kitchen," she said.

We sat in her white kitchen chairs, and she looked at me nervously.

"Is Mr. Perez home?" I asked.

She shook her head. "He's traveling with his work as a sales representative for Q-Fib, a company that sells laser equipment for cosmetic surgery. He's in Chicago right now. W-what is this about?"

"It's about your daughter," I said, folding my hands on the wooden table.

"Cassandra?" her voice became high pitched as she said the name.

I nodded. "Yes."

"W-what about her? Is she in some kind of trouble?"

"Mrs. Perez... I'm... so sorry to have to inform you that earlier this morning we recovered the body of a young girl in the area by South Brevard Avenue and Tenth Street. We believe it is Cassandra, as an officer on scene was able to identify her, but we will need your positive identification to be certain."

She looked puzzled. "Cassandra? But... but she's at school. No, no, no. You must have gotten it wrong."

Her fingers fiddled with the phone in her hand.

"Mrs. Perez, when was the last time you saw or heard from your daughter?" I asked. "A call or a text?"

She swallowed. "Well, I... I just... it was this morning, see?"

She opened her text messages and showed me.

Good morning, sweetie. I hope you'll have a great day. Don't forget you have track meet this afternoon. Love, Mom.

"I see you texted her, but not her answering," I said. "When was the last time you saw her?"

She seemed confused. Shock was beginning to set in. You never knew how next of kin would react in these situations, when giving a death notification. Some got aggressive, others paralyzed. I once had to take a mother to the ER to be treated for shock.

"I... I saw her yesterday, in the afternoon," she said, her voice shivering. "I kissed her on the cheek, and she left."

"What time was that?"

"Just before three o'clock."

I wrote it down on my notepad. "Did you hear from her later in the day?"

"She... she had a babysitting job and said that she would be home late. So, no. I texted her good night at about ten and went to bed."

"Who did she babysit for?" I asked.

"She had several families she helped out."

"Do you know who she went to babysit for yesterday?"

She looked confused. "I think it was for a lady who my husband set her up with recently. I don't know her myself, but I can get her name and number from Pete as soon as I talk to him."

"Okay, and we will need a list of her best friends as well and their phone numbers. They might know more of her whereabouts before her death."

Mrs. Perez stared at me, her eyes in shock, while the word hung in the air. *Death.*

"Yes, yes, of course."

I looked at my notepad.

"Did she answer your text last night?"

Mrs. Perez scrolled back in her messages. "No. I guess..." She paused. "She didn't. But I didn't ask her a question, only said good night, sleep tight. It wasn't that strange, I thought."

"And this morning?" Tom asked. "Didn't you notice that she wasn't in her room?"

Mrs. Perez looked up at us, then shook her head. "I... I mean no. She usually gets up at the crack of dawn to go to school. She runs track and they practice at six a.m., before it gets hot out. I just assumed that she had already left."

Mrs. Perez stared blankly into the air. "I was wondering why she didn't answer last night, but I just thought she was being a teenager, you know?" She was talking faster now, and I could almost feel the panic building in her body. Her breathing grew heavier, and she clasped her chest as if she was in pain, but I knew it was just the realization settling in.

I nodded. Yes, I knew a little too well what it was like having teenagers.

"So, what exactly are you telling me?" Mrs. Perez asked with a light whimper.

I reached across the table and touched her hand gently. "We will need you to come with us to identify the body."

Tom leaned forward. "Do you have anyone, a relative or a close friend, we can call and who can go with you?"

She seemed so lost, it broke my heart. A tear escaped her eye, and she wiped it away, but more came and it was soon hard for her to stop them. Her hands were shaking, and her breathing had become ragged.

"It's okay to cry," I said.

She sniffled and wiped her cheeks, then looked briefly toward the ceiling while biting the tears back.

"I have a sister. She works downtown at Café Surfnista. She can go with me."

"Okay, give me her number and I will call her and have her meet us," Tom said. "You shouldn't be doing this alone."

Mrs. Perez nodded. Her eyes were filling, but she was obviously fighting her tears. I don't think I would have been able to stop them if I were in her situation.

"And then maybe you'll want to call your husband," Tom said.

"We can call him for you, if you prefer," I said.

She shook her head. "N-no. I will do it."

She breathed heavily to calm herself down, then looked up at me. They had taught us that it was okay to show emotion when doing death notifications, but I knew that if I did, I probably wouldn't be able to stop.

"What happened to her?" Mrs. Perez asked.

"She was found in the retention pond. We don't really know a lot right now, but the autopsy will—"

"Autopsy... so you think she was killed?" she said with a small gasp.

"We don't know that as of right now, but yes, we do suspect foul play," Tom said.

"We will know more after the autopsy," I repeated.

Mrs. Perez shook her head slowly. "I just don't... I can't... are you sure she's not in school? She always goes to school. Maybe you got the wrong—"

I shook my head. "We called them. She didn't show up today."

"So, she was dead already yesterday? I don't understand."

"We don't know when time of death occurred yet, but we will know more soon. For now, I just need you to come with us to the morgue."

TEN

BILLIE ANN

I was back at the police station, writing my report, when the Chief came to my desk. It was late in the afternoon, and Tom and I had just come back. I was exhausted. Mrs. Perez had identified her daughter at the morgue, and that wasn't easy to watch. There were crisis counselors there who then took care of her, while we went back to open up the case. But to be honest, I wasn't feeling great.

"I need your help," he said.

"Sure, boss, what's up?"

He sat at the corner of my desk. "It's a little delicate."

"Okay?"

"There's a woman. She came in a couple of hours ago to report her child missing. I haven't had the time to talk to her myself, but Steele talked to her earlier."

Now he had my full attention. "A missing child?"

"Yes, but the problem is that... well, we think she's a little"— he made circles by his temple—"a little crazy."

"Why? If a child is missing, then why aren't we all over this?"

He exhaled. "Well, the thing is... we can't find out anything about this child."

I frowned. This made no sense. "What do you mean?"

"Supposedly she has a four-year-old girl named Emma. But she has no information to support that the girl even exists. And get this, the woman doesn't have a driver's license or any form of ID, so we can't run a background check."

"That sounds a little strange."

"Yes, it does. The child is not registered anywhere, no preschool, the woman doesn't have a birth certificate, heck, she doesn't even have a photo of the child on her phone to show us. I had Officer Steele go with her back to her home and look in the neighborhood, but when he talked to the neighbors no one had ever heard or seen the kid. I don't know how to deal with her. I can't just dismiss her. But I can't send out an Amber Alert either because I have no proof she exists or even a photo to send out. She wants me to start a search party, but how can I?"

"But you think she's lying? You think that she doesn't have a child?" I asked, puzzled. It all sounded very odd to me.

"I think she might be a little... um... confused, if you know what I mean," he said, rolling his eyes.

"You think she invented a child and now she can't find her, so she thinks she is missing?"

He exhaled again. "Like I said. It's a delicate matter. One that I would like to go away. We've got a lot going on here today."

"And you think me talking to her might help?"

"I don't know how to deal with her. She keeps claiming that she has a child, and that she has been kidnapped, and no one knows how to help her. You're a woman, can't you...?"

He made a noise with his cheeks, like I was a horse that he needed to move forward. It pissed me off. But he was my boss, so I didn't say anything. I respected Doyle greatly and had worked with him as my Chief for the past three years.

"Talk to her?" I asked. "Woman to woman?"

"Yes, do that. Whatever it takes," he said. "So, if you do find solid evidence that there really is a child who has gone missing, we have to take her seriously. If not, then we might need to take her to psychiatric emergency to be evaluated. I'm leaning more and more toward that solution."

"Of course, Chief. I will take a look at it."

He rose to his feet with a smile. I received a friendly clap on my shoulder. "Great. I knew I could count on you. She's in the lobby downstairs."

ELEVEN

MARISSA

Marissa looked at her fingers. She was tapping them nervously on her leg. The woman behind the counter in the flowery top smiled at her again. It was one of those phony smiles, showing compassion, yet not really meaning anything.

Marissa got up and approached her again. She could tell by her expression that the woman was annoyed by her, and the fact that she was—once again—coming to talk to her, but she did it anyway.

"Any news?" Marissa asked, while biting her nails anxiously.

The woman shook her head. "They will send someone soon."

"You said that an hour ago," Marissa said. "My child is gone. Please have someone help me."

"I assure you we're doing everything we can, but it's a busy day," the woman said.

Marissa nodded. She had said that an hour ago too. An officer entered through the front door and walked past her. Her heart started to beat faster. She never thought she'd go to the police. She didn't trust them, didn't believe anyone could help her. But this was Emma, she had to act, she had to get help.

"Please just take your seat, ma'am," the woman said. "Someone will be with you soon."

The phone rang and she picked it up, while Marissa went back to sit in the black plastic chair.

"Cocoa Beach police," she chirped like she had done a thousand times that day while Marissa had been waiting.

They're not gonna help you.

Marissa tried to calm herself down. The fact was, she had no idea what else to do. How to deal with this.

They won't believe you.

Marissa exhaled deeply, then decided it was no use. She would be better off trying to find her daughter herself.

She had risen to her feet and walked toward the door, when the elevator dinged behind her, and the doors opened. A woman entered the lobby. She was small, skinny, and looked like she was in the Army with her short buzz cut. She had beautiful amber eyes, a unique blend of yellow and orange, set in a tanned face.

"Marissa Clemens?" she said and looked at her.

Marissa paused. She let go of the door and faced the woman. "T-that's me."

"Let's talk for a minute, shall we?" the woman asked. "We have a small office in the back here where we can sit."

Marissa nodded. She still felt compelled to run away, but the fact that it was a woman, made her feel more comfortable.

"O-okay."

"I'm Detective Billie Ann Wilde," she said and shook Marissa's hand as they sat down. Billie Ann looked at the papers in front of her. "I understand your daughter is missing?"

"Y-yes, Emma, she's four years old."

Billie Ann nodded. "And where was Emma when she went missing?"

"She was playing in the backyard of my house. I looked away for a few minutes to do laundry and then she was gone. I know you need a picture of her, and a birth certificate, but I don't have them. I just need your help. Please? You have to believe me. Please have your patrols search for her. She has strawberry blonde hair and was wearing a pink shirt with sparkling unicorns on it. And a tutu. A blue tutu."

Billie Ann looked at the form in front of her that Marissa had filled out. "And your house is on South Brevard Avenue, correct?"

Then she paused. Billie Ann stared at the address for a few seconds, then shook her head. She closed the file.

"You know what? How about you take me to your house and show me where she went missing?"

TWELVE

BILLIE ANN

It was a long shot. I knew it was. But I felt bad for the poor woman in front of me. A part of me really wanted to believe she was telling the truth. There was something odd about the whole situation, and when I realized that she lived close to Cassandra Perez, like right down the same street, a couple of red flags went up. My gut told me it wasn't a coincidence.

I took her back to her house in my police cruiser, and I parked it out front. As I walked up her driveway, I could see the tech team were still working at the scene behind her house, down by the pond.

"Thank you for taking me seriously," Marissa said as she opened the door and let me inside of the home.

"You said she disappeared yesterday, right?" I asked and walked in. I closed the door behind me.

"Yes, she was playing out here in the back, and there was a squirrel and then... I don't know what she did after that. I worried she had gotten to the pond somehow..."

She stopped as we walked through the living room toward the kitchen. I scanned the room. It had a nice light beige carpet on it. No spills of chocolate milk or juice. There was a TV, two recliners, and a mirror on the wall. A sign said, *Welcome to the beach*. A pair of adult slippers were on the tiles by the door, next to a pair of adult flip-flops.

But no children's shoes.

There were no stuffed animals or dolls abandoned in the middle of a tea party by the TV. No sippy cups left out, or Crayola crayons on the dining room table. As we entered the kitchen, I noticed no photos on the fridge, or drawings made by a child's hands. Nothing but stainless steel surfaces, all polished and clean. There were no small greasy fingers on the counters. Not on windows or mirrors either.

"She was right out there, and I was watching her through the window here, while peeling potatoes and then—"

"Why did you wait so long?" I asked.

"What?" She gave me a puzzled yet frantic look.

"Why didn't you come to us yesterday when you realized your daughter was gone?" I asked, beginning to think the Chief was right. There was definitely no child living here. This woman was mad as a bat. She had to be.

"I... I..." she seemed to be searching for the answer, but not finding it. "I wanted to wait and see if I could find her myself, or if she came home and then I... then they pulled out Cassandra out of the pond down the street, and I thought for a second it was Emma. But then... well, I guess I realized she wasn't coming back and—"

"You knew Cassandra?" I asked.

Marissa looked at her fingers. "You have to believe me. My daughter is missing. I don't know what to do. I fear something awful has happened to her."

Was she just a cuckoo head? A lot of times murder cases pushed them out of their hidings. I don't know how often I had someone confess to a murder they didn't do. Often, they truly believed their own story, they truly thought they had done it. It was sometimes hard to convince them they hadn't.

I placed a gentle hand on her shoulder. "Marissa? Maybe we should go to the psychiatric emergency room, huh? They can help you there."

She stared at me. Her eyes grew wide with terror. "You think I'm crazy? That I'm lying?"

I bit my lip. I knew she probably believed her own story, and maybe she even had a child once then lost it. But she wasn't sane, that was for sure.

"I think you might be in need of some help," I said. I had barely finished my sentence, when I spotted a pair of small pink Crocs in the grass.

"What's that?" I asked.

Marissa swallowed. "Her shoes. It's all that was left of her when she disappeared. And to answer your question from before, then yes, I knew Cassandra. She was my babysitter."

THIRTEEN

BILLIE ANN

I had been calling all of Cassandra's friends, and their parents, since I got back to the office. Once I'd informed them of her passing, I'd been asking them about her whereabouts these past days leading up to her murder.

Meanwhile Scott and Tom took care of talking to the two other families Cassandra was babysitting for. After visiting one of them, Tom came back to the station and sat down across from me. I lifted my gaze from my computer.

"I sense you've got something," I said.

He exhaled and leaned back in the chair. "I just spoke to Mrs. Cornwell, who Cassandra babysat for twice a month, and it actually became quite interesting."

I nodded. "Go on."

He rubbed his chin. "She told me that Cassandra had been babysitting their seven-year-old daughter for about six months, and that she was very fond of her. She was trustworthy and the kid was always in bed on time, and that they had a special bond."

"But?"

"But... the thing was, that once I dug into it a little, Mrs. Cornwell started to cry."

"Was she sad about Cassandra?" I asked, thinking that would only be natural.

"Yes, that too, but there was something else."

"Like what?" I asked, getting intrigued.

"She said she had often worried that her husband, Eric, was overly familiar with Cassandra. He would always drive her home after she was done babysitting, and also did so on Saturday night, before she went missing on Sunday."

"What did she mean by overly familiar?"

"I asked her that and she said that it was like she could tell that her husband liked her, that he lit up when seeing her, and they would talk a lot. She kept telling herself that it was just in her head, but now that Cassandra was missing, she worried that maybe she had been right. She had suspected her husband of having an affair."

"With Cassandra?" I said, feeling appalled.

"She didn't want to say it, but she said she worried about it," he said.

"Did you talk to the husband?"

"Not yet."

"We need to talk to him as soon as possible."

Tom nodded. "Of course. I'll try to get ahold of him ASAP."

I nodded and smiled. "Good job, Tom."

He smiled back and went to his own desk. "Thanks, boss."

We had sat in silence for a few minutes, when Scott made a noise. "Eh, boss?"

"Yes?"

"Marissa is dead," he said, cutting straight to the chase.

He lifted his gaze from his computer, and his eyes met mine across the room.

"Say that again?"

"Marissa Clemens died nine years ago."

"Excuse me?"

"She's dead. She doesn't exist. Or rather she did. Marissa Clemens was seventy-two when she died."

I stared at him. "Couldn't that be another Marissa Clemens?"

"Not in Cocoa Beach," he said. "Or even Brevard County."

He went quiet, like he waited for me to fill in the blanks. But I couldn't. A frown grew between my eyes.

"Are you serious?"

"As serious as a heart attack."

"But that makes no sense," I said. "She doesn't exist and neither does her child? How is that possible?"

"I am not sure," he answered. "Remember how we found out that she didn't have a car or a license? Now get this, I called the hospital in Cape Canaveral where she said she worked. She doesn't work there. I then called all the surrounding hospitals, and they haven't heard about her either."

"So, she isn't working as a nurse? And she isn't registered anywhere? How does she make money? Does she even work?"

Just then, the Chief opened the door to his office and stepped out, slamming it against the wall. He glared at me, and I could tell he was in a mood.

"Wilde, get in here, now."

Tom and Scott both sent me a look of encouragement as I got up from my desk and hurried past the Chief and into his office. He closed the door behind him. His movements were aggressive.

"Sit."

I did. I had a feeling I knew what this was about.

"Listen, Chief—"

"You're starting a search party for a child who doesn't exist?" he said, sitting down. "You don't think we have enough of a caseload as it is? You wanna add a little more searching for ghosts?"

"Listen, Chief, I went to the woman's house, and you're right, at first glance it didn't look like she had a child, but I believe her. There were these pink Crocs in her yard."

"Oh, that settles it then," he said, rolling his eyes.

I bit my lip to calm myself down and not say something that I might regret later on. The Chief had a way of being very condescending toward me whenever he had the chance, and it bothered me. He could be to others, as well, but not as often as with me.

I was always *honey*, and *sweetheart*, and *pretty little thing*.

I gazed out the window from his office and my eyes met Scott's. He sent me an encouraging thumbs-up and a smile. I smiled back, feeling good knowing that my team had my back. I knew they did.

I sat there trying to maintain my composure. I wasn't going to let anyone question my instincts. I needed to help this woman. I just felt I did.

He continued. "I mean, there's no way this woman could have bought those shoes even if she didn't have a child, or maybe even stolen them from somewhere. Have you thought about that, huh, Wilde? Some people will go a long way to convince you they're telling the truth. I'm telling ya'. I have seen my share of crazy stuff in my day. You will too when you've been around as long as me."

I shook my head. No. I couldn't think like that. I couldn't be this cynical. I saw those Crocs, and the moment I did, I instantly knew there was a girl who had worn them recently. And that girl was nowhere to be found. Were there a lot of strange things about this mother and the fact she had no identification, no pictures or any toys lying around? Absolutely. But I had to follow my gut on this one. I felt very strongly that this was important. A little girl's life was at stake. I couldn't take that lightly. I simply refused to.

"Chief, I know it might seem like a long shot, but what if

we're wrong?" I said. "What if there really is a child out there who is in danger? Could you live with yourself if something happened to her? I know I couldn't."

He let out a sigh and leaned back in his chair, his eyes piercing through mine. He clicked his tongue and seemed to be mulling it over. I felt annoyed. We were wasting precious time by just sitting there, doing nothing. Debating whether or not we should use resources on this.

A missing child, for crying out loud!

What was there to discuss?

"And what about the Cassandra Perez case, huh?" he asked, tapping his finger on his wooden desk. "I think that should be our priority now. Someone killed that young girl and threw her in the pond. She was strangled and dumped like trash. It's not right. It makes me so angry. These things aren't supposed to be happening in my town. Not in *my* town. I want this solved, and the killer off the streets. As soon as it gets out it will terrify our little community. I want this killer caught before panic spreads around here. That's your job. Not looking for missing toddlers that only exist in the mind of a weird woman."

"I can do both."

He looked at me like he didn't quite believe me. I wasn't giving up. I knew I could persuade him.

"I think the cases are connected," I added. "The mother claims Cassandra was her babysitter. She's wrapped up in this somehow, and I'd never forgive myself if a little girl was truly missing and I did nothing to find her. Neither would you."

He eased up. I seemed to have caught his attention with this new information. His phone started ringing and I could tell he wanted me to get out of there, so he could take the call.

He grunted, annoyed. "Fine. You have until the end of the week. That's all I can agree to."

I clenched my fist. Finally, he gave in. "Thank you, Chief. You've made the right decision."

"But that's it. If you don't find anything by then, I want you to drop this and focus on your other cases. And no focus is taken from the Perez case, do you hear me? It's a top priority right now. Absolutely top. Nothing above it."

"I hear you, Chief. I want this killer caught too. Believe you me."

"Then get to work."

I nodded, grateful for the opportunity. As I stood up to leave, the Chief lifted his hand and stopped me. He had grabbed his phone, but hadn't picked it up yet. It was still ringing in his hand.

"Wilde, one more thing."

"Yes?"

He looked at me from above his glasses. "If you're wrong about this and it turns out to be a dead end, I don't want to hear any excuses. Is that clear? You'll be facing the consequences. I hope you realize this."

"Yes, Chief."

With that, I left his office, determined to prove him wrong. As I walked past Tom's and Scott's desks, they gave me a look of support, but I could tell they were worried about me. I was taking a huge risk, and if it didn't pay off, it could jeopardize my entire career. I wasn't that concerned. Not for me at least.

I was, however, extremely worried about Emma.

FOURTEEN

Then

Officer Damian quickly became a regular houseguest. They all enjoyed his visits, even Kitty's mom, who would invite him over for dinner at least once a week, mostly in the weekends, so they could drink beers in the living room of their mobile home all night long.

Kitty loved it when he came over. She would get to stay up late, and it was like everyone changed around him. Her mom and stepdad would be in a better mood, and they wouldn't yell at her so much, or at each other.

As the months went by, Kitty found herself looking forward more and more to Officer Damian's visits. She would stand by the window and watch as he drove up into the driveway, then feel the excitement rush through her body as she saw his face approach. He would always come bearing gifts—a new book for her to read, a cute pink teddy bear he just bought in the dollar store on the way there that was "staring at him, begging him to take him to the prettiest girl in the area," and loads of beers for her mom and stepdad to share. She loved how he always seemed to know just what to bring.

One evening, as they sat in the living room watching *American Idol*, Officer Damian leaned over and whispered in Kitty's ear.

"Hey, I've got a surprise for you, pretty girl," he said. "I managed to snag some tickets to Disney World for this weekend. How about you and I go together on Saturday?"

Kitty's heart skipped a beat. She had never been to an amusement park before, even if they lived close to a lot of them, but it was way too expensive for her mom. And Disney was the one she wanted to try the most. All the kids in her class had been there and some even went once or twice a year. The thought of spending the day with Officer Damian made her feel beyond giddy with excitement.

"Yes, please!" she exclaimed.

"But we have to make sure it's okay with your mommy," he said and looked at her sitting on the couch next to Cole.

Kitty stared at her mother, eyes growing wide with anticipation. Would she say yes?

"Please, Mommy, can I go? Please?"

Her mother looked at her, her eyes glassy, beer still in her hand. Then she smiled. Her voice was slurred, but Kitty heard the words loud and clear. "Of course. Go. Have fun."

Kitty jumped to her feet. "Yay! Did you hear that, Officer Damian? I can go."

He smiled at her excitement. "I heard it. I'm so happy."

She clasped her hands together. "I can't wait. I can't believe it. We're gonna ride the roller coasters, and eat cotton candy, and... and... eat candy and..."

"Say a proper thank you to him for being so nice," Cole said. "Go sit on his lap, girl."

Officer Damian's face lit up. He signaled for her to come closer. Kitty hesitated. She wasn't sure she dared to.

"It's okay, girl," her stepdad said and ushered her along. "Remember he's a cop, you'd better do what he says."

That was right. He was the police and you had to do what they said. It was true. She had been taught that in school.

"Don't wanna get in trouble with the law, now, would you?" he added, and he winked at his friend. "Go ahead."

Kitty swallowed and bit the side of her cheek. She felt nervous. She really, really liked Officer Damian and was afraid of doing something wrong.

"Come, pretty girl," he said and reached out his arms. "Come closer."

Kitty looked briefly in her mother's direction, like she wanted to make sure it was okay with her. She didn't want to do something that she didn't approve of. She didn't want her to get mad at her. But her mother had dozed off. Her eyes were closed, and she was breathing heavily, her head leaning on the backrest of the couch.

Cole laughed as Officer Damian reached out for her and pulled Kitty up into his lap. She sat there, nervously, but also feeling happy. He really did like her, didn't he? She liked him too. A lot.

FIFTEEN

BILLIE ANN

"I can't help you if you don't help me."

I stared at Marissa in front of me. I had asked her to come down to the station so I could get some more information about Emma and, hopefully, find out the truth about her and who she was. But so far, we had been talking for half an hour and I still didn't know anymore. We were sitting at my desk, and she kept staring at the wall behind me with all the pictures of our police department's history and the Chiefs we'd had since it was established in 1947. It was like she was avoiding my gaze on purpose, and it made me feel like she was lying to me again, or at least unwilling to tell the truth. I didn't know how to help her.

"I don't know what to tell you," she said.

"Okay, let's try again."

I pinched the bridge of my nose, feeling tired, even if I was on my third cup of coffee. Joe and I had been up most of the night arguing again. After the initial information had settled, he was starting to show some anger toward me; he just wanted to know "if it was all a lie." It didn't matter how many times I told him I loved him, he didn't believe me anymore. And then he began saying that he was still praying every day for me to come back to him. He was praying for it to be a phase, and for me to realize that.

That hit me even harder than the anger and frustration. He was asking me to stop being me, basically. Asking God to change who I am.

"It's not going to go away," I told him. And now it was my turn to be angry. It wasn't his fault that I hadn't been able to admit this to myself. That I had suppressed this side of me for this many years, in order to survive. Of course, it wasn't. But it wasn't my fault either. And he made me feel like it was. Like I had deceived him.

"I still don't understand why you don't have any pictures of your child, or any birth certificate," I said to Marissa.

"I lost the birth certificate when we moved here."

"And how long ago was that?"

"I don't remember. Three years I think."

"And where did you move from? Where was Emma born?"

"Up north, in Florida somewhere."

I sighed. Again, she was giving me vague answers. It was all I had gotten from her, and I was beginning to feel like she didn't even want me to help her. Every time I tried to dig deeper, she would evade the question and give me some ridiculous answer that I couldn't use. I still knew so little about her. But I did know that she had lied to me—and that concerned me. Was she just wasting my time? Did Emma even exist?

"And the dad?"

She shook her head. "He's not important."

"He might be, though. Could he have taken Emma? Children are usually abducted by their own parents."

Her fingers were touching her water bottle nervously. She was picking at the label, ripping it, and leaving small pieces of paper on the table. Her eyes were avoiding mine. There was something she wasn't telling me, but why? That's what I didn't understand.

"Do you have any enemies? Anyone who might want to hurt you by taking your child?" I asked.

She shook her head. "No one knew Emma existed."

"And that's what I don't understand," I said, growing more and more frustrated with this woman. "Why did you keep her a secret? Why can't we find you anywhere? Are you afraid of someone?"

Her eyes hit the floor. It was obvious she was uncomfortable. Still, she didn't answer my questions. I exhaled and continued.

"Cassandra was Emma's babysitter, you told me. What was your relationship with her? With her parents?"

Still no answer.

"Cassandra was likely killed on the same day Emma disappeared. Do you have any —"

Marissa shook her head. She rose to her feet abruptly, pushing her chair backward with a loud noise, interrupting me.

"Can I leave now? I have to get to work."

I leaned back in my chair, disappointed at this. "You're free to go anytime you want. But you're not making my job easier by not telling me everything."

She walked away and, hugging herself, she reached the door. Then she stopped. She turned to look at me.

"I kept her a secret because I was scared someone might take her. That's why."

I sat up straight. "Who? Who would take her?"

Her eyes looked into mine. I saw a deep fear there that almost frightened me. This girl was scared. I just couldn't figure out what she was so terrified of and why she couldn't tell me.

"I'm here to help, Marissa. Can't you just tell me?"

She seemed to be contemplating it for a few seconds, and I

almost thought she would, but then a dark shadow went over her face, and she shut down.

She shook her head, and said, "It's all been a mistake. I'm sorry. I shouldn't have come to you in the first place. It was stupid of me to think the police could help me. Just forget it."

And with that, she left.

SIXTEEN

ASHLEY

The evening went better than expected. Ashley Wittman had been slightly nervous before her date with the guy, Bryan. Not so much because online dating was new to her, it wasn't; she had been trying to find love online for years now, with no luck. No, she was nervous, because she had been talking to this guy for several weeks now and she already knew she liked him. She liked his personality, and he was well-educated and, on top of that, he was very, very handsome. At least in the picture. She had talked to him on FaceTime as well, many times, and knew he wasn't as handsome in real life as in the profile picture, but it was close enough.

He could be the one. This could finally be him, the man I have been waiting for.

She looked at herself in the mirror one last time, before leaving her condo. The thought was exhilarating. But it also terrified her. She was afraid to hope, she was afraid to think like that again, because she had been disappointed so many times.

But as the night went on, Ashley found herself becoming more and more attracted to Bryan. They talked about every-thing and anything, and she found herself laughing and smiling more than she had in a long time. The restaurant they had chosen was cozy and intimate, and the candlelight flickered across Bryan's face in a way that made her heart skip a beat.

As they walked toward her car after a lovely dinner, Bryan took her hand in his and gave it a gentle squeeze.

"I had a really great time with you tonight," he said softly.

Ashley smiled up at him, blushing slightly. Why did she suddenly feel like a high school girl?

"Me too," she replied.

Bryan leaned in closer, pushing a stray strand of hair away from her face. His eyes searched hers for an answer before slowly closing the gap between them. Ashley felt her heart flutter with excitement as their lips met for the first time. She melted into him, feeling a spark of electricity course through her veins as his hands found their way to her hips. He deepened the kiss, his tongue exploring her mouth as he pulled her closer. Ashley moaned softly, wishing that this moment could last forever.

They pulled apart, both of them breathless. Bryan leaned in and whispered in her ear, "Let's go back to my place."

Ashley hesitated for a moment. It was soon, but something about Bryan made her feel like this was the start of something special. She nodded, and Bryan took her hand once more, leading her toward his car.

The drive to his place was filled with anticipation, and Ashley couldn't help but steal glances at Bryan as he drove. Was it just her or was he more handsome now than when they first met earlier in the night? There was something special about him and his confident demeanor only added to his allure.

It was getting harder to keep the hope down.

Easy now, tiger. He could be some weirdo who lives with his mother. Or maybe he collects dolls' heads.

When they arrived at his condo, Bryan led her inside and immediately pulled her into a passionate kiss. There was no mother and no decorated dolls' heads on shelves or on display in glass monitors under spotlights. Ashley decided maybe she had been too paranoid. This was it; this was the time to throw herself in, full blown, with no holding back. She decided, for once, to give herself over completely.

It's now or never.

Ashley moaned into his mouth, her body pressing against his as he lifted her up and carried her toward the bedroom. The way he carried her made her feel light as a feather.

As soon as they entered the room, Bryan's hands were all over her, pulling at the fabric of her dress and leaving a trail of kisses down her neck. Ashley's fingers tangled in his hair as he undressed her, and soon they were both completely naked and tangled up in the sheets.

Bryan's touch was electric, igniting a fire within Ashley that she had never experienced before. Not even with Alex, who she dated for more than three years. This was different. More intense. He knew exactly how to touch her, where to kiss her, and how to make her moan with pleasure. The way he looked at her, with pure desire and passion, made her feel beautiful and wanted in a way she had never felt before.

As they explored each other's bodies, Ashley couldn't help but feel like this was more than just a hookup. There was a connection between them that she couldn't quite put her finger on, but it was undeniable. Bryan felt it too, she could tell by the way he kissed her and held her close.

Like he never wanted to let her go.

Hours passed by as they made love, forgetting the world outside of the bedroom. They were lost in each other, in the pleasure and in the moment. When they finally collapsed in each other's arms, sweaty and exhausted, Ashley knew that this was just the beginning. There would be many more nights like these. Exhausting and exhilarating nights.

· · ·

Later, Ashley opened her eyes to see him lying beside her, expecting the sight of his sleeping handsome face to make her smile.

Only he wasn't there. His side of the bed was empty.

She searched the room for any trace of Bryan. Had she done something wrong? Her mind raced with questions, each one more terrifying than the last.

Just then, she heard the sound of water running from the bathroom. Relief flooded through her as she realized he was just taking a shower. She lay back down, her heart still pounding as she tried to calm herself.

You're being silly as usual, Ashley. Just silly.

But as the moments ticked by, Ashley's anxiety began to grow once again. Bryan had been in the shower for an awfully long time. She couldn't shake the feeling that something was wrong.

Finally, unable to take it any longer, Ashley got out of bed, put on Bryan's T-shirt that he had thrown on the floor and walked to the bathroom. She hesitated for a moment before knocking softly on the door.

"Bryan?" she called out tentatively. "Are you okay?"

There was no response, no sound from inside the bathroom. Ashley's heart sank as she pushed the door open slowly.

The sight that met her eyes made her gasp in shock.

SEVENTEEN

BILLIE ANN

We frantically searched for answers to Cassandra's whereabouts before she was murdered, feeling our time and resources slipping away. Everywhere I went, I found people who had seen her the day before she was murdered, but no one had noticed anything amiss. The last person to have seen her on Saturday night was Mr. Cornwell, and so far, we hadn't gotten anything out of him. Tom had interviewed him, but he was at work that day in Publix and several coworkers gave him an alibi, along with surveillance cameras showing him at the store on that day. But his shift ended at two thirty and he didn't have any alibi for the time after, as he said he was taking a stroll on the beach before returning to his house at four thirty. He was still of interest to me.

Scott and Tom had checked Cassandra's usual spots, like the local mall and the arcade, the library, and the park, talking to people there, asking them questions about her. I even went to the high school, but the principal said she hadn't noticed anything out of the ordinary. Cassandra was a straight-A student who always showed up and was known to be a good friend to everyone. Nothing seemed off. The only person I hadn't spoken to was Cassandra's father.

When I arrived at their house, it was Mrs. Perez's sister who opened the door. She told me to walk into the living room. In there, I was met with a heartbreaking sight; Cassandra's mother was sobbing quietly in the corner of the living room while a man, who I assumed was Cassandra's father, stood still as a statue, his gaze empty of emotion.

I cleared my throat, but they didn't look at me. I walked to the father and reached out my hand.

"I'm Detective Billie Ann Wilde," I said.

He didn't shake my hand, and he didn't turn to face me.

"Are you bringing any news?" he simply asked.

I exhaled. This didn't feel good. I so wanted to help them find closure, and to know what happened to their precious daughter. But I had gotten nowhere still. I needed more information.

"Not yet, but I can assure you we're working very hard on—"

He lifted his hand to stop me. "Spare me your reassurances. We want to see results. Our daughter was brutally taken from us, and we want to see justice done. Is that too much to ask?"

I shook my head. "Of course not. That's why I am here. I was wondering if Cassandra had any more friends that she would hang out with?"

"She was with her track team a lot," the mother answered softly. "They had practice every morning and meets sometimes in the afternoon. They would also go to competitions together on the weekends, sometimes out of the area."

"Could you give me a few names of her closest friends on the team perhaps?" I asked.

The mother nodded. She wrote three names down on a Post-it note then handed it to me.

"Thank you," I said. "There was another thing."

"Yes?" Mrs. Perez said.

"The girl who Cassandra was supposed to babysit on the night she was murdered. How well do you know her and the mother?"

Mrs. Perez looked confused. "I have never met them. Like I said, it was Pete who got her that job."

"Do you know her well?" I asked Mr. Perez.

The father turned around and looked at me, his eyes heavy with sorrow. He shook his head. "She lives down the street, by the pond. To be honest none of us have ever seen the child, but I spoke to the mom, and she said she was looking for a babysitter and I suggested Cassandra. I asked her to go over there and talk to the woman and that's how she got the job."

"Why are you asking about her?" Mrs. Perez said. "Do you think this woman might have hurt our daughter?"

"I don't know who did hurt Cassandra, but I need to look into all possibilities, as you probably understand."

"I'm sorry, but we don't really know them at all," Mrs. Perez said.

"Okay," I said. "I will let you know if anything new comes up."

I had turned to walk away, when Pete Perez stopped me before I could leave.

"Please, find who did this to her," he pleaded softly, his voice full of grief. I believed he was heartbroken.

I nodded and stepped out into the night, determined to bring closure to this devastated family and, as if on cue, Dr. Phillips called me in for the autopsy.

I had no idea what he was going to tell me, but I spent the drive to the medical examiner's office thinking about all the leads that had already reached dead ends. We interviewed the locals in the surrounding areas, people walking their dogs in the street nearby or driving by the pond, just to hear if they had seen anything, in regard to Cassandra. But no one had. People were very nice and helpful, and most had heard about the finding of Cassandra's body and were terrified by it. Yet no one had seen her later than when her mother sent her off for her babysitting job.

I had a few tips from locals that I had Tom and Scott follow up on. They said they saw Cassandra on her bike around town, but that was on the day before she was killed.

There was something odd about the fact that Emma disappeared on the same day Cassandra died, and that they lived on the same street. She was her babysitter, and the Perezes had told me that she was supposed to have taken care of Emma on the evening of the day that the little girl disappeared.

I had combed through every record I could find, trying to find any evidence that might prove that Emma actually existed. But none of the neighbors had ever seen her, and that became a puzzle to me. Even the Perezes said they had never actually seen the child. How was that even possible? The yard was closed in and surrounded by very high bushes, but the girl must have left the house every now and then, right? Going to the park and playground? Someone had to have seen her. According to her mother, she had never even been to the doctor, which I found very strange. When my children were that age, I ran to the doctor once a week, or so it felt. They were sick all the time.

"What about shots?" I had asked. "Who gave her the shots?"

"I don't believe in them," Marissa had answered. "They make children sick. They are no good for them."

I knew of other parents who felt that way, so I couldn't exactly argue against it, but it still puzzled me that she never even took the child to see a pediatrician.

"She was never sick," was her response to my concern when I asked her about it during our first interview. "There was no need to."

I had talked to the personnel at the nearest hospital in Cape Canaveral, in case Emma had somehow ended up there, or to at least let them know to keep an eye out for her if someone brought her in. I scoured social media for any clues. I posted in local Facebook groups letting them know to keep an eye out. I had a drawing made by a professional, from Marissa's early description and memory of her daughter, then sent it out to the local media outlets, and I posted it in local social media groups, hoping to get something.

But everything came up empty.

Chief Doyle's words rang in my ears. To keep searching for a ghost was a long shot, I knew that, and one that could cost me dearly. Yet I couldn't let it go.

I couldn't shake the feeling that there most definitely was more to this case than met the eye.

I thought of Cassandra's family, waiting for answers, while arriving at the medical examiner's office. I felt a strong sense of responsibility, knowing that whatever the report said, it would be my job to deliver the news. I clenched my hands around the steering wheel, steeling myself for whatever lay ahead.

I stepped out of the car and a chill ran down my spine. The air was thick and heavy with a nauseating smell that reminded me of death and decay. As I made my way to the entrance of the morgue, the gravel crunched beneath my shoes.

The door creaked open, and I stepped inside, feeling a chill in the air. Inside was a small room filled with cold metal tables and fluorescent lights. There was a strange stillness in the room that seemed almost eerie to me. Maybe it was just the situation.

I walked farther into the room, my footsteps echoing off the walls. In the corner, a figure emerged from the shadows, shrouded in a white coat. It was Dr. Phillips.

He motioned for me to come closer and handed me a yellowed piece of paper. It was the autopsy report. I would also receive a digital copy, but this would do for now. I followed him into the autopsy room. The smell of antiseptic filled the air, and I could feel my sense of unease grow. I looked around the room. The walls were a dreary white, the air thick with an oppressive silence. We walked in single file, my footsteps echoing off the tiled floor. As we approached the autopsy table, I saw her.

Cassandra Perez.

Her body so small it seemed to barely reach the edges of the table. Her skin was pale, and she had a peaceful look on her face, as if she had been sleeping.

Dr. Phillips approached me, his hands encased in gloves. He touched her neck and then turned to me, his face a mask of sorrow.

"She's been strangled," he said quietly.

I felt my throat tighten, the tears welling up in my eyes. I couldn't believe that this sweet young life had been taken away so cruelly. It just wasn't right.

Dr. Phillips's voice was a whisper as he told me the details of her death. All I could do was nod my head in silence, my heart breaking for this family who had lost their daughter. All I could think was that it could have been me. It could have been me getting the news that I was never going to hold my daughter again.

"There were no signs of rape," he said.

"So, it's not a sexual motive; that's a relief, at least," I said.

"She definitely died from asphyxiation," he said. "But not with the use of hands or a rope or cord. I believe it was a belt that was being used. It was tied around her neck and then tightened. There were pressure marks, bruises, which were similar from that of a belt buckle, a big one."

"Oh, wow," I said. "That's brutal. So drowning is definitely not an option?"

"She was dead when she entered the water, no doubt about it, as there was only a little water in her lungs," he said.

"Time of death?" I asked.

"Death occurred between three and four o'clock the day before she was found," he said.

"Right about the time she was supposed to arrive at Marissa's house, so Marissa could go in for her shift," I said.

Dr. Phillips sighed. It felt deep. He was a renowned medical examiner, who had done so many of these over the years. But this one was getting to him; I could tell as wrinkles grew deep in his weathered face.

"I sometimes wonder... what this world has come to, when anyone can do something like this," he said with a soft exhale. He shook his head sorrowfully.

The chill in the air seemed to penetrate my very bones as I left him and the morgue. I walked back to my car, happy to leave this place behind me, but wondering about the details of this case.

Whoever had killed Cassandra, had probably done so on her way to the babysitting job. But why? And was it the same person who had taken Emma? It was highly plausible. I had to find that girl before it was too late. I was beginning to wonder if Marissa could be a suspect.

The next day I received a call.

EIGHTEEN

BILLIE ANN

It was Rose from the reception desk on the other end. "I have a woman on the line for you. I think you should take it. Sounds urgent."

"Okay, put her through."

"H-hello?"

"Hello, this is Detective Billie Ann Wilde, who am I speaking to?"

A sniffle was followed by a cough. "I don't really know who to talk to, but I know y'all are looking for a young child, right?"

"That's correct. Have you seen her?" I asked.

A silence followed, and I wondered for a second if it was just another prank call. We have had a lot of those lately.

"I think so," she said. "She looked a lot like her if you ask me."

Now she had my attention. "What do you mean? Where?"

"I... I saw a man with a child who fits the description that has been in the media," she said. "He was dragging her along against her will. She didn't seem like she wanted to go with him at all."

"How did the man seem?" I asked.

"Agitated and nervous."

"And where was this?"

"I saw him dragging her by the arm earlier in the day toward a house on Ninth Street. I don't know if it is her, but the picture on the TV caught my attention and I thought I'd let you know. It has been nagging at me ever since."

"Thank you so much. I'm very happy you did," I said and hung up. I stared at the address she had given me. It was right near where Cassandra and Emma both lived. It was worth following up on.

I drove down A1A and stopped at Ninth Street, on the corner where the woman said she had seen him. Then I stopped the engine and sat in a parking space next to it. There were three houses, all small beach bungalows that were usually rented out as one or two bedrooms, often to surfers who just needed to cross the street to get to the beach and those alluring waves.

As I sat there thinking about my own children when they were Emma's age, and how adorable they had been, yet quite a handful, the door to a garage opened and a car backed out. It was a black SUV, and a man fitting the description the woman had given me was sitting in the driver's seat. He had long blond hair in a ponytail and was tall and lanky.

But there was no child in the backseat.

I watched him drive off, then got out of my car and walked closer. I was staring at the house, when I heard the unmistakable sound of a child crying.

It was coming from inside of the garage.

NINETEEN

Then

When Saturday morning finally came around, Kitty woke up early and got dressed in her favorite sundress and sneakers. She couldn't wait to go to Disney World with Officer Damian. She was so excited, she had barely slept, and after she ate breakfast, she stood by the window and stared into the street, jumping at every car that drove by, thinking it was him.

When he finally drove up, she couldn't wait. She opened the door and ran to him. He pulled her into a deep hug.

"Are you ready to go?" he asked, smiling down at her. "Well, it looks like it. What a beautiful dress, almost as pretty as the girl wearing it."

Kitty nodded eagerly and blushed, following Officer Damian out to his car. As they drove to the amusement park, they talked about all the rides they were going to go on and the food they were going to eat. Kitty had never had cotton candy before, or caramel apples, but had heard about them, and always wanted to try them. Damian promised he would get her all of it.

"And Dippin' Dots," he said. "You gotta have some Dippin' Dots too."

"And I wanna meet Mickey, and Minnie, and—oh—Daisy, and all the princesses. Belle is my favorite," she exclaimed.

That made him laugh out loud. "Of course, she is. Because Belle means beautiful, and that's what you are. I'd say that you're even prettier than her. I hope you know that."

Kitty's eyes grew large. She couldn't believe he would say that. That was a very nice thing to say, and she didn't quite know how to respond. No one was prettier than Belle. She blushed and looked out the window, butterflies fluttering in her stomach. She felt like a princess herself. She wished this day would never end. She never wanted to go back to the mobile home park and her parents, who always yelled at her.

When they arrived, Kitty's eyes widened in awe. The park was huge, with roller coasters, water rides, and much more. It was truly as magical as she had imagined. Famous characters were greeting them everywhere. She met Donald Duck, Goofy, and even got to hug Daisy. Later on, Cinderella came waltzing down the street, and Kitty ran to her and got another hug, and Damian took a picture of them together. She got to visit Mickey's house, where both he and Minnie were. She rode the train around the park. She ate cotton candy for the first time and had a caramel apple, all at the same time.

Kitty was practically bouncing with excitement. They raced to the biggest roller coaster they could find, and Officer Damian held tightly on to her hand as they rode the loops and twists. Kitty screamed with delight, and Officer Damian laughed.

After a few hours of riding rides and eating junk food, Officer Damian decided to take a break and sit on a bench with Kitty. As they rested, he reached over and took her hand in his without saying a word. He just held it, and Kitty smiled.

It felt nice. Very, very nice. Officer Damian was such a kind man, and Kitty wished that he was her stepdad instead of Cole.

She looked up at him, endearingly, and he smiled. "All right, kiddo. One more ride, and then we'll need to head back."

"Aww," she said and looked at him beggingly.

He gave her a look. "No, I promised I'd have you back by late afternoon."

"Please can we stay a little longer, please?"

He narrowed his eyes and looked into hers. "What am I going to do with you? Okay, I'll tell you what."

She felt excitement again, as she could tell she was persuading him. She knew she could.

"What?"

"I could call and tell your parents that we're running late due to the *horrible* traffic and then we can stay for *two* more roller coaster rides, how about that? And maybe we can pop in at the Beast's castle and see if Belle is there? A pretty girl like you should at least meet her favorite princess, right?"

She literally jumped in happiness. "Yes, please oh please, yes thank you, thank you."

She had gotten ready to walk away, to run for the line to the roller coaster before he changed his mind, when he stopped her, grabbing her hand.

"Uh-uh," he said, then pointed at his lips.

She paused. His grip was tight on her wrist. What did he want?

"I deserve a proper thank you, don't you think?" he said.

She smiled nervously. She stared at his lips underneath the mustache. There was a little bit of pink cotton candy stuck to the bottom of it.

"Just a little kiss," he said with a grin.

She stared at his lips again, then leaned forward and kissed him, closing her eyes, feeling her heart race in her small chest.

TWENTY

BILLIE ANN

I rang the doorbell first, then knocked hard on the front door when no one answered.

"Cocoa Beach police, open up!"

I could hear the child crying, and it was driving me crazy. I waited patiently, but there was still no answer. I looked around the porch, scanning for any signs of forced entry. The door was locked, so I pulled out my lockpick set and went to work. As I worked on the lock, I could hear the child's cries growing louder, and my heart raced with urgency.

Come on, Billie Ann, come on!

Finally, I heard a satisfying click, and I pushed the door open. The house was dark and quiet, except for the sound of the child's cries. I drew my gun and called out again, "Cocoa Beach police, is anyone here? Hello?"

Suddenly, I heard footsteps rushing down the stairs, and a woman appeared in front of me, her eyes wide with fear. She saw the gun and paused with a light gasp. She was holding the crying child in her arms, and I could see the bruises on the child's face.

"What's going on here?" I demanded, my voice stern.

The woman began to sob. "He hit her again. He's been hitting her for days. I didn't know what to do. I was too scared to call the police."

I took a deep breath, trying to contain my anger. I looked at the woman and child, tears streaming down their faces as they clung to each other. It reminded me why I went into the force in the first place, to protect those who couldn't protect themselves. Domestic abuse happened often, and my involvement could escalate the situation for this woman if I wasn't careful.

"Is he your husband?"

"Y-yes."

"Where is he now?" I asked.

"He's just left," she whispered, "but he'll be back soon. He just went for smokes."

I nodded, signaling for her to stay put.

"Please don't take my babies away."

"Babies? You have more than one?"

My heart ached as I saw the desperation in the woman's eyes. I lowered my gun, trying to ease her fears.

"I'm here to help you and your children. Tell me, where is the other child?"

She glanced toward the door to the garage.

"In there?"

She nodded with a small whimper. "She's been in there for two days now."

Oh dear God.

I approached the door to the garage, keeping my gun at the ready. I could hear the faint sound of crying coming from behind the door. I took a deep breath, bracing myself, ready for anything. I tried the door handle, but it was locked. I pulled out my lockpick set once again and successfully picked the lock. The door creaked open, and I was hit with a musty smell. It was scorching hot inside.

I was met by a sight that made me want to scream in rage. I

found a little girl, no more than four years old, huddled in the corner of a dog crate. The crate had a lock on it. I could tell she was sitting in her own urine and feces. The entire room smelled so bad I had to breathe through my mouth. I was almost in tears as I knelt in front of her. She was crying softly, tears streaming down her face. I approached her slowly, trying not to scare her. Her eyes looked at me, terrified.

"Hey there," I said softly. "It's okay. I'm here to help you."

The little girl looked up at me with big, scared eyes. She didn't say anything, and I could tell she didn't trust me. Who could blame her? Adults weren't safe to her.

"I'm gonna help you get out, okay? I'm not gonna harm you. I once had a little girl like you, but now she's a big girl," I said while picking the lock on the cage. I could tell that the sound of it frightened her. It was probably usually the sound that meant he was back and ready to hurt her again. I bit my lip to force back my tears. Who would be this cruel to a poor child?

The lock clicked open, and I pulled it off, then opened the gate. The girl didn't come out at first, but then her mother came to the doorway, still holding the girl's little sister, and seeing her, she started to move.

"It's okay," her mother whispered. "You can come out. He's not here."

I reached out my hand toward her, and she took it. I felt relief as I led her back into the house along with her mother and sister. They all looked up at me with a mix of fear and hope.

"Everything's going to be okay," I said. "I'm going to get you out of here and someplace safe."

Tears were streaming across the mother's face. She hesitated. "I'm scared. He will find us. I know he will. He's clever like that."

"I won't let him," I said. "Please come with me. For your children's sake."

She paused, still thinking it over, fear rushing over her face.

I knew how she felt. I remembered what it was like to have your freedom taken away from you. To be forced to do something you knew was wrong. To feel ashamed. I'd had someone who was supposed to protect me do the opposite before...

"I will take you to the shelter," I said. "There's one in Rockledge, about half an hour away, that I know is good. They'll provide for you, help you start again. He won't be able to get to you there. Okay?"

She nodded, her eyes still unsure. "O-Okay."

Just as we reached the front door, we heard the sound of a car engine approaching the house. The woman gasped, and I knew we had to act fast. He was parking outside and coming in through the front door.

"Go to the back porch and hide with your children. I'll handle him," I said, my voice firm and authoritative. I couldn't show them that my heart was right now racing in my throat and all my own memories of abuse and violence rushing through me, reminding my body of what happened, how difficult it was for me to fight back, even if I had always thought I was strong.

Because I froze. In shock.

I had been taught self-defense—I knew how to take down dangerous criminals, but when it came to protect myself from the man I thought I could trust, the man who had been like a father to me, I froze. I simply couldn't manage to use any of my training all those years ago.

And it haunted me still.

Why didn't I fight back?

That was the question always lingering on my mind. *Why didn't I?*

I had no answer. All I knew was that I said no. When he leaned toward me, right before he placed a hand over my mouth, I said the word, "No."

I didn't see it coming. I never would have thought he would do such a thing to me. We had been partners, friends, almost family. Joe and I had been to dinners at his house, with his wife. He had taken me under his wing, promised to train me.

I guess it was the shock that made me paralyzed.

But boy, if I could ever go back. The things I would do to his face.

The woman's eyes stared at me in terror, tears streaming down her face. I took a deep breath, steeling myself for what was about to come. The man stepped in through the door. He glared at me, obviously surprised to see the police badge that I was holding up.

"What the hell is going on here?" he growled.

The sound of his voice made me shiver. I had heard the same tone in my old partner when he realized I had told our Chief what happened. He had attacked me in the hallway and yelled at me. It was that same anger I now heard in this man in front of me, and it scared me.

I didn't respond, but I held my gun up, ready to defend myself if necessary.

The man's eyes flickered to the open door, and he took a step toward it. "Where's my family?" he snarled.

I raised my gun higher, now pointing it directly at him.

"Stay back," I warned. "Your family is safe. You need to come with me."

The man sneered. "I'm not going anywhere with you. Who do you think you are? You have no right to interfere in my family."

But he was wrong. I had every right to interfere, because he had been abusing his family. No one had the right to do that, and it was my duty to protect them.

"Put your hands up," I commanded. "You're under arrest."

The man's eyes widened in surprise and then fear. He knew he was caught. He raised his hands slowly, but then suddenly lunged toward me, trying to knock the gun out of my hand. I reacted quickly, sidestepping his attack and grabbing him by the arm. With practiced ease, I twisted his arm behind his back and forced him to the ground. He struggled, but I held him down firmly. I didn't freeze up. I didn't let him intimidate me. Finally, I was able to react, to do the right thing in a situation like this.

"Stop fighting," I ordered. "It's over. You're going to jail."

I handcuffed him and stood up, keeping my gun aimed at him, reading him his Miranda rights, until my backup arrived.

As they took him away, I turned to the woman and her children. They were huddled together, watching me with wide eyes. I walked toward them slowly, trying to ease their fears.

"It's all over now," I said softly, feeling relieved and slightly proud of myself. "You're safe."

As I drove home later that evening, after finishing my report, I could no longer keep the tears at bay. I let them roll and soon I was crying heavily inside of my car. I drove up into my street, and parked in my driveway, then bent over the steering wheel and let it all out, all the fears, all the anxiety and anger about this world and the injustices I had to face every day.

And I still hadn't found Emma. Or put Cassandra's killer behind bars.

TWENTY-ONE

ASHLEY

Ashley stared at the dead body on the floor. The water in the shower was still running. He was lying on the white tiles with his eyes open wide, his body twisted in an unnatural position. Ashley's heart raced as she tried to process what had just happened. She slowly stepped closer to the body, her eyes fixed on the almost purple bruises around his neck.

She knew immediately that he had been strangled. She had watched her share of crime shows, enough to know what that looked like. Her mind raced as she tried to piece together what could have led to this.

How did it happen? Was someone here while I slept? Who did this?

The shock paralyzed her, and she just stood there, frozen, staring at the man she had kissed, held, liked—hours before. He was gone. She was quickly drenched in sweat by the horror of what she was looking at.

Call the police. Grab the phone and call them.

She was about to turn around and walk back into the room to get her phone, when she paused.

They'll think I did it. They'll think I murdered him.

As Ashley stood there, panicking, she noticed something strange. The window was open, despite the hot night air outside. She shivered as she realized that the murderer could still be in the apartment.

Get out. Get out now.

She was slowly backing away from the body, when she heard a rustling noise from behind her. She spun around and found herself face-to-face with someone wearing a ski mask.

In his hand he was holding a belt with a big shiny buckle.

TWENTY-TWO

BILLIE ANN

Joe had a strange look on his face when he came home. I had made dinner and eaten with the kids, wondering what held him up at work.

If he was even at work still.

Joe was in construction and had his own company, which usually meant he could come and go as he pleased. It was a huge help for us because I never knew what my day looked like, and he could pick up the kids and drop them off if needed. Right now, his company was working on building a new hotel on the beach, and it was a big job, but usually he would always be home for dinner at least.

Just not today.

"Oh, hi," he said, almost like he was surprised to see me home, and closed the door behind him. "We're drinking wine now on a weekday?"

"I just had a rough day," I said and sipped my wine.

Joe walked closer, then scoffed. "If you say so."

I frowned. Joe's tone was dismissive, and I could tell he was upset. His eyes avoided mine, and I could feel the tension building in the room.

"What's that supposed to mean?"

"Whatever."

He left. I followed him. "Hey, what was that? We can't even talk anymore?"

"You chose that, not me," he said with a sniffle. "You're the one deciding to ruin a perfectly well-functioning family."

"Well-functioning? Maybe it wasn't so well-functioning for me," I said.

"Oh, wow," he said.

I bit my lip. I really wasn't in the mood for this right now. He looked at me. I saw deep disdain in his eyes and that hurt.

"Did you sleep with a woman? Did you cheat on me?"

I was taken aback.

"No!" I said quickly, quietly.

He ran a hand through his hair. "It's just really hard thinking about you with someone else."

I exhaled. "I know. But I haven't."

"But you want to. And you're going to."

He was tearing up, and it broke my heart. My voice cracked as I spoke.

"Listen, Joe. I'm sorry for all of this. I really truly am."

He paused and bit back his tears. "It's not fair. I went through cancer with you, I feared you would die, I held your hand through chemo and held your hair when throwing up, while terrified I'd lose you. I saw you lose your beautiful hair and all I could think about was that you might die. And yet I lied. I told you sweet little lies about how your hair didn't matter. That I didn't love you because of your hair, and that I didn't care. Of course, I cared. You losing your hair reminded me every day that you might die, that I might lose you. But you didn't die. You survived. And now I am still losing you? It's not fair."

I stared at him, trying hard to breathe. I felt awful. No, it was more than that. It crushed me completely to see him like this. Breaking his heart, the way I did, was the hardest thing I ever had to do.

I hate myself for doing this.

I wanted to tell him how sorry I was, how awful I felt. I wanted to tell him that I loved him, that I hated being this selfish. But I never got around to it.

I felt like screaming and crying at the same time. This was so tough. Why did everything have to be so freaking hard?

Joe had turned around and left me to go upstairs, slamming the door behind him, when my phone vibrated in my pocket. It was Chief Doyle.

Now what?

"I need you," he said.

TWENTY-THREE

BILLIE ANN

Please let it not be another child, please don't let it be another child. Please don't let it be Emma.

I drove through the rain and darkness toward the apartment complex on the beach downtown. My heart was racing, and I could barely breathe, worried that another child had been killed. I couldn't bear the thought.

Chief Doyle had been very vague on the phone and didn't know much, only that I needed to be there. They suspected it was murder. But what exactly waited for me there, I didn't know, and I feared the worst as I drove toward the beach and the condos there. It was one of the newer condominiums, built within the past three years, the ones that cost about a million dollars each and came with spectacular views of the Atlantic Ocean.

As I reached the apartment complex, I parked my car and made my way toward the entrance, passing the patrol cruisers in the front with their flashers on. The sound of the rain drowned out every other noise, and the gusts of wind made it difficult to walk. I shuddered, partly from the pouring rain soaking me and partly from the fear that gripped me.

I took the elevator to the third floor, where I found the door to the apartment I was looking for. I took a deep breath before approaching, my heart pounding in my chest. The door opened, and I was greeted by Officer Steele. Big Tom was already there, and he greeted me with a nod.

"You always get the lucky calls, huh?" I said to Steele. "What have you got?"

"It was a neighbor who walked by in the hallway and saw that the door to the apartment was open. As it was late, she worried that something was wrong and knocked on the door, before walking in. She heard the water running and found the door to the bathroom open, then peeked inside, while calling out for Bryan, the occupant's name, worried that he had fallen or something. She found him in there, already dead. She recognized him as her neighbor right away. Tom has spoken to her and taken her statement."

I nodded. "Male? Adult?"

"Yes. Dr. Phillips is in the bathroom with him. He told me you could go straight in when you got here."

I touched Officer Steele's arm gently. He gave me a tired look.

"Thank you."

I went to the bathroom, where Dr. Phillips was standing bent over the body. It was a relief that it wasn't another child, I had to admit, but still hit me hard. Any life taken too soon was unbearable.

"Detective Wilde," Dr. Phillips said with an exhale. "We need to stop meeting like this."

It was an old joke that he had used many times before. Still, I smiled at it politely. I stepped closer to the body. The man was young, probably in his early thirties. He was lying on the floor, naked, with his eyes wide open, staring up at the ceiling. Bruises on his neck told me everything I needed to know.

They were similar to Cassandra's and that terrified me.

"What do you know?" I asked, trying to keep my voice steady. I didn't like what I was looking at one bit, that was for sure.

"We won't know with certainty until the autopsy," Dr. Phillips said. "But it looks familiar, right? I'd say he was strangled with a leather belt with a big buckle. His body is clean and hair still wet, so I assume he was in the shower, then was attacked when he came out. Killer came up from behind and used the belt to strangle him."

My heart sank. It was a tragic end for a young life.

"Do we know who he is?"

Dr. Phillips nodded. "His name is Bryan Henderson. The neighbors identified him. This is his condo."

I closed my eyes and took a deep breath, trying to stay focused. I had seen too much death in my career as a detective, but it never got any easier. I nodded. "All right. We need all evidence bagged and secured. If this killer left any DNA behind, I want it found."

I said the words to Tom as I stepped back out into the bedroom. I walked around the bed and noticed it had been slept in. It was ripped up on both sides, and the sheet messed up on both sides as well. There were smears of makeup on the pillow on the right side. I took a picture with my phone for myself. Then I spotted a hair, a long blond one. I signaled for Steele to bring me an evidence bag and put it in and sealed it. I handed it to him.

"Bryan wasn't alone last night. Someone was here with him," I said and lifted a wineglass up from the side of the bed. It had visible smears of lip gloss on it. I handed it to Steele to secure it safely. I then found a bra on the floor, which he secured as well, using tweezers to pick it up. I spotted a dress on the floor.

"I'd say he had female companionship. And said female was in a hurry to get out of here. She didn't even have time to get dressed. I bet you her phone and maybe even wallet might be here somewhere too."

TWENTY-FOUR

Then

Kitty's mom left early for work that morning. Her stepdad was already gone as usual, for his job at the auto shop. Her mom looked at her just before she left, then kissed her cheek.

"You'll have to walk to the bus by yourself. I think you're old enough. Can you do that?"

Kitty nodded. "Of course."

Kitty put on her favorite pink dress and grabbed her backpack. Her mom had forgotten to make her lunch, so she smeared some peanut butter on a piece of toast, put some jelly on top, and put it in a bag, all while eating cereal. She also grabbed a bag of chips from the pantry and a pack of cookies, taking advantage of the fact that her parents weren't there to tell her not to.

Smiling happily, she walked up the small hill toward the bus stop at the end of her street. It was hot out, and she became sweaty quickly. She passed the swampy area close to their house and gasped lightly. She had seen a gator in the water a few weeks ago, and she had run to the other side of the street. The branches heavy with Spanish moss seemed like they were reaching for her, and she picked up the pace. After ten minutes of walking, it seemed like the bus stop was even farther away than when she started. She was feeling so hot and tired already.

Kitty looked up at the scorching sun and wiped the sweat off her forehead and upper lip. She wondered if she should have worn shorts instead of the pink dress, but she loved the way the dress fluttered when she turned. Suddenly, a car pulled over by her side, and the window lowered.

At first, she didn't pay them any attention; she had been taught not to talk to strangers and knew better than that. But then a familiar voice called out her name.

"If it isn't pretty Kitty?"

She stopped and smiled. This was no stranger. "Officer Damian!"

"Please, just Damian," he said. "What are you doing out here all alone in this scorching heat?"

"I'm walking to the school bus," she said.

"Oh, you haven't heard?" he said.

"Heard what?"

"School is canceled for today. The AC broke down, and they can't teach when it is this hot."

She felt lost. "School is canceled? But what...?"

"How about I take you out for an ice cream instead, huh? Doesn't that sound way more fun? No one wants to do anything in this heat anyway, am I right? I'll call your mom and let her know where you are. She'll be happy to know that you're safe with me."

Ice cream did sound good. Very good actually.

"Can I get cookies and cream?"

That made him laugh. "You can get any ice cream you want to, baby girl. Any flavor you crave."

He reached over and opened the door for her, so she could get in. Kitty stared up the hill, at the other kids who were waiting for the bus. She felt bad for them that they didn't know that school was canceled, and that you could go get ice cream instead.

She got into the car, and they took off. She looked out the window at the kids from her school, who were still standing there, like it was any ordinary day.

Little could she have known it was the last time she would see them.

TWENTY-FIVE

BILLIE ANN

"Right there, stop."

I pointed at the screen, and the man clicked the mouse. His name was Blake, and he was the president of the board of the condominium where we had found the body of Bryan Henderson. He was also the one responsible for the cameras that had been put up around the building. He hadn't been home himself when the murder took place, so he hadn't seen anything helpful. But I was hoping the cameras had.

"There she is," I said and tried to get a good look at the face of the woman walking into the building with Bryan Henderson earlier this same night. I recognized the dress she was wearing as the same blue one I had found on the floor. I took a picture of the screen with my phone, then asked Blake to send all the files to us so we could go through them.

"Okay, that's her arriving," I said. "Can you fast-forward it a little, so we can see when she leaves?"

He nodded, pushed his glasses back up in place and clicked the mouse. He was an elderly man, but seemed to be on top of what he was doing. He kept rolling the footage, but nothing happened. The next-door neighbor who found the body came home and entered through the main entrance. I recognized her after I had interviewed her. But there was no sign of the woman who had been with Henderson.

"That's odd," I said, "try to go back again."

We went back and then ended up with the same result. No footage of the woman leaving the building.

"That's it," Blake said and took off his reading glasses. He looked up at me with a shrug. "That's all there is, I'm afraid."

I pursed my lips, deep in thought. Something wasn't adding up. If the woman had entered the building with the victim, why wasn't there any footage of her leaving?

"Are you sure there's no other footage?" I asked Blake, my eyes fixated on the screen. "Maybe from another camera angle?"

"We have a camera in the parking lot as well, let me check."

I waited impatiently, tapping my foot on the ground. Blake's office was cluttered with files and paperwork, and the stale scent of coffee lingered in the air. I couldn't help but feel a sense of unease.

"No, nothing there either," he said. "Only of them entering. Not leaving."

"Are there any other exits?"

He shook his head slowly. "Only the fire escapes."

"Are they surveyed by cameras?"

He shook his head with a frown. "Our HOA budget only allowed for these two cameras. I'm sorry, Detective. I wish I could be of more help," he said, his voice apologetic.

I sighed, feeling frustrated.

"Okay, thanks for your help, Blake."

He nodded, and I made my way out of his office, trying to make sense of this new development. Why had this woman not used the main entrance when leaving? Because she murdered Bryan Henderson and didn't want to be on camera? Perhaps.

As I walked down the hallway toward the elevator, I felt a

presence behind me. I turned around, but no one was there. I shook my head and continued walking, feeling paranoid.

This whole case was getting to me in a weird and uncomfortable way.

In the elevator I looked at the photo of the woman on my phone. I would have to go to bars and restaurants tomorrow and ask them if they had seen her with Bryan, maybe there would be some surveillance footage of them together. I had to find her, and fast. Either she was the murderer, or she had seen the murderer. Either way she was an asset to me. One I couldn't afford to lose. Bryan Henderson had been murdered the exact same way as Cassandra Perez, so this was by far the strongest lead to finding her killer and, hopefully, the person who had taken Emma as well.

TWENTY-SIX

BILLIE ANN

I got a few hours of sleep, once I returned to my house. I stayed in the guestroom downstairs, as I didn't want to wake up Joe, and if I was being honest, it was just as much for my own sake. I didn't want to talk anymore. I didn't want to face his anger and reproach again. I was too exhausted for that.

My golden retriever, Zelda, was the only one greeting me when I came home, and I let her sleep in my bed with me all night, bringing me great comfort. I loved that crazy dog so much.

The next morning, I hung out with the kids over breakfast, taking my time because it was after all Saturday, but I never saw Joe. He didn't come down, so I had to prepare breakfast on my own and walk Zelda before I could leave for work. I showered downstairs and grabbed a clean button-down shirt from the laundry room.

I glanced toward the stairs as I grabbed my belt and badge and then retrieved my gun from the safe and strapped it on. I was still hoping he would come out and maybe tell me to have a good day at work, but he didn't. Instead, I texted him that I had left for work and that there was coffee in the pot.

Then I left. Coffee in my YETI cup, I drove to the police station, where Tom and Scott were waiting for me.

I sat at my desk and sipped my coffee, then turned on my computer. I stared at Tom, he looked exhausted, but I guess I was one to speak. It had been a long night for the both of us. It was the weekend, but we had no time to rest.

"Any news from the forensic department?" I asked. "Anyone had time to look it over?"

Scott raised his hand. "I came in early and went through it."

"Did they find the woman's phone and purse?" I asked. "Or a wallet?"

He shook his head. "Nothing but Bryan Henderson's things. His phone, car keys, credit cards, computer, and so on."

"They didn't find this woman's phone? Or purse?" I asked, leaning back in my chair, feeling baffled. If this woman had been running out of this condo so fast, she didn't put on her dress or bra, then how the heck did she remember her phone and purse?

"Nope. Just the clothing."

"So, we have no way of identifying this woman?" I asked. "How about his phone? Any texts from her?"

He shook his head. I felt frustrated. I had been so certain we would find something that could lead us to her. "She left the condo without clothes, but had time to grab her belongings?"

Scott shrugged. "Maybe she never took them there. So, she wouldn't be identified."

"Scott has a point," Tom said. He placed his hands behind his head and tipped his chair backward, reminding me of my teenagers. "If she planned this all along, she would never leave something so important behind."

"Okay, so have there been any reports of a naked woman

running around in the streets?" I asked. "Maybe with a purse and phone but no clothes?"

"There was no shirt on the floor," Tom said. "She might have put on his. Maybe to draw less attention to herself. A dress and high heels might be something people notice. Maybe she also knew we would be looking for a woman in that dress because we have the surveillance footage."

"So, you're saying she had it all planned out," I said.

"Yes. That's why she took the other exit. So, we wouldn't see her on the surveillance cameras. She's being smart."

I tilted my head. "I'm not buying it."

"Why not?"

"I saw the footage of them entering the building. She's not a very big woman, and Bryan was a big guy. She would have to be very, very strong in order to strangle him with a belt."

Tom shrugged. "Some women are strong as heck. Just sayin'. The fact is, we don't see anyone else arrive or leave on the cameras, do we? So, if there was someone else, then how did this person get in and out?"

"Same way that the girl left?" I said. "Undetected. Out of the sight from the cameras."

"She's got a point," Scott said.

Tom grumbled something I couldn't hear.

"Okay, let's say I run with it," I continued. "Would that mean that this woman has killed Cassandra too? And taken Emma?"

Tom shrugged. "I guess that's what we're looking at, right? She might be a victim too, and we just haven't found her. I know it hurts to hear, but we still gotta consider the possibility."

I exhaled. I knew he was right.

"We need to find this woman. And fast. Tom, how about you go down to the local bars and restaurants in the area and ask them if she was in there last night, and if she was with Bryan

Henderson? Ask for any surveillance footage if they have cameras.

"And Scott, you go talk to Bryan Henderson's colleagues and friends. Let's get to know this guy and his relationship with this woman. Maybe they'll know who she is. Even better maybe they'll know *where* she is."

TWENTY-SEVEN

BILLIE ANN

"Got it!"

It was the end of the afternoon that I received the message. We had grabbed coffee and a snack at Café Surfnista, which was located down the street from the police station and had just come back when I saw it.

"What do you mean?" Tom asked.

"I know who she is," I said with a smile. "The woman on the footage. God, I love social media."

"Okay, rewind for a second," Scott said. "For those of us who aren't as bright as you."

"I posted the photo that I took of the girl with Bryan Henderson in our local Facebook groups and someone wrote to me privately that she was her neighbor. The neighbor is up in Boston now. She is a snowbird and only comes down here for three months during wintertime with her husband and dog, but the girl lives there full-time, she says. I got the address and everything. Her name is Ashley Wittman. And she has a prior. For stealing a car with her friend."

Tom rose to his feet. "What are we waiting for?"

. . .

The condominium where Ashley Wittman lived was located with a view of the Banana River on the backside of our barrier island. It was where you could watch the gorgeous sunsets at night over the mainland, and where dolphins and manatees could be spotted in the water regularly. Every day the Dolphin Tours would go by, helping the tourists see those playful and alluring animals, while telling the town's history.

As we drove toward her condo, I couldn't help but feel a sense of excitement and anticipation. Finally, we were getting somewhere in this case. The sun was setting, casting a pink and orange glow over the water, and the palm trees swayed gently in the warm breeze. I couldn't help but feel a little envious of Ashley's view. It was absolutely gorgeous.

When we arrived at the condo, we were met with a gate and a camera. We rang her door number on the intercom, but no one answered, so we tried a couple of others. Tom flashed his badge to whoever answered the camera phone, and we were buzzed in. We made our way inside the building. Ashley lived on the top floor, so we took the elevator up.

When we knocked on her door, there was no answer. I had gotten her phone number from her neighbor, and we tried calling, but her phone was off. We decided to wait for her to come back. We could see the sunset from the platform, and it was even more stunning from up there.

Still there was no Ashley Wittman.

Tom looked at the door, got impatient, then knocked again.

"Cocoa Beach police, open up."

As he knocked harder the third time, the door slid open. It wasn't locked. He gave me a look, lifting his eyebrows, then stepped inside the hallway.

"Ms. Wittman, this is Cocoa Beach police. We'd like to ask you a few questions regarding Bryan Henderson. May we come in?" he asked, keeping his voice firm but polite.

Still no answer. He shrugged. "I don't think she is here. Let's just go back... wait a second."

There was alarm in his voice. He grew pale and his eyes widened as he looked at me. I stepped closer, hand lightly resting on the grip of my gun. Sweat sprang to the back of my neck.

"What? What do you see?"

He gave me a look of concern, then pointed and mouthed. "Blood."

My heart rate skyrocketed. I took a step inside and stood next to him. He was right. On the wall by the door was a light switch with blood smeared all over it. Bloody fingers had been touching it, and the wall around it. It had happened recently. It looked fresh.

Tom quickly scanned the entrance while I examined the light switch and took pictures of it with my phone. There was no sign of a struggle in the condo, but the disarray of the furniture suggested a hurried exit. A basket by the entrance had been pushed to the floor, and keys, sunglasses, and phone charging cords were spread all over the tiles. There were bloody fingerprints on the walls and door handles. My heart sank at the thought of where this blood came from. There had been no blood on the body. Bryan had been strangled. So, was the blood Ashley's? Had she been hurt somehow? Maybe while running away? But what was she running from? Why was she running? Because of what she had done? Or was it the killer?

I was leaning toward the latter. Yet I wasn't taking any chances.

"Let's split up and search the rest of the condo," I said quietly to Tom, pulling out my gun. "Be careful."

Tom nodded and headed toward the living room, while I moved toward the hallway leading to the bedrooms. The silence was deafening, the only sound was of our own footsteps on the marble tiles.

As I approached the first door on the left, I noticed it was slightly ajar. I pushed it open with my foot and stepped inside, keeping my gun ready. My heart was racing in my chest.

It was a small room with a queen-sized bed and a dresser. There was no one there, but the room was in disarray, with clothes strewn about and drawers pulled open. I walked toward the bed. I spotted a white T-shirt on the carpet and touched it with my foot. It had huge bloodstains on it. The T-shirt was a man's, judging from the size of it, and my guess was it was most likely Bryan's. Ashley had been wearing this when running from his place. As I moved inside of the bathroom, I noticed something else that made my heart throb.

It was more blood. Inside of the sink. Lots of it. On the porcelain sides, and on the soap dispenser. The towel hanging on the wall also had bloodstains on it.

Someone had washed blood off their hands recently.

"I'm calling it in," I said and grabbed my phone. "We need the techs to get in here ASAP, so we can determine who this blood belongs to."

TWENTY-EIGHT

Then

He had a nice house. When Kitty arrived at Officer Damian's place, he held the door open for her so she could go in. Inside a woman stood by the stove. She smiled at Kitty when she saw her.

"Welcome," she said.

Kitty looked at Damian, puzzled. "Who is she?"

"That's my wife," he said. "Her name is Linda."

Kitty looked disappointed. "I didn't know you had a wife."

He smiled and touched her cheek gently. "But now you do."

"Do you want anything?" Linda said. "A soda? Gatorade?"

Kitty nodded. "Blue Gatorade, please. That's my favorite."

"Then that is what you'll get."

Officer Damian's wife poured Kitty a glass of blue Gatorade before retreating to the living room. Kitty took a seat at the kitchen counter, her eyes scanning the room. It was a nice house, and she felt comfortable there, but it was still hard for her to believe that Damian had been hiding a wife from her all this time. Why had he kept her a secret?

Damian reached out and took her hand, his thumb rubbing circles over the back. "You don't have to be jealous. I only have eyes for you, Kitty."

She raised an eyebrow. "Really?"

He leaned in, his lips brushing against her ear. "Absolutely. You're the one who's captured my heart. You are the prettiest girl in the world. At least to me."

Kitty felt her cheeks flush as Damian pressed a soft kiss to her neck. She couldn't deny the attraction between them and the way his touch sent shivers down her spine.

"Also, there are things that my wife can't help me with. I have needs that she can't fulfill. That's where you come in."

Kitty stared at him. His piercing eyes felt like they saw straight through her. She wasn't sure she understood what he was saying.

"When is my mom coming?" she asked, feeling uncomfortable all of a sudden.

He kissed the top of her hand. "Come on, Kitty. Don't tell me you don't love me anymore?"

She tilted her head. Love? What did he mean? Kitty knew that she loved her mom, and sometimes her stepdad; occasionally when he wasn't drunk, she liked him. But did she love Officer Damian the same way?

"When am I going home?" she asked.

Damian smiled and shook his head. "You're staying here tonight. I just spoke to your mom, and she said it was okay."

Her eyes lit up. "Like a sleepover? Does that mean I don't have to go to school tomorrow? But I didn't bring any of my stuff."

"It's okay," Damian said. "We have stuff."

She sipped her Gatorade. "Oh, okay. Cool." She stared at the front door.

Damian saw this and walked to it, then locked it. The sound of the door clicking made her gasp.

"It's okay," he said. "Don't be scared. I'm a police officer, remember? Gotta protect my family against criminals. Can't have no robbers and burglars and such come in here and hurt my loved ones, okay?"

"I'm family?" she asked, puzzled.

He nodded. "Yes, Kitty. You are now. You live here with me. You're part of this family. Our family."

"But I already have a family," she said, suddenly feeling panic set in at the thought of not going home to her mother. "I... I have a mom. I miss my mom. I want to go home now, please."

He shook his head. "I'm sorry, sweetie. Your family didn't want you anymore. That's why they sent you here. They want you to come live with me. You belong to me now, you hear me?"

Belong to him? What did that mean? Why was he sounding so angry all of a sudden? He never sounded like that before.

Kitty tried hard not to, but she couldn't help herself. She began to sob. Tears ran down her cheeks, and her torso was jerking.

"No, no, no crying," he said, lifting his finger in the air. "There will be no crying in this family, do you hear me?"

That just made her cry even harder. She didn't know what else to do. She felt so helpless. Soon Officer Damian lost his temper, and he slapped her across the face. Kitty gasped and stopped crying immediately. She stared at him with eyes wide, her cheek burning from the slap.

"Now you shut up, do you hear me?" he said, panting.

Kitty looked into his eyes. They had changed. They didn't look at her the same way, like he thought she was pretty. No, they were angry and harsh and cold as stone. Kind of like Cole when he got very drunk. He could get mean like that. Well, not completely like this. This was more. She knew she needed to get out of there. She took her Gatorade and spilled it on purpose on the wooden floors.

"What the heck? Oh my God, you're clumsy!" he growled.

He went to get a towel. When he turned his back at her, she sprang for the front door. She grabbed the lock and flipped it, then opened the door and leaped outside. But as she did, an arm grabbed her around the neck and pulled her back. Officer Damian then took out a stun gun and tased her. It felt like a stunning jolt, like putting a finger to a light socket or on the fence when feeding the horses at the farm down the street, only this didn't stop. It continued. Shocks of electricity shot through her small body till the pain made her pass out.

TWENTY-NINE

BILLIE ANN

It was late before I made it home. I drove through the town in the darkness, wondering about Ashley Wittman and where she could be. I had finished my report on the murder of Bryan Henderson, and I couldn't—for the life of me—figure out what his connection was to Cassandra or Emma. Tom had done a great deal of work, and we could strike out several leads. Bryan Henderson didn't work with anyone in connection to the girls; he had no relation to the Perez family or Marissa; he had never stepped foot at Cassandra's school; and he had no links to the area where they lived, or where Cassandra's body was found. Nothing seemed to connect them. A neighbor had called in and told us that she had seen a man come and go regularly from Marissa's house, and I couldn't help wondering if Marissa had a boyfriend she hadn't told us about.

In a moment of exhaustion Tom suggested that our guy was just a random murderer who killed for the fun of it, toying with us, by choosing victims that were very different and had no connection. Then he once again questioned whether or not Emma even existed.

That's when I decided it was time for us all to go home. We were tired and nothing good came of that. We needed rest.

I had driven up my street and into my driveway, when I realized my mother's car was in my spot.

What's she doing here?

I wasn't exactly in the mood for company and especially not hers.

I exhaled and braced myself, then walked inside. I spotted Joe sitting at the dining room table, a beer in front of him. My mom was in the kitchen doing the dishes. The house smelled like food, and I saw that there was a meatloaf on the counter.

"Mom?" I said, putting down my keys. "What are you doing here?"

"Joe asked me to come."

She smiled. It came off as very forced and uncomfortable. I knew that smile. She wanted to talk. She had that look in her eyes—of compassion, but also like she was about to tell me the hard truth about something.

"Come sit."

I felt like a child in trouble. I opened a bottle of white wine, poured myself a glass, and then sat down at the table with Joe and took a long sip. I knew my mother well enough to know that the conversation she was about to have would be a heavy one.

"Did the kids eat?" I asked.

Joe nodded. "Your mom cooked. They're in their rooms."

"Good."

"Sweetie, we need to talk," my mother said, sitting down at the table across from me. Her voice was soft, but I could hear the edge of worry in it. She looked at my wineglass with concern, and it made me feel guilty.

I sat up straight, bracing myself for whatever was coming. "Okay, it's been a long day, so I'm really tired. You know, with trying to solve a double homicide and all that. But by all means.

Let's talk now. No time like the present, right? What's going on, Mom?" I asked.

Joe looked up at me, his eyes sympathetic. I didn't want his pity.

"What's going on?" I repeated.

My mother exhaled. "Honey. Joe has told me everything."

I frowned. "Everything? What do you mean?"

I sipped my wine.

My mom's lips shivered nervously. "He's told me... he's said that you and he are... um..." She paused, unable to get the words out. I knew she was against divorce and thought people today didn't do enough to fight for their marriages, like she had done with my father. I knew this was going to be a blow for her, and that was probably why I hadn't been able to tell her yet. I needed to deal with my own emotions first.

"Separating, yes," I said. "I was going to tell you but haven't gotten around to it yet. We haven't exactly seen each other in a while."

She looked at me like she felt sorry for me, her shoulders slumping, her head tilted, eyes concerned. Like I had just told her I had been fired or lost someone dear to me. It almost seemed condescending, and it infuriated me. Why did she have to worry? Couldn't she just be proud of me for once? If for nothing else, then for the hard work I'm doing? Trying to stop a murderer?

"Yes," she said, bobbing her head. "He told me that."

"Okay," I said. "I can understand why you're upset, but in all fairness, I was going to tell you eventually. I just wanted to do it face-to-face. And I wanted to tell you so myself, but apparently Joe thought he could just blurt it out—"

She placed a hand on my arm. "He told me everything, Billie Ann. And I'm grateful he did."

Everything? As in *everything*?

My eyes grew wide. I stared at her, then at Joe, then back at her, baffled at this news.

"Excuse me?"

She nodded again. "Joe told me the reason why you are splitting up. And I want you to think about this carefully, Billie Ann. Do you hear me? These things are not something you play around with."

"These things? What things, Mom?" I asked, feeling myself getting worked up. I wasn't surprised at her reaction, but it still angered me. I wanted her support. She was my mother, and I craved it. Of course, I did. I think anyone in my situation would want that.

"Now there is no reason to take a tone with me," she said, her lips growing tight. "I'm only here to help."

I shook my head in disbelief. "Help? Help with what?"

"Help you to not destroy your family over something so silly, Billie Ann," she said with a light snort.

"Did you just call the fact that I'm gay silly?" I asked. It was so ridiculous I almost laughed. Maybe I would have if it wasn't my own mother talking to me. The very woman whose acceptance I really wanted.

"It is silly, Billie Ann. You're not a lesbian. Look around you. You have a husband and three lovely children."

"I do have that, but I'm still a lesbian, Mom. Besides, you aren't much better yourself. I know your secrets, Mom—you think you successfully kept things from me and Andrew?"

My mom winced. She didn't like anyone speaking about my little brother.

"I'm allowed to say his name, Mom."

I took a deep sip of my wine. I was so furious, I could barely sit in my chair. How could Joe do this to me? How could he tell my mother like this? How could he out me to her?

"No, you are not a lesbian," my mom said, after a few breaths. I knew mentioning Andrew would make her feel awful, but I guess that's why I did it. It didn't stop her, though, and she continued, nostrils flaring as she spoke.

"Will you stop with that nonsense."

Her deep disdain made me feel sick to my stomach. I bit back my anger. "You can't tell me what I am, Mother."

"I'm sure you think that you are... *that*... I don't doubt that at all, Billie Ann. But you're just going through a crisis right now. It's perfectly normal. We all go through those things. So, you felt attracted to a woman? It's a phase, and soon you will wake up and realize what you have done, that you have ruined a perfectly well-functioning family, and then what? How will you get it all back? Being attracted to another woman once in your life is normal. But it passes."

"Yeah, well, it has been going on for me since I was a young teenager, and it hasn't passed, how about that for a phase, huh, Mom?" I said, finishing my glass. I pushed my chair back, got up and poured myself another glass. I stood by the sink looking out into the darkness at the swaying palm trees by the canal I lived on. I didn't want to look at those two sitting in my kitchen. I didn't want to talk about this anymore.

"Nonsense," my mom said. "You dated Ricky in high school, remember? You were heartbroken when he broke up with you."

I turned to face her. "I only dated him because everyone wanted me to. I felt pressured into it. I never cared about him. And guess what? I never even slept with him. Because I didn't want to. He kept pushing for it, but I couldn't do it. Because the very thought made me nauseated. That's why he broke up with me. Because I kept saying no to him. How about that?"

She scoffed. "That's not true. You didn't sleep with him because you were a well-raised Christian young lady, who knew she had to wait till she was married. We had taught you that."

I tilted my head. "Yeah, well, I kissed my best friend Monica in the bathroom at prom, and believe you me, I wanted to do more than that, if I had dared to. But I didn't. Because I had been taught that what I was, who I was, was wrong. That's what they said to us in church, Mom. That we were wrong. That I was sick and suffering from sin. That I would go to hell. That God despised me. That I was under the influence of the devil. How do you think that made me feel? How was I supposed to stand up and tell you who I was? How could I not marry a man when I was taught that was the only right thing to do?"

My mom went quiet for a few seconds. She looked down at her hands, then back up at me, while I sipped my wine.

"There are treatments available, Billie Ann," she said, her voice growing stern, like I was some unruly teenager who didn't listen. "I know this is all just because of what happened to you, that awful incident with your former partner. It has made you hate men. You're in pain because of that, and that's understandable, but there is no need to let it ruin your life, your beautiful family. Think about the children. There are clinics that can help. Or maybe we can ask Pastor Stan to help you. You remember him, right? I know he's done stuff like this before. It's just a phase, Billie Ann. It's all about how you act on it. You don't have to go down this path. It's a choice and right now your choices are about to hurt a lot of innocent people. People you love and care for. We can help you."

I stared at her, unable to speak. I couldn't believe her. I couldn't believe that she was actually saying these things to me right now.

"Why won't you listen to me, Billie Ann?" she continued. "I'm your mother. I know my daughter, and she is not some lesbian. Homosexuality is an abomination. Read Leviticus eighteen, verse twenty-two."

That was it for me. I was done. I went to the front door and opened it.

"I want you to leave. I can't deal with you, and this, right now. Please."

My mom looked at me in disbelief. Then she turned to face Joe. He shrugged and said with a sigh, "At least we tried."

"I can't believe you'd ask your own mother to leave your house," she said as she passed me. "After all that I have done for you."

"If you can't accept me for who I am, then I can't be around you," I said. "It's as simple as that. Oh, and I have a Bible verse for you too, Mom. Galatians six, verse seven. 'Do not be deceived. God is not mocked, for you will reap whatever you sow.' You sow hatred, Mom, that's what you get back."

She looked at me, almost with disgust, and it made me feel so sick, so vulnerable. But I didn't let her see that. I bit my sadness back, and as she walked out, I closed the door behind her. Then I looked at Joe who was standing in the doorway to the kitchen. I shook my head.

"Wow. Just wow, Joe."

I went to the guest room, and closed the door behind me, then fell to my knees on the floor and cried.

THIRTY
MARISSA

Riding down the road made her heart race. Marissa felt dizzy, and sick to her stomach, as she pulled over to the side of the street and got off her bike.

There it was. The house.

She was breathing heavily as she stared at the front yard and the red door. It was still early in the morning, and they were all sleeping. But soon they would get up and the place would be busy.

She could imagine exactly what it sounded like. She envisioned every step, every voice, as she would lie awake and try to listen to them, to no avail. Small feet tapping across the wooden floors. Voices—some were crying, some yelling at each other. Voices that would grow older as the years passed and sound different. It was the sound of life. Of children.

How she longed to hold them, to kiss their hair and smell them. She missed the closeness, the breastfeeding, the connection, the love. The deep and wonderful love she had felt for them.

And then it was gone. They grew older.

Oh, Emma, where are you, my baby? I need you to come home. I need to be with you. I need you with me. My body, my entire being longs for you.

She leaned her head forward and let the tears stream down her cheeks.

"I can't do this anymore. I can't be without you," she cried. "I can't lose you too."

Marissa felt like she was suffocating, like everything was closing in on her. She sat there on the curb for a moment longer, the weight of her grief crushing her chest. She couldn't shake off the feeling of loss that had consumed her after Emma had gone missing. The raw pain was still there, pulsing through her veins like poison.

With a deep breath, she wiped away her tears and looked up at the house again. Suddenly, something caught her attention. There was a light on in one of the windows on the second floor. She squinted, trying to make out any movement inside.

Her heart skipped a beat when she saw a figure moving around behind the curtains. It was small, childlike.

Marissa held her breath. Her heart was pounding so hard that she could hear the blood rushing in her ears. Seeing this child, she couldn't stop smiling. She felt a surge of hope and adrenaline coursing through her veins.

Emma.

Tears rushed down her face, and she got to her feet. She walked across the street toward the house, staring at the little girl in the window, forgetting where she was.

"Emma?"

She was staring at the window, when suddenly a dark figure came up behind the child. The sight made Marissa shudder with fear. She couldn't breathe as the man took the little girl's hand and pulled her away from the window.

Then she was gone.

Marissa kept staring at the empty window, before running back to the bike and getting back on it. She stepped hard on the pedals and screamed in anger and frustration, then took off, tears of anger rushing down her cheeks.

I'm gonna get her back. No matter what it will cost me, if I have to die while trying, I will get her back!

THIRTY-ONE

BILLIE ANN

I arrived at Marissa's house hoping for some answers. I desperately needed to talk to her. I had been calling her for days, but she didn't answer her phone. I had been trying hard to sort out why she was suddenly so distant, so elusive. It was odd to me. I needed her help with this case—to interview her again. I needed to know if she knew Bryan Henderson. I had to figure out if there was a connection between them. And I needed to know who this guy who had come to her house was.

My knocks echoed through the street that was strangely quiet except for a few chirping birds, probably because it was still early Sunday morning. I thought I could catch her before she took off for work, in case she was working today. But no one answered much to my surprise. I waited with my heart in my throat. I was worried about her. I feared something had happened to her.

After a few moments I heard the sound of tires on asphalt. When I turned, I saw Marissa riding her bike toward me, and into the driveway, her head down and her face obscured by shadows, a cloud of sadness all around her.

"Marissa?" I said and approached her.

She saw me just as she got off her bike. She stopped for a second, then quickly averted her gaze and began to walk toward me without a word. She walked right past me as if I didn't exist.

"Marissa?" I said again.

I followed her, calling out to her, but Marissa kept walking and wouldn't turn around.

Finally, I stopped and shouted at her. "Marissa! You can't just ignore me. Why won't you talk to me?"

She paused by the door, head slumped. "You can't help me."

"What do you mean?" I said, feeling frustrated. "It's literally all I am trying to do. Help you. I'm working night and day to find your daughter. I arranged for search parties that combed through the area for days, we have an Amber Alert out, everyone in the town knows to look for her. I have my entire team all over this, even if they think I'm nuts. I put my career on the line for you. I know no one believed you at first, but I do, Marissa. I believe you. But I can't do this if you won't help me. Can we talk, please? I'm sure we can..."

I paused, as it dawned on me all of a sudden. The realization came as a deep shock to me. I almost refused to believe it, but it was the only explanation for her sudden change of demeanor toward me. She had been begging me to believe her, and now all of a sudden, she wasn't? She no longer needed my help?

It all made sense now.

"You know where she is, don't you? You know who took her."

Marissa stopped in her tracks but didn't turn around. She stood still for a moment, her shoulders trembling. Then, in a voice barely more than a whisper, she said, "Please, just leave me alone."

"No, Marissa, if you know where your daughter is, then we need to—"

I approached her, reaching out my hand, hoping to make her change her mind and start talking to me.

But I had no such luck.

She opened the door and disappeared inside, closing it firmly behind her.

As I watched her go, the truth suddenly dawned on me. Marissa had seen something—or someone—that had scared her into silence. She was hiding a terrible secret, and I had to find out what it was.

THIRTY-TWO

BILLIE ANN

"Can we talk for a minute?"

I knocked on the door to Mr. and Mrs. Perezes' house the next day. I felt angry and confused by this entire case, and now I was suddenly doubting my investigation. I had been thinking about it all day the day before, and all night. Maybe it was a coincidence that Cassandra was murdered on the same day that Emma disappeared. If I couldn't speak to Marissa, I needed to find out if Bryan was connected to Cassandra.

There was one thing that I was fairly sure of. The same person had murdered Cassandra Perez and Bryan Henderson. It had to be. It had been a week now since Doyle gave me the ultimatum, and I feared he would take me off the case, if I didn't provide anything by the end of the day.

It was Mr. Perez who opened the door. He had that look in his eyes that I had seen before in parents losing a child, of despair and grief. It was heartbreaking.

"Can we talk for a minute?" I repeated, my voice barely above a whisper. "I need to ask you some more questions."

Mr. Perez hesitated for a moment before nodding and stepping aside to let me in. The house was warm and cozy, contrasting with the icy feeling in my gut. I followed him to the living room, where Mrs. Perez was sitting on the couch, her eyes fixed on a TV show.

"Is everything okay, dear?" she asked, glancing up at him. Then she saw me and sat up straight. "Detective Wilde? What are you doing here? Are you bringing us any news?"

I opened my mouth to speak, but my voice caught in my throat. How could I even begin to explain what was going on in my head? The doubts, the fears, the suspicions—they were all jumbled up inside me, and I couldn't make sense of them. It was so frustrating. I wanted to help these people. I wanted them to get closure. But the fact was, I was far from being able to provide them with any answers at all. Or any comfort.

It broke my heart. Mrs. Perez was holding a cup of tea in her hand. Her face was creasing in worry, and a deep frown grew between her eyes.

"I just had a few questions about the case," I said, taking a seat across from her. "I was hoping you could help me."

"I'll do my best," she said, setting down her tea. "What do you need to know?"

As Mrs. Perez spoke, I couldn't help but admire the way her hair fell in soft waves around her face. She had a gentle and calming energy about herself, and it was a stark contrast to the tension that filled the air. I could feel my heart beating faster, and I tried to focus on the task at hand. I really wished I had news for them.

"There's been another murder," I said.

Mr. Perez sat down next to his wife. They grabbed each other's hands.

"Oh dear God, no," Mrs. Perez said, her voice breaking. "Please tell me it wasn't another child?"

I cleared my throat. "Not this time, no. A man. In his early thirties."

They looked briefly at each other in shock. Mrs. Perez

spoke, while her husband just stared at us, a look of disbelief on his face.

"That's still so young. Is it related to Cassandra's murder you think?" she asked. "It must be because you are here, right? Oh lord, what is happening in this town?"

Her husband clapped her gently on her hands to calm her down. "Let's hear what the detective has to say, Malia."

"Yes, yes, of course," she said. "I'm sorry. Do continue."

"We believe it might be the same murderer, yes," I said. "Cause of death is very similar. And that brings me to why I am here."

I found a picture of Bryan Henderson that I had on my phone and showed it to them.

"Do you know this man?"

They both leaned forward to look at it, and I noticed Mr. Perez winced slightly, then grabbed his side.

"No," Mrs. Perez said after studying the picture. "I have never seen him before. I'm sorry."

"Mr. Perez?" I said and looked at him. He was very quiet and seemed lost in his own thoughts for a few seconds while looking at the picture. "Do you recognize this man from anywhere?"

He looked at it closer, then shook his head. "No, no. Don't think I do. I'm sorry."

I narrowed my eyes and scrutinized his face. Something about him felt off all of a sudden.

"Are you sure? Because for a second there you looked like you knew him?" I said. "Do you want to look again?"

He shook his head. "No need to. At first when I looked at it, I thought it was someone I knew, but that wasn't him."

His wife placed a hand on his arm. "Pete has never been very good with faces."

I nodded, still looking at him. His eyes avoided mine. "I see.

His name is Bryan Henderson. Does that name mean anything to you?"

They looked at each other, then back at me. Mrs. Perez shook her head. "I'm sorry we couldn't be of more help," she said.

I rose to my feet. "If you suddenly remember something, then give me a call. Anything, okay?"

They both nodded.

Mr. Perez walked me to the door. He held a hand to his side as he opened it. I was about to walk out, when I hesitated.

"Are you in pain, Mr. Perez?" I asked. "I see you holding a hand to your side and wincing."

"Yeah, I hurt myself on my bike a couple of days ago. I fell. I may have broken a rib or at least bruised it."

I looked at where he was holding his hand.

"The ribs are usually higher up," I said.

He stared at me, eyes wide. "Well, maybe it's something else then. I should probably have it checked out. Thank you for stopping by, Detective."

He closed the door as soon as I stepped outside. I stood for a few seconds and looked at the yard, wondering why that visit felt so strange. Something was off.

I had barely finished the thought before my phone rang. I picked it up and rushed toward my car, with it pressed against my ear.

"Hello?" I said, holding the phone between my shoulder and ear, while opening the car door.

"Hello, Mrs. Wilde? This is Diana Schmidt, from Cocoa Beach High."

I paused and grabbed the phone in my hand, forgetting all about getting into the car. I only got calls from Diana if one of my children was sick or that one time when William got into a fight.

"Yes? Is something wrong?"

Diana cleared her throat. "Well, I just wanted to let you know that Charlene hasn't been to any of her classes today, and usually you call in first and let us know if she is sick, so I was just wondering if—"

"If I knew she was absent? Well, no, I most certainly didn't."

"It's just so unusual for her," Diana said. "She's always here."

"She should be," I said, my heart beating faster in my chest. "And you say she hasn't been to any of her classes? Not even this morning?"

"No, ma'am."

"Thank you," I said and hung up with a deep exhale. Worry began to creep in as I got into the car and took off. Diana was right. This was very unlike my daughter. I didn't like this one bit.

THIRTY-THREE

Then

Kitty opened her eyes with a small gasp. She felt hot, soaked in sweat, even if she was only in her underwear and a T-shirt that was three sizes too big. She lifted her head to look around.

Where am I?

She was lying on a metal bed in a dimly lit room. The only source of light was a flickering fluorescent bulb, dangling from the ceiling. Next to the bed was a rusted metal table, and there was a single wooden chair in the corner. Her head throbbed from the aftereffects of the stun gun, and she could feel the bruises on her neck where Officer Damian had restrained her.

Why would he do this to me? Why? I thought he loved me?

She tried to move her arms and legs, but they were strapped tightly to the corners of the metal bed with nylon cable ties. Panic set in as she realized that she was a prisoner. Her mind raced with questions, but all she could muster was a feeble whimper.

"Help."

Kitty fought her restraints, trying to free herself from the metal bed. Her wrists and ankles ached from the tight bindings, and she could feel the nylon digging into her skin. She wriggled desperately, but it was no use.

"Mom? Mommy?"

She said the words but knew there was no mom there. She was all alone. No windows she could look out of and see where she was. Just those dark black walls surrounding her. They were covered with some material that she remembered she had seen before. One time when she was invited into a radio studio, where her friend Julia's mother worked. They had the same foamy materials on the walls. To stop the sound, the mother had told her when she asked. As she looked at it, heart throbbing in her small chest, she knew exactly what that meant.

No one can hear me.

Anxiety spread in Kitty's heart as she realized that escape was impossible. Tears welled up in her eyes and streamed down her face. Where was she? How did she get here? What would happen to her next?

The questions swirled around in her mind like a never-ending loop, filling her with fear and dread.

She cried out for help, even though deep down she knew it was futile.

"Mommy!" Kitty screamed, desperation deep in her voice. But there was no answer. No one could hear her cries for help.

Kitty lay motionless on the dirty mattress, feeling so helpless, so lost and so, so scared. She had been taken from the safety of home and put into a nightmare she could not get away from. What was going to happen to her? Would she ever see her mom again? Her only hope was to pray for some sort of miracle, but even that felt like clutching at straws. All seemed lost and Kitty's heart sank deeper into despair with each passing moment.

Please help me. Please someone help me.

A door creaked open, and for just a second, she thought her

prayers had been answered. She lifted her head and stared toward it as a figure emerged from the shadows. His piercing blue eyes seemed to bore into her very soul. The sight of him terrified her, and she lost all hope.

As the figure walked closer, she tried to pull herself up, but her restraints kept her firmly in place. Her heart raced as he drew nearer, and she could feel his breath on her skin. He didn't say a word but simply stood there staring at her, his eyes cold and unforgiving.

She tried to speak, to beg for mercy, but no words came out of her mouth. He seemed to sense her fear and smiled cruelly, knowing that he had complete control over her.

She closed her eyes, tears streaming down her face. She knew that she was trapped, at the mercy of this cold and heartless man.

But then, as he stepped into the light, she saw a glimmer of kindness in his eyes. He approached her slowly, his footsteps quiet against the cold concrete floor. She could feel her heart racing, but she forced herself to remain still.

"Are you all right?" he asked softly, his voice gentle as he sat on the edge of the bed beside her. She hesitated before nodding slowly. He reached out and touched her cheek, and she flinched at his touch. But then, something about the warmth of his hand made her relax.

"It's all right," he whispered. "I'm not going to hurt you. You can trust me. We are family, remember?"

She looked up at him, searching for any signs of anger, but found none. Slowly, she began to relax.

He touched her hair. "As long as you are a good girl, and do as I tell you, then there is no problem."

She was small, but she was no dummy, and she had a will as strong as steel. Her green eyes were full of suspicion as she looked up at the imposing figure in front of her. He towered over her, tall and broad, but there was a gentleness in his voice that didn't fit with his intimidating stature.

He touched her nose with a finger, and she flinched slightly, but he only smiled showing off his white teeth. She used to love seeing him smile. Now it filled her with fear.

"Can we agree to that?"

Slowly, she began to relax. He seemed sincere, and she wanted to trust him. She really wanted to.

"Okay," she said finally, her voice barely a whisper. She was so thirsty and wanted to ask for some water. And food. She was starving. She would do anything for something to eat.

He smiled again and winked at her.

"That's my girl."

Kitty stared at Officer Damian, heart still racing rapidly in her chest, yet feeling oddly comforted. He then smiled and lifted up a bag of McDonald's.

"I hope you're hungry. I brought food."

THIRTY-FOUR

BILLIE ANN

I called Charlene and left a bunch of messages while driving back to the station. Of course, she wasn't answering. She was skipping school, probably up to no good with her friends.

This was so not what I needed right now.

And it was unlike her. That was the part that concerned me. She was the good one. She usually always took care of her schoolwork and chores. She always got good grades and never skipped. I left one more message, telling her to call me back NOW. Then I hung up and called her father. It was the first time I had spoken to him since he'd betrayed me and outed me to my mother. I really wasn't ready to speak to him, as I was still furious, but this was important.

"Joe? Do you know where Charlene is?"

I could hear the noise of construction in the background. He was still at work. He sounded distant. "She's in school, no?"

I exhaled and rubbed my forehead in frustration. "No, she is not in school, Joe. They called and said she hasn't been there all day."

He went quiet.

"Well, that's not good. Have you tried calling her?"

"Of course, I have. She doesn't pick up and she turned her location tracker off, so I can't use Find My Phone to track her."

He exhaled. "She's sneaky, huh? You know what? She's just being a teenager. It happens. We're just not used to her doing stuff like this."

It happens. Is that all you have to say?

"Well, it shouldn't be happening," I said. "This is not okay. She needs to know this. She can't just skip school without telling us. Especially not now that we have a killer on the loose. This is terrifying to me. What do we do?" I hadn't told Joe about the case, but he'd have seen it on the news.

"Listen, it's Charlene. She's a smart girl. I'm sure she will be fine. She'll be home later today pretending like she was in school, and then we'll have to talk to her, tell her that they called and that we know she is lying. She'll tell us she's sorry and that it will never happen again. She'll probably cry a little. But it will be okay. I promise. Cut her some slack. She's probably just acting out a little. I'm sure she can sense that something is going on with us."

"So now it's my fault?" I asked.

"I didn't say that."

"That's what you meant."

"You can't expect our children to not react to this, Billie Ann. Charlene is a smart kid. She probably already knows we're separating. She could easily have heard us talking. Listen I gotta go. I have a five o'clock meeting later today with the architect. I'll be home afterward."

We hung up. I parked in front of the station and turned the engine off. I felt bad. No, I felt absolutely awful. Was Joe right? Was this affecting my children already? I couldn't bear the thought. How could I do this to them? What kind of a mother was I being to them?

How can I not? They want to see me happy. I'm teaching them that it's okay to choose happiness.

I took the elevator up to the third floor and got out. Tom and Scott were sitting at their desks as I walked in. Tom lifted his head and saw me.

"Well, you look like sh—"

I lifted my hand. "I'm gonna stop you right there. I do not want to hear it. I don't have time for it."

"Sorry, I didn't mean it in a bad way. You seem like you're in a bad mood or something."

I looked at them both, deliberately choosing to ignore his comments. Who cared what I looked like? Yeah, I was in a terrible mood. Could you blame me? It wasn't exactly a good day for me.

"I need to know everything we have on Cassandra's parents," I said. "I know we have gone through them before, but I want to dig deeper. Let's go over everything again. Especially her father. Background checks, do they have priors, where do they work, where did they used to live before they came here, who have they been married to? Heck, I want to know what they had for breakfast this morning. They both seem like they're hiding something, and I need to know what it is. Tom, you're on that one."

He nodded and sat up straight in his chair.

"Scott?"

Scott smiled behind the soft curls. I wanted to tell him he needed a haircut, but this wasn't the time.

"I need you to find all the information you can on Ashley Wittman, the girlfriend who disappeared. Does she have any connections to any of the others, to the Perezes or Marissa Clemens? If they used to play tennis together or be Girl Scouts together, I want to know, okay? If her sister's husband works for any of them, I need to know. Okay? Stuff like that. Details. The answer is in the details, you hear me?"

He nodded. "I'm on it. And the pediatrician's family? Do you want me to run backgrounds on them too? He wasn't married but his parents and siblings and all that?"

I paused.

"Pediatrician?"

Scott nodded. He snapped his fingers. "Yes, you know—what's his name—Bryan Henderson."

"He was a pediatrician? How come I didn't know that?"

Scott threw out his arms. "I thought you knew."

"No one told me this! You just said he was a doctor."

"Technically he *is* a doctor."

I grabbed my car keys and started to walk toward the elevator again. "But this is an example of an important detail," I said, turning to Scott. "These are the kinds of details I need to know."

Scott looked up at me, his expression unreadable as he gestured to the papers scattered around him.

"I'm working on it," he told me. "It's all here."

I took a deep breath, trying to contain my impatience. It was my fault; I had been distracted. I turned back around and continued to walk away.

"Where are you going?" Scott asked.

"To the pediatrician's office," I replied. "Text me the address and all the info you have on him ASAP."

With that, I stepped into the elevator and pushed the button, doing my best to not be mad at myself and my team for missing this important aspect. The doors closed behind me, and I was enveloped in the sound of the elevator's humming as it carried me down. I knew this information was important, and time was of the essence.

When I arrived at the lobby, I hurried to my car, my feet moving faster than my thoughts. This could be the missing link I was looking for. If Cassandra or Emma was one of Bryan Henderson's patients, then that would link them all together. It could be my missing piece.

THIRTY-FIVE

BILLIE ANN

I couldn't sleep. I literally paced back and forth in my living room, looking at the clock again and again. It was eleven o'clock. Charlene still hadn't made it home, and now I was getting seriously worried about her.

I had called all of her friends, and even spoken to their parents, and gone to some of her best friends' houses, but no one knew where she was. All they knew was that she wasn't in school today. I asked her best friend, Alexis, to keep texting her in case she would answer her and just not me. I had been driving around searching for her everywhere, down on the beach, downtown in all the restaurants and cafés where I knew she might go with friends from time to time. I was getting close to sending out a missing person report and had asked my colleagues on patrol tonight to keep an eye out for her. I had even called Chief Doyle to ask him what he thought I should do.

"She's sixteen. It's not unusual," was his answer. "Let's wait and see if she doesn't come home. She might just be with a friend that you don't know and fallen asleep there or lost track of time, or maybe she is drinking or smoking weed."

"Not my daughter," I said angrily.

"They all say that," he said with a chuckle.

I knew I would probably have said the same to any mother coming to the station reporting a teenager missing. But now that it was me, I found it reckless, and irresponsible, and I couldn't help thinking that maybe I could do more to find her. My daughter didn't run away or get herself in trouble. It wasn't something she would do. Was it?

Maybe Joe is right. With all that has been going on, I totally forgot to check in on the kids.

I felt a sadness overwhelm me. I hated feeling like this, I hated it so much. The guilt was eating me up.

"Where are you, Charlene?" I said while looking out the window at the street, waiting, hoping, and praying for her to suddenly show up.

Maybe she just needs some space. Give her that.

I felt like I was losing her. It hurt. I tried to think about the case, to get my mind on something else. Cassandra's dad had been strange, I thought, when I went to visit. I couldn't put my finger on it, but something was off. We had gotten the results from the lab and the blood in Ashley's apartment wasn't hers. They had taken hairs from her brush and made a DNA test matching it with the blood, and it wasn't a match. It wasn't a match with Bryan Henderson either. It meant that it belonged to a third person, and I could only assume that was the killer.

The pediatrician's office had been closed when I got there, so I'd decided to stop by the next morning instead.

I can't just stay here. What if my daughter is in trouble?

I shook my head, then grabbed my car keys and rushed outside. Joe was fast asleep in the bedroom, and I shot him a text to let him know I had gone to look for Charlene yet again. I didn't understand how he could sleep when our daughter hadn't come home. I for one couldn't even sit still.

I jumped into the car and drove down through our town's

main street, looking at the faces of people coming in and out of
bars and restaurants. Then I continued toward the beach. I had
been there earlier and found no sign of her, but it was worth
trying again. It was very hot out, so it would be the perfect place
to spend the night if she had nowhere else to go.

As I came to First Street, and parked there with the inten-
tion of going down to the beach, I realized I was at the building
where Bryan Henderson had been found murdered. I got out of
the car and looked at the backside of it, and I spotted the fire
escape.

*What if Ashley was running from the killer? How would she
have gotten out of the building?*

I approached the condominium, then looked up. That was
most certainly a way to get out of the building without being
seen by the cameras. I walked the length of the building and
was searching the ground when I came across an area with a
huge red spot on the concrete by the dumpsters. It had dried up,
but there was something else.

A piece of broken glass had been tossed next to the
dumpster.

It was covered in blood.

THIRTY-SIX

Then

The door to the room she was in was bolted shut as soon as Officer Damian left. He said he would come back the next day, and so he did, bringing more food, burgers and fries. The first thing she asked was if she could go outside.

"I can't let you go outside. I want you to remain safe," he said. "It's for your own protection."

Part of her believed him. Maybe because she wanted to. She had always liked him, and she didn't want to stop now. He had always been so nice to her. She almost felt like she loved him.

But then there was that other part, the one that told her he was keeping her a prisoner, and that he was going to hurt her if she didn't do as he told her to. Maybe he even would do it anyway.

"Be a good girl now." That's what he always told her. To behave.

"You'd better do as he tells you to. He is after all a police officer," her stepdad Cole had said. And she did. She always obeyed him. Because when she did, she was rewarded. She got to go to Disney World. She got ice cream and presents. She knew how to keep him happy, so if she just continued to do that, then maybe he would let her go one day. Maybe she would get to go home to her mother.

The sound of the door bolt shutting every time he left echoed like a gong in Kitty's mind, leaving her feeling more isolated than she had ever been. She had been in the shed for days now, and Officer Damian had offered no explanation as to why, even if she kept asking him about it. Every day he would bring food, but his presence only brought more questions.

"When will I see my mommy?" she asked.

"Don't ask so many questions," he answered.

"How long will I stay here? When can I go home?"

"You live here now."

"But...?" and that was usually when she began to tear up. Did this mean he would never let her go home? That's when she began planning her escape. She knew there had to be a way for her to leave. But she just didn't know how.

The morning of the fourth day, Officer Damian returned once again. He brought with him a bag of burgers and fries as usual. But before she could even taste the food, Officer Damian told her that there were pit bulls outside the shed, ready to attack any intruder. He claimed it was for her protection.

Kitty didn't know what to make of this news; she was torn between hope and despair. Part of her believed he was telling the truth, while another part of her feared it was just a way to keep her from trying to run away. Nonetheless, she remained still, silently waiting for him to leave.

Still, Kitty was left with one burning question. What did Officer Damian want from her?

THIRTY-SEVEN

BILLIE ANN

I called the forensic tech unit and had them come down to the condominium and secure all the evidence. I told them to comb through the dumpster in case there was more evidence inside of it, and to seal the bloody area on the ground so they could take samples of it. To see if it matched the blood on the glass and in the apartment.

I walked down to the beach. I took a flashlight from my glove compartment and checked the time; it was already two in the morning.

The night was calm, and with only a few streetlights in sight I could make out faint silhouettes of people walking around in the distance. Some used flashlights to light their way, or maybe look for turtle nests or crabs. I started calling Charlene's name, even though I knew deep down that she wouldn't answer me. I searched around the dunes with my flashlight, hoping that maybe I would find her hiding somewhere. But after what felt like an eternity, there was still no sign of her. Nothing but empty sand and some scattered bits of trash here and there.

My heart sank as I feared what could have happened to her. Tears started rolling down my cheeks as I walked back to my car, feeling completely broken inside. I drove home, exhausted yet still worried about what might have happened to Charlene. As much as I wanted to believe that she was okay, something inside me told me otherwise.

I couldn't shake off the feeling of dread as I pulled into my driveway. My mind raced with all the possibilities of what could have happened. Was Charlene hurt? Lost? Worse, was she...?

Don't even finish the thought.

I tried to focus on what I could do to find her. I had put out an ALPR hit for the license plate number of her truck and hoped that it would show up somewhere. But so far nothing. I grabbed my phone and called her again, praying that she would answer. I don't know why I thought this time would be different, but it was my last resort. I had run out of ideas what to do.

Come on, Charlene, come on answer the darn phone!

After several rings, it went straight to voicemail again. I had walked up toward the door, shoulders slumped, my stomach in knots, when I heard tires on the asphalt coming down the street. I turned to see Charlene's truck as it slowly drove toward me.

What on earth?

I stared at the red truck as it trundled up the street, my heart pounding. I squinted, trying to make out who was inside. It was definitely Charlene's truck, but that didn't mean she was driving it. When the truck pulled up in front of my house, I saw that Charlene was indeed behind the wheel.

My first thought was relief. But then I noticed that she was alone and there was something strange about her eyes. She didn't look happy or relieved to see me, instead she looked determined. She stumbled out, and as I tried to approach her, I was startled by the dazed look on her face.

She was drunk.

"Charlene?" I asked, feeling so many conflicting emotions. I was relieved to see her, alive and well, but as that feeling subsided, it gave away to another. Anger. Here I had been worried about her all day, and she showed up drunk? At almost two thirty in the morning, on a school night?

She paused and looked at me. Her speech was slurred. "Oh, hi, Mom."

I tried my best to contain my anger. "What's this, Charlene? What is going on here? You're driving around drunk?"

She shook her head. "No, I would never."

"Where have you been? Do you know what time it is?"

She could barely stand still and was swaying from side to side. I felt like I was going to explode. But she was too out of control to have a real chat right now. It would have to wait.

"Charlene, go to bed. We will talk about this in the morning. You hear me?"

She saluted me like she was in the Army.

"Loud and clear," she muttered before she turned and walked inside the house, unsteady on her feet.

I watched her go and sighed; I was relieved, but I was not looking forward to having that conversation in the morning.

THIRTY-EIGHT
BILLIE ANN

Charlene was sick in the morning when she woke up. I heard her throw up in her bathroom, then walked in to help her, and to hold her long blonde hair. She gagged and gasped, then sat on the floor, head leaning on the shower door, sweat sticking to her forehead.

It was tempting to say something like *that's what you get*, or *that'll teach you*, but I didn't think it would go down well. She was definitely sick from the drinking, and hopefully this would be a lesson for her on its own.

"I'm sorry, Mom," she muttered between breaths. "I'm sorry I'm such a disappointment."

I exhaled and sat next to her, then pulled her into a hug. "You're not a disappointment, sweetie. I worry about you, you know? You scared me like crazy last night."

"I know. I'm sorry."

I rubbed her back soothingly as she leaned against me. She smelled like alcohol and vomit, but I didn't care. She was my daughter and I loved her, even when she made mistakes.

"You don't have to apologize, Charlene," I said. "But you do need to take responsibility for your actions."

She nodded miserably and wiped her mouth with the back of her hand. "I know. I messed up."

"We all make mistakes. Now I will have to punish you, though," I said.

She nodded, hiding her head between her knees. "I knew that was coming. So, what will it be?"

"You're grounded for two weeks," I said. "You will only go to school and come home right after. No skipping classes again and no drinking. I need to regain my trust in you. Is that understood?"

"Two weeks?" she whined, all of a sudden seemingly better. "Two weeks? But then I'll miss Peyton's birthday party this Friday."

I shrugged. "That's what happens."

She rose to her feet, then looked down at me still sitting on the floor. "That's not fair, Mom."

Now I was getting angry. I rose to my feet. "Not fair? How's that not fair? You were driving your truck while intoxicated. You could have killed someone. You could have gotten a DUI. This is very serious, Charlene."

She was in tears now. "Ugh, you're just so... you and Dad are... ugh, I HATE you. Don't you think I know what is going on, huh?"

"What do you mean?"

"That you and Dad are separating? Don't you think I know this?" she asked. "I hear you late at night. I hear you discuss things and get angry at each other. I see that you sleep in the guest room. I'm not stupid, Mom."

"Okay, no, you're not stupid, but what does the fact that your dad and I are having some disagreements have to do with you getting drunk and driving across town? And skipping school and scaring us half to death because we don't know where you are?"

She shook her head angrily. "I know what you are, Mom. I heard Dad tell Grandma the other day. It's disgusting."

My heart sank as I heard my daughter's harsh words. It made me want to cry. But I held it back. I squared my shoulders and met my daughter's gaze.

"What I am—who I am—is not disgusting, sweetie," I said, firmly, steadying myself, pushing back the desire to cry and scream at the same time. "And you should never have found out that way. I was planning on talking to you about it."

I could feel the heat rising in my face. Charlene crossed her arms and looked away; her anger barely contained. I took a deep breath and spoke again, keeping my voice gentle but firm. "I understand that you're upset, but I need you to respect me, no matter what. What I am may not be to your liking, but I'm still your mother and I deserve your respect."

She scoffed. "I won't respect you for being some dyke."

My eyes grew wide. My daughter had never talked to me like that before. "Excuse me? That's three weeks of being grounded, young lady." I struggled to keep calm and contain my anger as she looked at me angrily. I had to remind myself that she was just a child. My child. I was the adult here. But it wasn't easy. "So, you'd better be careful that I won't ground you for the rest of high school."

"Yeah, right."

I sighed, feeling a deep sadness. This was not who Charlene was. She was just acting out. I put my hand on her shoulder. "You don't have to accept my choices, sweetie. But you need to accept that they are mine to make."

Then she left the bathroom, and I watched her climb back into bed, crawling under the covers. I shook my head, cleaned up the vomit in the toilet bowl and flushed. I couldn't believe her. For a second, I felt like she understood the seriousness of the situation, but apparently, she didn't.

Yet as I left her room, I couldn't help feeling devastated by her comments. They were hurtful.

Tom called as I walked down the stairs, to get my keys and go to the station. I had asked him to go check out the pediatrician's office for me, and to ask if either of the two children were Bryan Henderson's patients.

"Neither of them was in their files," he said. "I spoke to the nurse there and she searched in their system to see, but their names didn't pop up. Not Emma or Cassandra."

I walked outside, slamming the door shut behind me, leaving a note for Joe, telling him to let Charlene sleep and to walk Zelda before leaving for work. I had taken the younger kids to school, because I knew Charlene was in no state to go today.

"That can't be right," I said, feeling frustrated and disappointed. I had been so certain that Bryan's job was the missing link. Now where did that leave me? Back to square one? Was Doyle going to confront me today? Demote me? Or just take me off the case? Who was going to get Emma back to her mother then? I wondered if I could convince him to let me keep searching for her. Seeing how scared Marissa was, I knew the girl had to be in danger. She needed to come home to her mother.

THIRTY-NINE

MARISSA

Two can play that game.

Marissa had been taking it lying down all of her life. Never complaining. Never putting up a fight. Well, those days were over now. It was time for her to stand up for herself. To show the world what she was made of.

She didn't own much. She could barely provide for herself and her daughter. She had no influential friends either, or even friends who could help her. And she knew she couldn't trust the police. They were useless and hadn't proven her otherwise so far. But she had her wits. She was smart. And she was stubborn. Once she set her mind to something, she didn't rest until it was accomplished. She hadn't always been like this, but lately, she had discovered that side of herself, and that's what she used when planning her next move.

To get Emma back.

She parked her bike outside of the house where she had seen a little girl in the window, for a couple of days, keeping an eye on every movement inside, writing down every time someone left and when they came back, making sure to keep her distance so no one would see her. Soon she had prepared an entire schedule for their daily life, and now it was time to see when she could make her move.

Marissa dug deep into her resolve and started making plans. She had a few ideas, but she wanted to make sure they were airtight. After days of researching, plotting, and planning, she settled on a strategy.

As she stood in the street, watching the house, she felt a sense of satisfaction. This was her revenge. She had lost Emma, and now it was time to take her back. She had planned every detail, every move, and every step. She felt alive with power, ready to strike at any second she got the chance.

Finally, the moment arrived. The last person left the house. She hurried toward the front door, her heart pounding with excitement and fear.

She had brought everything she needed with her. A small hammer and a mask to cover her face. She slipped on the mask, and then smashed in a window next to the front door with the hammer. She waited for a few seconds to make sure that no one in the neighborhood, or inside of the house—in case she had miscalculated, and they hadn't all left—reacted to the sound of glass being smashed. Nothing happened, and she figured the coast was clear.

It was dark inside, but she could see well enough. She walked through the living room, taking note of everything she saw. The pictures of the children, with their parents, some of them only with the dad, while fishing or going hiking. She paused for a second and studied them, feeling her heart drop even further.

Then she remembered why she was there.

She looked toward the stairs, where the children's rooms were and the master bedroom. But then she spotted the backyard through the kitchen window.

The shed.

Where no one can hear her cry or even scream.

Heart throbbing in her throat, Marissa went through the kitchen and headed toward the back door leading to the long yard, gasping lightly at the sight of it, while placing a hand on the handle.

She opened the door, then walked outside on the back patio, spotting the shed all the way at the end of the backyard. It was covered by bushes and tall trees, but she knew it was there. Taking in deep, calming breaths to keep herself composed, she approached it, heart knocking against her ribcage, and hands shaking in fear.

FORTY

BILLIE ANN

"I can't believe every lead is a dead end," I muttered, feeling my frustration rise.

Tom and Scott were sitting opposite me at my desk, the three of us desperate to find the thread that would lead us closer to a resolution. We had been going through the case and the evidence we had all morning, trying to connect the dots between the scattered information we had gathered. But nothing seemed to fit, no matter how hard we tried. We had no suspects in Cassandra's disappearance—just her father acting strangely, but he was alibied. We had no new links to Emma, nothing to connect either girl to Bryan. No positive IDs for the blood in Ashley's house. No surveillance cameras had brought up anything of interest—just Ashley and Bryan on a date at a local bar. And no one had heard from Marissa.

It simply wasn't good enough.

I felt a wave of exhaustion wash over me as I slumped in my chair. Tom and Scott exchanged a meaningful glance, and I knew that they felt the same as I did. We had to find something soon, or else this case would be lost forever.

And my career washed down the drain with it.

"What are we missing?" I asked. "What is it we're not seeing?"

"I'll tell you what you aren't seeing," sounded a voice from behind me. I turned and spotted the Chief. He was holding a piece of paper in his hand that he placed on the desk in front of me.

"What's that?" Tom asked.

"I was curious," Doyle said. "I couldn't figure out how a woman like Marissa Clemens, with being a single mom and a nurse, with her income could afford to live where she did. So, I called the county and asked for some info."

"And what did you find?" I asked and leaned forward to look at the piece of paper he had placed in front of me. Chief Doyle was looking at it over my shoulder, casting a long shadow.

I looked up at him. He smiled. I had always believed he was quite good looking. He was a tall, broad-shouldered man, with a booming voice and a stern demeanor. He had lost his wife some years ago, before he came to our station. People said he never got over it and hadn't dated since. I still saw her picture on his desk when I was in there. They looked very happy together. It had been a home invasion. Some drug addict, looking for money, shot her in her own home.

It was a tragedy. One you could still see on his heavy burdened face, even if it was years ago.

"Is that what I think it is?" I asked.

He nodded with a smirk. "Yup. This is the deed to the house she lives in. She never paid a dime to live there. That's your connection right there."

I lifted the paper and stared at it to be completely sure I was getting this right.

"Then who did?" Tom asked, leaning forward.

I looked up and my eyes met his. "Pete Perez. Cassandra's dad. He owns the house, but his name is also on the loan."

"And he paid all the mortgages," Doyle said, determined.

"Something is going on between the two of them. But no matter what it is, then there is a connection, an important one. So, I guess we're still working that angle, Wilde."

Tom wrinkled his nose. "And why would he do that? Did he have an affair with her or something like that?"

I rose to my feet and grabbed my phone in hand. "A neighbor did say she saw a man come and go at Marissa's house. Maybe it was him? I say it's time to call him in for a little chat." I paused and looked at my boss. "I thought you didn't believe that Marissa Clemens had a child?"

"We haven't found evidence that she didn't either," he said. "Plus, I believe in you. And your gut. That's enough. You've done good work on this case so far."

That made me smile. Chief Doyle had been head of the police department for nearly five years. He had a reputation for being uncompromising and by-the-book when it came to crime, but his resolute fairness was also well known. It wasn't often Chief Doyle gave out compliments, so when he did, I could be certain that he meant it. And I was allowed to be proud of it.

FORTY-ONE

Then

Kitty woke up from a deep sleep, her head pounding and her chest heaving. The only sound was the faint thumping of her heart and the scratching of a branch against the walls on the outside of the metal shed. It was hot inside of it, almost unbearably so, and she was sweating heavily, her hair falling into her face, soaked.

Kitty heard a loud clank and the door to her room creaked open, flooding the small space with sunlight. She bolted upright in her bed, expecting to see Officer Damian and his piercing blue eyes staring down at her, as she had been accustomed to over these past many weeks, or was it maybe even months? She no longer knew. She couldn't keep track. The only thing she knew was that he would come to her at least once a day, bringing food, and they would talk. Sometimes he would kiss her and hold her and tell her she shouldn't be afraid. Other times he would slap her across the face and yell at her for making him do this to her, making him keep her like this.

"Why do you have to make me love you?" he had yelled often.

She didn't know how to answer that, and all she could do was cry. She had gotten no further in planning her escape. She was still strapped to the bed, only untied when she was eating, and going to the bathroom. She couldn't even examine the door to see if there was any way of opening it from the inside. And even if she did succeed, and made it to the outside, then there were the dogs she had to worry about. She had never seen them, but pictured them sitting out there, in front of the door, waiting for her, drooling, showing their sharp teeth as they growled at the door.

It was terrifying.

A shadowy figure appeared in the doorway. Kitty gasped lightly, thinking it was him again, that he was coming for her, and then instantly wondering what mood he would be in. Usually, she could tell by the look in his eyes the moment he stepped inside. But much to her surprise, this wasn't him.

It was his wife.

Linda stepped inside, carrying a tray with a glass of chocolate milk and a pink teddy bear sitting next to it, leaning on its side. Kitty recognized her from the first day she had come to the house, and she braced herself for the worst. Why was she here? What did she want? Had she come to hurt her?

But instead of aggression, the woman looked sad.

She sat down on the edge of the bed, like Damian usually did. She put the tray down and untied Kitty's hands, then handed her the glass of chocolate milk. Kitty grabbed it and drank it greedily. She was enjoying something she hadn't had in a long time. So far, she had been living off nothing but burgers and fries and sodas, and barely enough of it to keep her alive.

She was constantly starving.

Linda sighed and sat with her hands folded in her lap.

"I'm sorry we are doing this to you," she said softly. "Believe me it doesn't make me feel very good."

Kitty stared at her. Officer Damian had said the same thing several times before as well. How sorry he was for doing this to her. He had even cried once and she'd had to comfort him and tell him it was okay, that he was just doing it out of love, and for her own good. That's what he had told her at least, and over the weeks she had started to believe him. He wasn't a bad man, and his wife wasn't bad either. They meant well. They wanted her to be safe.

Linda reached over and stroked her hair gently.

"It's not fair to you," she continued, almost breaking into tears. "I feel awful. I feel so, so terrible."

Kitty couldn't stop looking at her. She had tears in her eyes. Kitty felt sad now too. Maybe they didn't mean so bad? After all, they did treat her okay. She was getting food and stuff, and now a teddy bear?

Kitty stared at it. It was pink and fluffy and had a rainbow on the front. It reminded her of her favorite teddy bear from home, only this one was newer and had bigger eyes.

Linda saw her looking at it. She took it and lifted it up. "Do you like it? You want it?"

Kitty nodded eagerly. She loved teddy bears more than anything. Maybe even more than her Barbie and Ken dolls. Maybe. It was hard to say in this moment because any toy would make her happy, anything that could help her pass these long, lonely hours alone in the shed, anything that could make her feel safe. She had longed for something to hold when sleeping. Something soft to make her feel good.

Linda handed it to her. "Here. I brought it for you. Hoping it might cheer you up a little."

Kitty's face lit up. She grabbed the teddy bear with both hands and hugged it, feeling happy for the first time since she got there.

"Thank you, thank you," she said.

"How about we let your hands be free from now on, huh?" she said. "So, you can hug the bear while sleeping? I'm sure Damian won't mind if I ask him."

Kitty felt such deep relief. For some reason she really wanted this woman to like her.

"Would you, please?"

"Of course. There's no need to have you tied up. The door is bolted shut anyway from the outside."

"Thank you. Thank you."

Linda smiled gently. "I can see why my husband loves you so much. I have to admit it makes me jealous from time to time. Some days I have been wanting to come over here and hurt you, because of it. She paused and Kitty stared at her, mouth open. Then the woman smiled and tilted her head.

"But of course, I won't. Don't be scared."

Kitty stared at her, hugging the teddy bear a little too tight. She didn't know if she was supposed to feel sorry for the woman or fear her.

Maybe it was a little of both.

Linda averted her eyes and grabbed the tray. "My husband loves you. I can see it in his eyes. He's never looked at me that way."

Kitty was too stunned to speak, and she just nodded in response. Linda gave her one last regretful look before turning and walking to the door. With one hand on the door handle, she said, "I'm sorry. I just wanted you to know."

Then the door closed, and the silence returned.

FORTY-TWO

BILLIE ANN

Pete Perez was already seated in the room when Big Tom and I walked in. He was a small man, with a face lined by age and worry, but his eyes still held traces of the young, carefree man he had once been. He was nervous and fidgety, shifting position constantly as we sat down, and twirling a ring around on his finger, as if he were trying to distract himself from some invisible pain.

"Mr. Perez?" I said.

He looked up and our eyes met. I could tell he was anxious. "Yes?"

"We have called you in today to ask you a few questions."

He nodded. "Of course. Is something wrong?"

"No, nothing is wrong, Mr. Perez. Just routine."

He nodded. "Oh, okay. 'Cause I already told you; I was away on a business trip when Cassandra was murdered. I know you always look at the close relatives first when investigating a murder. And I have an alibi. I have hotel receipts and airline tickets to prove it."

I smiled again. "We know. We have everything on file."

He sniffled. "That's good. That's good."

He sipped the water I had given him in a small plastic cup.

"Mr. Perez, what is the nature of your relationship with Marissa Clemens?" Big Tom asked.

He lifted his glare and met Tom's. "I already told you I didn't know much about the woman living across the street. I never even saw her child. I've told you this."

"But that's what I don't understand. Your daughter babysat her daughter?" I said. "How can you not know her? Your wife told us that you helped her get that job."

"She did? Yeah, well, I guess I did. Technically. I didn't do a lot though. I just met the woman in the street one day and she mentioned that she needed a babysitter, and asked if I knew anyone I could recommend. I just told Cassandra about it and asked her to go over there and talk to her. Cassandra did it by herself really. She had so many babysitting jobs around the neighborhood; she was very popular."

I leaned forward folding my hands on the table. "Mr. Perez. This would be way easier if you could just tell us the truth."

He looked startled. "What do you mean? I am telling the truth. I maybe have spoken to her a few times in the street, but that's..."

I pulled out the paper with the deed of the house from the county and slid it across the table for him to look at. He stopped talking and stared at it.

I pointed with my finger, then stated for the recording, "I'm showing Mr. Perez evidence eight A." I looked at him. "This is your name, right? On that line here?"

His shoulders slumped, and he became less guarded. "Y-yes."

"Okay, let's try it again then," I said. "What is the nature of your relationship with Miss Clemens?"

"I... I don't know how to answer that."

"You paid for her house," Big Tom said. "You own it and paid her mortgage."

"Yes, that is true. The house is mine. I used to live there before I met my wife. We needed something bigger when Cassandra was born, but wanted to stay in the neighborhood, and so we bought the one across the street."

"So, Marissa rented that house from you?" I asked.

He nodded.

"For the purposes of the tape, Mr. Perez has confirmed..." I paused. "There's nothing wrong with that, except she didn't pay any rent, did she? We've been through your bank records. No deposits or transfers from her. She could never afford a house like that on her nurse's salary."

He swallowed and looked up at me, suddenly looking like an even smaller man, almost a young boy.

"Listen," I said, trying to sound friendly so he would start talking, "if you had an affair with her, it's okay."

He stared at me, his nostrils flaring. I could tell he was ready. He knew he had to start talking. There was no other way out. He shook his head.

"No," he said, his voice breaking. He put his hand to his side, as if he was in physical pain. I took notice of it, thinking about the glass by the dumpster and the blood in Ashley's condo.

He was silent for a moment, then added softly, "I swear. It was nothing like that. Please, you must understand. I was just trying to help her. That's all. Her and that sweet little girl."

I looked up and met his eyes. This was the first time someone besides Marissa confirmed that Emma actually existed.

"So, have you met the girl?"

FORTY-THREE

MARISSA

Be still my heart, be still. Please.

Marissa stared at the door to the shed, heart throbbing loudly in her chest. She felt dizzy, almost overwhelmingly nauseated. She closed her eyes briefly to steady herself, then reached out and pushed the bolt aside, slowly, making sure she didn't make a sound and let anyone know she was there.

Careful.

As the door swung open, fear and dread stirred up inside of her, making her chest tighten. She felt such turmoil inside, she almost closed the door again.

She stared into the small room and, taking in a deep breath, she entered the shed, a shiver running down her spine. She could hear something inside and quickly spotted what it was.

Emma.

It was her. It really was. She was huddled in the corner, trembling and crying. Hiding her face, leaning her head on her pulled-up knees. Marissa could barely contain the joy of seeing her daughter again, and it almost paralyzed her at first.

"E-Emma?"

Her voice was barely a whisper; it was hoarse and strained.

Her eyes were filled with tears, and she could barely get the word across her lips, no matter how much she wanted to. She pulled off her mask.

"It's me. It's Mommy."

The girl stopped crying and looked up at her. The sight of her blue eyes and strawberry blonde hair made Marissa's heart skip several beats, and she could barely breathe.

"It's me, Emma."

For a second, she feared the girl didn't recognize her, and it overwhelmed her with sadness. But the moment their eyes met, Emma burst into a smile, a gorgeous wonderous smile, and said, "M-mommy?"

"Yes, Emma, it's me. I'm here. I found you."

After Marissa removed her restraints, Emma, giggling happily like she always did when seeing her mother, embraced her. Marissa closed her eyes and held her tight, so tight she realized she had to be careful not to hurt her. She was just so happy, so relieved to finally be with her again, to feel her close. She rocked Emma gently in her arms, murmuring words of comfort as she stroked her hair, smelling the top of it, and kissing her chubby cheeks, tears streaming down her own as she did.

Finally. Finally, they were together again.

"Where were you, Mommy?" the girl asked, tilting her head.

Marissa smiled and hugged her again, her heart aching for her daughter's pain but also with guilt for causing it.

"It doesn't matter. I'm here now. I will never leave your side again. Let's go."

Barely had she said the words, when she heard a sound coming from behind them. Marissa spun around with a gasp, only to see the door slam shut behind her. She ran to it and hammered her hands on the soundproofed material. She tried to open it, to push it, but it had been locked from the outside.

Panic rose fast within her as she realized that they were locked in.

"Help! Help!"

No matter how much she pounded and shouted, no one answered. No matter how much she pleaded, no one came to her aid. Marissa felt a chill settle over her as she suddenly understood that they were both prisoners.

FORTY-FOUR

BILLIE ANN

"You're telling me that you met Marissa Clemens's daughter?" I had to repeat the question, as it was important to me that we fully understood each other.

Mr. Perez, sitting in the interrogation room, nodded, his eyes avoiding mine.

"I was trying to help them. They were running away from something."

Running? My mind was spinning. "Okay, let's take this from the beginning, shall we? When did you first meet them?"

Mr. Perez took a deep breath before beginning his story. His hands were clammy, and he wiped them on his jeans, while his eyes darted around the room nervously.

"It was four years ago," he said with a sniffle. "I came home, my wife and Cassandra were out of town, visiting my mother-in-law who was in the hospital in Atlanta, Georgia, where my wife is from. They flew up there on a Thursday and were going to stay the entire weekend to be with her, as she was very sick."

He exhaled and took a sip of water. I studied him, wondering if he was a very good actor or was actually telling the truth.

"You gotta understand," he added, setting the cup back down, "I have only been lying to protect her."

"I understand," I said. "Continue. You came home from work and then what happened?"

He cleared his throat. "I remember coming up into the driveway and thinking it was odd that the gate to the fence wasn't closed properly, as it usually was. I walked up and closed it, then thinking it was probably nothing, I went back inside the house and poured myself a glass of wine. My wife doesn't like it when I drink on weekdays, but because she was away, I thought I could treat myself a little. I ordered a pizza and went to the living room to watch TV. It was once I sat down in the recliner that I saw something in the yard, out the window."

"What was it?" Tom asked when Mr. Perez paused.

"The lights turned on," he said, biting the side of his cheek.

"What do you mean?"

"You know I have those sensor-controlled lights in my back-yard that will turn on if there is movement out there."

"So what? I have those too and usually it's a cat or a possum or a raccoon at that time of night," Tom said, leaning back in his chair. It creaked with his weight.

"And that's what I thought it was. We've had a racoon living out there underneath our shed, and it had babies, but it keeps going into our trash and leaving a huge mess. They can be so annoying. I wanted to get rid of it, and finally thought I had the chance."

"So, you bang on pots and pans to scare it," Tom said. He had come a long way since I first started training him, but he still had a lot to learn. Especially about interview technique and not interrupting the suspect when they were finally speaking. It wasn't because he was rude, he just got a little overly eager sometimes, I had noticed.

"And that's what I did. I grabbed a couple of pans, went outside, and started banging to scare them away from my property. And that's when I noticed something else. A shadow in the window in my shed. A big one. Once I saw it, it disappeared. So, I walked back to the house and grabbed my rifle, thinking it had to be an intruder, maybe some homeless person. I wasn't going to shoot, just scare them away. I opened the door to the shed and imagine my surprise when I saw what was really in there."

"Marissa and her child?" I asked.

He shook his head. "Almost correct. It was Marissa all right, and she hadn't given birth yet. But she was about to."

"She was in labor?"

He nodded. "Yes. She started to scream in pain. Her eyes were begging for my help. I didn't know what to do. I had watched my own wife give birth, but that was at a hospital. So, I told her I could take her there, but she told me no. No hospital and no police. I could see on her face that she was bruised badly, so I knew she was running from something, and understood that it was important for her not to be found. Besides, the baby was coming, fast, so there was no time."

"You helped her deliver the baby?" I asked.

He nodded. "I was so scared, so afraid of doing something wrong, but the baby almost slipped right out of her, and that was it. She took the girl on her chest and started breastfeeding immediately—she knew what she was doing, she was, for want of a better word, calm. I cut the cord, then took them both back to the house, where they got washed up. I had some of Cassandra's old baby clothes in a box in the closet upstairs, or rather my wife had saved them because she wanted a second child, but we never succeeded. I gave them to Marissa so she could dress the baby. Then she slept in my guest room for two days, and I called in sick for work.

"Once I knew my wife would be coming back, I had to figure out what to do with Marissa and the baby. I still had the house across the street and had been using it for Airbnb. It was empty at this point, so I told her she could stay there as long as she needed to. She told me it was extremely important that no one ever know she was there or that she had a child. She made me promise to never tell anyone and said she would be killed— they both would—if they were found. I felt protective of her, after all I had helped deliver her baby. I wanted to help her out. So, I did. I made sure they got settled in the house, and then went and bought groceries for them and such. Until she started to make her own money. Once Cassandra started babysitting, I suggested her to Marissa, because I knew she struggled with childcare when she was at work. Cassandra was my daughter, so she trusted her that she wouldn't tell anyone about them." He exhaled. "It torments me every day that I couldn't protect them or my daughter. I wanted to tell you about this, believe me I did, but Marissa begged me and made me promise not to. She was so terrified, and she said her life would be in danger if I did."

"And you have no idea whom it is they are running from?" I asked. "Has anyone come to her house, threatened her, or been keeping an eye out for her? Have there been strange cars in the street, parked there?"

He shook his head. "No. Believe me I have been wondering about the same thing for every day since Emma disappeared, and since my daughter..."

He stopped, tears springing to his eyes. He winced in pain and held his side again.

"Tell me, how did you get that injury?" I asked.

"I was working in my yard," he said. "I think I just strained a muscle."

I stared at him, taking note of the fact that this wasn't what he told me the first time.

"I thought you fell on your bike?" I asked.

"Oh, yeah, well, that too," he said. "I did both, silly me. I just don't know which one made me bruise my rib."

Once again, I noticed he wasn't holding his hand where the ribcage was.

"Can we ask for a DNA sample before you leave?" I asked. "Just a quick swab of your mouth."

"Yes, of course."

"Thank you, Mr. Perez," I said and got up. "We will let you know if we have any more questions."

He nodded, sweat springing to his forehead. He wiped it off with his hand. "It's hot in here, huh?"

"Not really," Tom said and got up to follow me.

"Ah, I guess it's just me then."

Tom held the door for him, watching him closely as he walked past him. "I guess so."

He shut the door, and Scott came to get Mr. Perez and take him to another room where he could do the swab.

Tom came up behind me, and said, "I don't believe a word that man just said. He is lying faster than a horse can run. Did you notice how he was fidgeting and constantly shifting in his seat?"

Chief Doyle had been listening in on the interview and came toward me, shaking his head. "I ain't buying it either."

"Why not?" I asked.

"You're telling me he helped deliver a baby in his shed and never told anyone, let alone his wife, about it?"

"Marissa asked him to keep it a secret. She was scared. Of what we still don't know," I said.

The room went silent, and I looked between the two of them, unsure of what to say. I didn't really know what to make of it yet, and now I felt uneasy. Doyle had always been the more reserved one, never too quick to come to judgment, and I had respected that. Lately, however, he seemed to have taken a hard line against anyone who lied to the police.

Doyle ran his fingers over his face, shaking his head. "Maybe so, but the whole 'I was just trying to help' act," he said, making quotation marks with his fingers, "is too much. He's trying to come off as so innocent, when clearly he is not."

"Was he maybe just trying to help her?" I asked cautiously.

Doyle walked past me, tapping me mockingly on the shoulder. "He slept with her, I'm telling you, Wilde. If you can't spot him lying, then we need you to go through some more training in interrogation technique. Don't let him ride you and wrap you around his finger. I thought you were better than that, seriously."

I sighed and looked down at the ground, feeling my cheeks flush. I hadn't expected this kind of reaction from Doyle.

I walked to my desk and looked at Tom next to me.

"I think the Chief is right," he said. "But we'll know more when the DNA results come in."

I sat down, looking at my notes. "He did definitely lie to us about how he got his injury. It was a completely different story from last time I asked him."

I exhaled and decided to go through my notes again. I couldn't help but feel like something was off about the whole situation. Very off. I was beginning to feel the weight of the case heavy on my shoulders. I needed to find out the truth, no matter how difficult or uncomfortable it may be.

FORTY-FIVE

BILLIE ANN

It was late before I went home. I was exhausted, and frustrated with this entire case, to put it mildly. Doyle was pushing for us to look deeper into Cassandra's dad; he said as of now he saw him as our main suspect, but I wasn't sure. People lied all the time. It didn't mean they killed anyone. Let alone their own daughter. I needed to know why. I needed a motive to believe it.

I needed also to find Marissa. I feared she had gone after Emma by herself. I felt certain she knew where she was and just didn't dare tell me for some reason. I couldn't stop thinking about her in that shed, giving birth all alone and how scared she must have been. I was worried for both Marissa and Emma now. I feared they were both in great danger.

I opened the door to the house and stepped inside, feeling the strains of exhaustion that had become my constant companion since taking on the new job as the head of homicide. I shrugged off my belt with my badge and gun and hung it up in the hallway, locking the gun in the safe and pausing for a moment to take in my home: the deep blue walls, the gleaming hardwood floors, the living room filled with books and toys, and the faint smell of cinnamon and homecooked meals.

At least when someone did cook, that was. Lately we hadn't really done much of that. It was too hard for both me and Joe. To pretend. It made me not want to go home. That and the anger I was still processing over him telling my mother the truth.

Making my way through the house, I spotted Joe in the garage, hunched over his old motorcycle, engrossed in whatever project he had going. That thing had never worked, but he loved to try to make it, especially when he had a lot on his mind. I put a hand on his shoulder, and he turned to face me with a start.

I smiled, even if it was forced. He returned my smile and eased up.

"Welcome home," he said, and I could tell from the look on his face that he hadn't even thought of dinner. Neither had I. Maybe we could just order something. DoorDash was our savior these days.

"How are the kids?" I asked, my voice almost a whisper as I glanced up the stairs.

"They're fine, I think," he said with a nod. "Charlene's on her phone in the living room, Zach is playing video games, and I haven't seen William these past few hours, as he has been in his room."

"Okay," I nodded. "How does Mexican for dinner sound?"

"Good. Good."

An awkward silence filled the room, and I decided to leave him alone. I walked to the kitchen and pulled out my phone, then opened the DoorDash app and ordered a bunch of tacos and burritos. The food came a little later and we all ate together, even if we might as well have been eating apart, as no one engaged in any form of conversation at all. I tried to ask them how school was today but received nothing but a shrug and "it was okay" from the boys.

That was it. At least I tried.

My guess was they sensed the tension between me and Joe, even if we tried hard not to show it, or to let them know. Kids knew. Kids always knew.

As I cleaned up after dinner, a tear escaped my eye. I wiped it away fast, but I couldn't help myself. I felt awful. I loved my family. What was I doing to them?

I'm making myself happy. I'm not doing anything to them. I deserve to be happy.

I knew it was the right thing to do, to follow my heart, but was it worth it?

"I'm going to bed," I told Joe when I was done. He was back in the garage fumbling with his bike project, and just grumbled something back that I couldn't hear. I went to the guest bedroom and closed the door, then crept under the covers and closed my eyes.

Sleep came and knocked me out fast.

FORTY-SIX

Then

Eight months had dragged on since Kitty was taken, and she was slowly beginning to lose hope of ever leaving this place again. She had been living in this small shed that got scorching hot during the day, with nothing but a thin mattress on an old metal frame bed, and a tattered blanket to keep her company. And of course, the pink teddy bear. But not a single scrap of sunlight had made its way in, and she spent her days in the light of one small bulb hanging from the ceiling, trying her best to sleep off the tedium. The only sound keeping her company was the low humming of the small AC unit in the wall. It was very old and didn't run very well, but at least provided some relief to her.

Her days were so incredibly boring, and the same thoughts ran circles in her head. But today, she sensed something was different. She heard voices coming from the other side of her walls, and a steady rhythm of footsteps growing louder as they got closer.

What's going on?

Heart throbbing, she sat up on her bed and stared at the door as she heard the bolt being pushed aside.

Was this good news? Or was she in danger?

When the door opened, surprise flooded through Kitty's body. There stood Damian, holding a silver tray in his hands. Curiously, it carried a plate with a homecooked meal—rice, beans, and stewed chicken—instead of the usual bag of burgers and fries. Behind him was his wife. She was smiling and nodding happily, and it frightened Kitty, because she always looked so angry and serious, or sad. Never happy. Never smiling. Never.

"You must be hungry," he said, setting the tray down on the bed. He looked at her with a strange kind of sympathy and untied her, while saying, "We brought you something special."

Kitty felt a wave of emotions—relief, confusion, and something else she couldn't quite explain. But she didn't want to say anything, so instead she started to eat. She looked at the plate in front of her and a tear rolled down her face as she tasted the food. It was the first time in so long that someone had given her something out of compassion, and she knew it meant more than just the food.

Linda sat down on the bed and took her hand in hers. "Sweetie, we came here to talk to you about something."

She glanced up at her husband, then back at Kitty.

Kitty had her mouth full of chicken and wanted to cry in happiness. This tasted so good, and she realized that it had been so long that she had completely forgotten how good a homecooked meal was.

"We know you're not very old," Linda said. "But you do know where babies come from, right?"

Kitty stopped chewing. She nodded, thinking of what had happened over the past few months, then ate more of the delicious food.

"Okay, good. That's good," Linda said. "Because the reason

why we're bringing you this food, is that we believe that you..." she paused almost tearing up.

Kitty didn't quite understand why she was getting emotional, so she frowned.

Linda cleared her throat. "Remember how we had you pee on that stick? Well, it came out positive. We believe that you are pregnant."

Kitty stared at her, food still in her mouth. She swallowed what was in there and the big lump struggled all the way down.

"Here, have some water," Damian said when she began to cough.

Tears sprang to Kitty's eyes, and she drank from the bottle of water. She took in a deep breath and her nostrils were filled with the stench from the bucket in the corner where she was to relieve herself. The taste of piss and feces came in her mouth, and she wanted to throw up, but bit it back.

She knew what being pregnant meant. Her mom had talked about it when Aunt Jane had been *knocked up*, as she called it. By some bastard, she'd said, who wouldn't even recognize the child. And then she had to raise the child all by herself. And she also knew she hadn't been bleeding for the past three months but thought nothing of it. Damian had been coming to her every day, and she had let him. Because that meant getting food, and he would also sometimes bring her candy, if she was extra good to him and let him lie on top of her, even if it hurt.

Damian stroked her gently across the hair. "I'm so proud of you, Kitty. I really am. I can't wait to see what our baby will look like. I'm sure it will be beautiful just like you."

FORTY-SEVEN

BILLIE ANN

The dream started out as a nightmarish blur that slowly became clearer. I was walking home along the same route I used to take, back years ago when I was a young detective. But something felt off. I had the distinct feeling that I was being watched, and I began to feel the hairs on the back of my neck stand up. I quickened my pace, but it felt like I was going nowhere. It was almost like the faster I tried to go, the slower I went.

Suddenly I was in a strange room, and I was being pinned down by someone I knew. I felt helpless, unable to move or fight back as he touched me. I could feel tears streaming down my face as I screamed for help, but no one could hear my voice. No one came to rescue me.

Time seemed to stand still as I struggled, and I felt a deep emptiness wash over me. I felt trapped, like I would never be able to escape this nightmare. I wanted to wake up, but I was stuck in an endless loop of despair and hopelessness. I begged him to stop, to leave me alone.

Next, I was walking through an unfamiliar city when I stumbled on a crime scene. On the ground, in a ditch, was a body, lifeless and cold. The body was crumpled and mangled in a way that was unmistakably unnatural. I knew who he was but couldn't remember his name.

Around his neck was tied a belt with a shiny buckle.

I woke up in a cold sweat, my body trembling and my heart pounding. As I lay there in my bed, I couldn't help but feel relieved. It hadn't been real. It had only been a dream. I kept telling myself.

It was just a dream.

But then it overwhelmed me. I started to shake heavily, and tears streamed across my face, soaking my pillow. I could barely breathe and sat up straight, hoping it would calm me down, but little did it help. Knowing I wouldn't be able to sleep anymore, I got out of bed, grabbed my phone and called my best friend Danni. She was sleeping, of course, so it went to voicemail. I hung up without leaving a message.

I couldn't say anything, I simply couldn't get the words across my lips, so I just cried helplessly.

I walked downstairs and outside to the porch swing, and I sat down.

I had finally stopped crying and was able to just sit there and try to shake the dream. My dream had been different from what really happened, but some of it was very similar. Like the feeling of being helpless, of feeling frozen and unable to move. Because of who he was. The feelings still sat with me if I let them, if I was alone and didn't keep busy. That's why I always made sure I had stuff to do. I couldn't stand feeling those feelings. I couldn't stand thinking about what had happened.

But what really bothered me about the dream was that it wasn't just about the rape. It was also about this case. It was getting to me.

You know why.

I exhaled. I did know why. Because it reminded me of the first case I ever worked on, back when I was starting out as a detective in the small town of Ridge Manor. The disappearance of a young girl. It was never solved because then everything happened, and I was suspended, and I was moved to another homicide department in another city. The case became a cold case because of it. She was never found.

"It's the belt buckle," I said into the night. "I forgot about it."

I know what I must do.

I stared into the darkness of the night, my hands growing clammy at the very thought. I knew exactly what I had to do, and it terrified me more than anything.

FORTY-EIGHT

BILLIE ANN

I can do it. Billie Ann, I can do it.

I took a turn at the light and found myself driving down the main street of downtown Ridge Manor. I didn't feel good at all. I felt terrible. My stomach was in knots, and my hands gripped the steering wheel tightly out of an instinctive sense of dread. I felt my heart race in my chest, and my breathing became ragged the closer I got to my destination. I tried not to focus on the task ahead.

Don't overthink this. Just do it and do it fast.

The town looked the same. Nothing much had changed since I was there last. Still same old empty streets, an occasional dead racoon or armadillo on the side of the road after being hit by a car, and pickup trucks passing me carrying cages for hog hunting in the back. When I was younger, I would go hunting in the swamp that the town bordered. I once caught a ten-foot gator and sold the meat to Daisy at the Southern Harmony Café, where we always went for lunch when on duty.

As I took the next turn, I could see the swamp in the distance, and my unease grew rapidly with each passing street corner. I felt my grip tighten around the steering wheel, and my knuckles turned white.

I had never thought I would be back here again.

I had bought a bag of Reese's peanut butter cups for the ride, and now I took the last one in the bag. I was stress eating. My mom would kill me if she saw me. She had always been on my case about my stress eating. I sighed when thinking of her. I hadn't talked to her since I had thrown her out of my house. I missed her but didn't really want to talk to her. She had really hurt me with her comments, and it was hard to get back from there. I wondered where my dad was in all this. Probably staying out of it as much as possible, as usual. He didn't want to get involved in our family drama, and I couldn't blame him.

Even if I could use his support in all this. But I knew my mom was in his ear about it and he would be betraying her if he showed me support. My dad had never been good at standing up to my mom, so I didn't see that happening anytime soon.

But I couldn't focus on my family problems right now. I had a job to do. I pulled into the parking lot of an old two-story house with a wraparound porch and a big magnolia tree in the front yard. It had been there since the beginning of the nineteen hundreds, and the story was told that they used to lynch people from it. It gave me the creeps. Always had. I took a deep breath, trying to calm my nerves, and stepped out of the car.

The heat hit me like a ton of bricks, and I immediately regretted not wearing shorts instead of jeans. I took a deep breath and looked around, letting my eyes scan the area. I didn't see anyone I knew, but that didn't mean they weren't watching me. This town had eyes everywhere. Nothing went unnoticed.

Not even a visit from one of its former cops.

I glared nervously at the house in front of me. It had been years since I was there last, but seeing it again made me stop breathing for a few seconds. I shook my head.

I can't do it. I can't do it.

I closed my eyes and steadied myself. Then I took in one more deep breath, before walking up the three steps to the porch. I opened the screen door and knocked on the door behind it.

Then I waited. Calming myself down.

Breathe, Billie Ann, breathe.

FORTY-NINE

Then

Kitty looked down at her protruding stomach, amazed at how big it had grown. Damian told her there were still two months to go. Would it really get bigger than this? It was already uncomfortable.

Thinking of it made her feel both wonder and dread.

Damian had said it would be fine, and she trusted him.

She closed her eyes and let the sunlight hit her face. Since she became pregnant, they had let her outside in the yard once a day for half an hour, so she could get some sunlight and vitamin D, Linda had said.

"It's important both for you and the baby."

The rest of the time she spent back in the shed, behind the bolted door. They had let her have a TV in there, but she couldn't watch the news and wasn't allowed to turn it on without someone being there to observe her. More than often, it was Damian who did that. He would sit on the bed with her, massage her feet when they cramped up, and they'd watch a movie or a show of some sort; and if she let him touch her, sometimes he would let her watch for longer, maybe an entire hour. It made the time pass faster in the shed, and she felt less lonely.

She had also gotten real food, homecooked meals, almost every night, now that she needed it for the baby. And vitamins, they would make sure she took those. Kitty thought they were being so kind, and she savored every moment of Damian's presence when he came to see her.

It made her feel special.

It was only when she was all alone in the middle of the night that she would sometimes think of her mother, and she would miss her. But those feelings usually passed again, after she cried for a little.

After all, she also cared for Damian and Linda, and they loved her so much. She liked being with them.

As she stood there, lost in thought, enjoying the sunlight and the kicking of the baby inside of her, a hand gently rested on her shoulder. She turned to see the smiling face of her Damian. He was holding a small, wrapped box and a single red rose.

"You're so beautiful," he said with a wink. "I have a little surprise for you."

Kitty's eyes widened. "What is it?"

"Open it and see," he replied, handing her the box.

Carefully, Kitty unwrapped the box and lifted the lid. Inside was a beautiful necklace with a delicate pendant of a mother holding her child. Tears welled up in her eyes as she looked at it in awe.

"It's so pretty," she whispered, feeling overwhelmed with emotion.

Damian gently took the necklace from the box and secured it around her neck. Kitty leaned into Damian and embraced him tightly, feeling a sense of comfort and security in his arms.

He really loved her, she thought, while touching the necklace. And together they were going to love this baby too.

FIFTY

BILLIE ANN

"What do *you* want?"

The words were harsh and almost spat at me. The woman in front of me in the doorway, with her piercing blue eyes and sharp jawline, looked like she meant business. I took a deep breath and tried to steady myself before answering. Seeing her again filled me with anxiety, and my hands began to shake.

"You can't be here, go away," she added, shooing at me with her hand, like I was a stray cat.

"Betty," I said with a deep exhale. "I need to talk to him. It's important."

She shook her head angrily. "No, no, no. He doesn't want to see you. Ever again. Now go."

"Betty, I wouldn't be here if it wasn't important," I said.

"I don't care. I never want to see you here again. This is private property. You know we have guns. Don't make me go get them."

I could barely breathe as I looked at her. I wanted to cry. Seeing her again brought everything back, and it hurt.

She shook her head. "How could you do this to him?"

"I didn't do anything to him."

"He took you under his wing. How could you?"

My heart was racing now, and I could hear the rapid pulse in my ear. I felt dizzy but managed to steady myself.

"He raped me, Betty. I had to report him."

"Oh, don't start with all that again. You know you wanted it too, just as much as he did. You just regretted it afterward. Don't give me that rape nonsense. You consented to it. Why didn't you report it, right after it happened then? Why did you wait?"

"Because I was in shock."

"No, let me tell you why you reported him. You were mad because you didn't get that promotion. He gave it to that Hansson guy instead. Was that why you slept with him, huh? So you could get the promotion? Well, congratulations. I hear you're the head of homicide now where you live. I guess you won. Meanwhile, my husband, the very man who got you to where you are today, who taught you everything when you were just a young kid, he's in a wheelchair for the rest of his life. Fired, and disgraced, ruined, and my life is ruined too. I hope you're happy."

"It was never my fault that he was hit by a truck. That had nothing to do with what happened between us," I said.

"Yeah, you tell yourself that," Betty said and tried to close the door.

I put my hand in it and pushed it back open.

"That's it, I'm getting my gun if you don't leave this property, now," she hissed.

"Betty, I need to... do you think it was easy for me to come here today, huh? Do you think I want to be here?"

"Yes, I do. I think you like this, and you want to rub it all in his face, but I ain't letting you."

"What's that commotion about? Why are you yelling?" The voice came from behind her. I recognized it immediately and felt a shiver in my spine.

Travis.

My former partner.

"It's her," Betty said and stepped aside so Travis could roll toward me in the doorway. It was the first time I'd seen him in his wheelchair, and it startled me. I had only heard from other people what had happened to him. He looked so different, yet his eyes remained the same.

Betty wheezed. "She won't leave."

"I need to talk to you," I said, my hands clammy, my breath unsteady.

"I told her we're getting the gun, so..." Betty began, but Travis lifted his hand and stopped her.

He glared at me, then smirked. "I'll talk to you."

"But...?"

"Shut up, Betty," he said. "I wanna hear what she has to say."

FIFTY-ONE

MARISSA

She could hear voices. Voices that were arguing close by. Marissa got up and put an ear to the door, to better hear. Emma was sleeping on the mattress; she had been sleeping a lot these past days. It was very hot in the small shed, and the air stuffy.

Marissa could feel beads of sweat trickling down her forehead as she strained to listen closely. The voices grew louder, they were definitely arguing. Their voices were laced with anger and hostility.

She turned around to look at Emma, who was still fast asleep. Marissa knew she had to keep her safe, no matter what. She tiptoed toward the mattress and gently touched Emma's shoulder. Emma stirred but didn't wake up.

Marissa made up her mind and went back to the door. She pressed her ear against it once more, and this time, she could hear them more clearly, but she couldn't make out what they were arguing about. The voices were too muffled and the words incomprehensible.

Yet she took the chance. She clenched her fists and started hammering on the door, while yelling, "HELP! Someone help us!"

She kept banging on the door and screaming for help, yet nothing happened. Marissa felt tired too and sat down on the floor. She wondered if the shouting had woken up Emma, but it hadn't. She was still lying there, sleeping heavily.

Like a little angel.

Marissa was happy to be with her again. If she was being honest, she preferred being a prisoner with her, over being on the outside without her. It was simply too painful. At least in here she could protect her.

Marissa could hear the voices again, but they sounded like they were moving away now. She gathered her last strength and started to bang again, while yelling, "Help. Please HELP."

Then she sank to her knees, sobbing. She couldn't believe she was trapped here. He brought them food every day, but usually just threw it at her, then bolted the door shut again. Every day Marissa tried to plead for her freedom. Every day she would scream and yell and plead for mercy, but none was ever given. She was stuck there, in this hot oven, with her child.

She wiped her nose with her hand and looked at her daughter. She had been sleeping for an awful long time now, it seemed.

A frown grew between Marissa's eyes.

That's not normal.

She got up and walked to her daughter. She looked so tiny, so pale from the lack of sunlight and proper food.

"Emma?" she said. She reached out a hand and gently touched her forehead, then pulled it back again with a gasp.

She was burning up.

She tried to wake her up. "Emma? Emma?"

She touched her cheeks, then kissed them, while calling her name. "Emma? Emma. Wake up, baby girl."

But Emma didn't wake up. She lay there, completely still, her red cheeks and forehead burning.

"Please, Emma, please," she cried and took her baby in her arms. "Please, Emma, wake up. Please, WAKE UP!"

FIFTY-TWO

BILLIE ANN

"We can talk out here on the porch. I don't want you in my house."

Travis rolled outside in his chair and closed the door behind him. I walked to the side, my heart still throbbing in my chest. Seeing him made everything inside of me hurt. His piercing eyes and the way they looked at me took me right back to that day. My body still remembered every detail of it, and especially the feelings that surrounded it. I could still hear him breathing on top of me, his mouth close to my ear, his heavy body weighing me down, hurting me.

"So, what do you want?" he said, folding his hands in his lap.

I swallowed and told myself I could do this. For Emma. For Marissa. "I... I am working a case and I need to ask you a question."

He scoffed. "What do you need my help for?"

"It's very... similar to the case we had, you know the one we worked on, together when—"

"When we had sex, and you went to the Chief and said I raped you, oh, I remember that very well."

I closed my eyes again and focused on breathing. Just breathing. Then I looked at him.

"There's a girl missing, taken from her home just like it happened back then."

"Kitty Durham wasn't taken from her home, you know that. She was on her way to the bus; someone saw her and told us. You gotta get those facts straight if you want to make it as a detective, Wilde."

"I know there's a difference. This girl disappeared from her backyard."

He scoffed again. "So what? Children go missing all the time. What does it have to do with the old case?"

"There's something else."

"I'm dying from tension here," he said sarcastically. "Do tell."

"The belt."

He stopped smirking. "What about it?"

"Kitty's stepdad, Cole Durham, dedicated his life to finding her, and led search groups and started a campaign for donations and everything. And then one day his wife, Kitty's mother, came home from work and found him dead, a belt wrapped around his neck."

"He killed himself. He felt guilty."

"But remember how we suspected that it wasn't suicide? We thought that maybe he actually found out what happened to Kitty, and he was murdered because of it?"

"That was your little theory," he said, grinning. "Not mine."

"No, the medical examiner questioned it too, remember?" I asked. "He said that he wasn't sure it was suicide. It didn't fit with the way the marks were on the neck."

He shook his head. "Not really. You know what? This was—what—like ten years ago?"

"Fourteen," I said.

"Yeah, it's ancient history by now. I don't really want to

think about those things anymore, and I think you need to leave it alone. You ruined my life, now go enjoy yours."

"But no one knew about the belt, but the two of us," I said. "We were the only ones there. You took the belt off and put it back in his closet, remember? But we asked his wife about it, and she said it wasn't his. She had never seen it before."

He shook his head. "I don't remember all those details anymore. It's a long time ago."

"I need to know who else knows about the belt and the buckle. Besides you, me, and Kitty's mom. I've been through the old case files, but you were the head of that investigation—I wasn't privy to everything that was going on. Someone is either copying this murder, or we're dealing with the same killer once again after a dormant period of fourteen years."

He shook his head. "No one knew. Just us. I really don't think Kitty's mom, that weak little woman, could kill anyone. So, I guess it's either you or me." Then he laughed. The sound of it made my skin crawl. He shook his head. "That's the best laugh I've had in a long time, ever since you ruined my life. Sorry, kiddo, I can't help you. The man killed himself."

He leaned forward and signaled for me to lean toward him. I didn't. I just stared at him. The smell of him alone made me feel sick. His word, his nickname for me. *Kiddo.*

"Let me ask you something," he said. "If I really did rape you then why didn't you scream? Why didn't you fight back? You learned self-defense. You could have at least tried."

I stared at him, my heart knocking against my ribcage, hands shaking heavily. I turned around and walked to my car, resisting the urge to run, tears springing to my eyes, unable to breathe.

He was right, I didn't scream or fight back when he pushed himself on top of me. I didn't scream because of who he was. He was my boss. He thought he was entitled to it. I was scared. I froze.

And he knew that had haunted me ever since.

FIFTY-THREE

Then

At first, she didn't think it was anything important. When Kitty felt the small jabs in her stomach, and it became rock hard, and then eased up, she thought it was just part of growing the baby inside of her.

Until she realized it didn't stop. It came back a little later, same sensation, same degree of pain, maybe slightly more painful this time. And then it stopped, and she could breathe again. Thinking it had stopped, she closed her eyes to relax, but then the sensation returned, only more powerful this time, and she groaned loudly. It came again and again and became rougher to get through, and she screamed in pain for the seconds they lasted.

When it stopped, it was like heaven, like every cell of her body relaxed at once and she became so peaceful.

But then it returned.

Then more came and after that more again. With briefer and briefer intervals. Soon she realized the seriousness of her situation. This had to be it, right? Her baby was coming. And she was all alone in the small shed.

Please? Someone? Help me?

Kitty tried to stay calm, but panic crept in as the contractions became stronger. She had no idea how long this would take and had no medical supplies or assistance. She didn't know how to do this.

She was alone and terrified.

As the pain intensified, Kitty remembered watching a movie recently with Damian where a woman gave birth. She tried to focus on her breathing, like the woman in the movie had done it, inhaling deeply through her nose and exhaling slowly through her mouth. It helped for a moment, but soon the contractions became too intense to ignore.

What do I do? What if I do it wrong?

She felt hot tears stream down her face as she realized that she might not make it through this alone. She tried to push the thoughts away, but they kept coming back. What if something went wrong? What if she couldn't deliver the baby? What if the baby didn't survive?

Just as she was about to give up hope, Kitty heard the sound of footsteps approaching the shed. She tried to call out for help, but her voice was weak.

The bolt was pushed aside and in came Damian. He looked at her, then gasped.

"Are you okay?"

She grunted and shook her head. "I don't think so."

He came to her and sat by the bedside. Kitty's face was slick with sweat as she groaned in pain. Damian grabbed her hand in his and gazed down at her with a mixture of fear and determination.

Kitty's voice was soft and hoarse from screaming as she said weakly, "Please help me."

He nodded. "We can do this. We can do this together."

Damian nodded his head and squeezed her hand tight, trying to give her strength. He spoke softly, assuring her that everything would be all right.

"I'm here for you."

She screamed again and, finally, after what felt like an eternity, there was a tiny, high-pitched squeal, and then a perfect, round little head appeared in the world.

Damian's eyes widened in amazement, and he exclaimed with tears, "Look how beautiful!"

Hands shaking, he lifted the baby from Kitty's body and brought it up to her chest. The small slippery lump of flesh felt magical against her body. Was this a real baby? Had she really made this creature inside of her? Kitty felt overwhelmed by the beauty of this new life—with its delicate, fluttering eyelashes, tiny fingers, and rosebud lips. She started to weep softly as she looked lovingly into its eyes and whispered the words, "Welcome to the world, little baby boy. Welcome."

FIFTY-FOUR

BILLIE ANN

The engine rumbled as I drove with the windows wide open. I raced in a fury through the streets, going back to Cocoa Beach, away from this place and all its bad memories.

I had been humiliated again, this time beyond repair. He had looked at me with such condescension, so sure of himself, so certain of what he could get away with. I had wanted to reach out and smash him in the face, to make him feel for just one second the heat of the fire that I was burning in.

But of course, I didn't.

Instead, I had said nothing, swallowed my pride, and walked away. But the anger was still there. It bubbled up inside me like a pot of boiling water on the stove. I screamed loudly inside of the car. I was so angry, so furious it felt like my blood was boiling.

"That bastard," I said, slamming my hands on the steering wheel. "That sick, sick bastard."

I found some Joan Jett and turned the sound up, screaming along to "Bad Reputation." I was angry at him, but also a little at myself for letting him get to me the way that he did. What had I expected? An apology? Him being remorseful or understanding? I knew better, but still had held on to some foolish hope.

The rage coursed through my body, like an electric current, making my skin hum and my heart beat faster. I was determined to take back control, to reclaim my strength and power. I would show him I was not afraid.

He had hurt me for the last time.

I had made it to the bridges when my phone rang.

"H-hello? Detective Wilde?" a small, still voice said.

"This is she, who is this?"

"My name is Darcy Mason," she said, clearing her throat.

"What can I do for you, Darcy?" I said as I reached the top of the bridge and could spot the cruise ships at Port Canaveral in the distance, towering like the massive floating high-rises that they were.

"I'm... well, I work... worked for Dr. Henderson," she said. "I have been debating whether or not to tell you this, but well... I think I should. The thing is that Dr. Henderson sometimes treated patients but didn't put their files in the system, if you know what I mean."

"I don't, no. Please explain that to me."

She exhaled. It was obvious she felt like she had betrayed her former boss.

"He had some patients, children, that he sort of treated for free. If they didn't have insurance. Like children who are here with their parents illegally, or maybe hiding from an abusive ex."

"Go on," I said.

"And Emma Clemens was one of those who came under that category. That's why her name wasn't in the system. She was brought to him by a neighbor who knew Dr. Henderson. I don't remember his name. I should have told your colleagues when they were here, but I just... I didn't want to jeopardize—"

"It's okay," I said. "It's understandable. But just so we're clear, what you're telling me is that Emma Clemens *was* Dr. Henderson's patient?"

"Y-yes."

Darcy's voice quivered as she spoke.

"That's extremely interesting to me," I said. "I'm very glad you did tell me this, Darcy. Because what you just told me is very important to my investigation. It's a good thing, okay? You didn't betray him."

The phone went deadly silent as my words hung in the air. I suddenly felt very awake and forgot about my anger. Darcy had revealed a key piece of information that could really help me, and even if I couldn't see the big picture yet, I sensed that some of the puzzle pieces had fallen into place. This was the connection I was looking for.

She broke the silence. "He was such a good man. Why anyone would ever hurt him, I just don't understand. They all loved him."

I couldn't help feeling a pang of sadness for Darcy, who clearly had been so devoted to her employer. I reached the barrier island and took the turn down A1A toward my town and the police station as I softly said, "We'll do our best to answer that question, Darcy. That's why I'm here."

FIFTY-FIVE

BILLIE ANN

As I entered the station the next day, my steps were light, and my heart was pounding. I had to push away my gut-wrenching meeting with my former partner in order to focus on the case.

A hush seemed to fall over the entire building as Chief Doyle rushed out of his office. There was an urgency in his stride. He signaled for me to follow him back in, and I obeyed, dread filling me as I crossed the threshold.

Now what?

The office was dark and smelled of stale coffee. Chief Doyle took a seat behind his large mahogany desk and gestured for me to do the same.

"Chief, I got some news on the way back here," I said. "The pediatrician was Emma Clemens's doctor. That's our connection. Cassandra was her babysitter; this guy was her doctor. I can't help thinking that it is almost like this killer wants to erase any trace of Emma. Does that make any sense? Like we didn't believe she existed at first, because there were no records of her, no birth certificate, and so on, and someone is killing off anyone who could confirm she was real."

He exhaled and rubbed his forehead. "Here we go again."

I was taken aback. "I thought you were onboard with this. What happened?" I asked him.

He sat up straight. "I called you in here for another reason. I need you to listen, Wilde."

I nodded, feeling like a child in the principal's office. "Yes, sir."

"We got a DNA test done on this," Chief Doyle said gravely.

He opened a drawer and pulled out a small bag, placing it on the desk in front of me. His face was lined with worry, so deep that it almost seemed like he aged right before my eyes. In the bag was a lock of hair.

"It matches the hair of Pete Perez, Cassandra's father."

I felt my stomach clench as I realized what he was implying. On the one hand, I desperately wanted to give Pete the benefit of the doubt; after all he had just lost his only daughter. But then there was also the pain in his side that had me worried, and the fact that he was lying about it. And the fact that he let Marissa live in his house for free. Could he really be behind Dr. Henderson's murder? Why?

With conflicting emotions coursing through me, I took the bag from Chief Doyle's hand and studied it closely.

"The hair was found in Henderson's apartment close to the body. They believe he might have fought for his life and then pulled it out of the head of his attacker."

"Why have I not heard of this before?" I asked.

He shrugged. "I don't know, Wilde. I don't know where you are half of the time these days. A lot of stuff was found in his apartment, and I can't even keep track of it, but this one is the only one that matches someone that can actually serve as evidence. Are you going to fight me on this? Are we going to have a problem here?"

I shook my head. "No, sir. Of course not."

"Okay, good," he said and sat back in his chair, folding his hands over his stomach. "Now bring him in."

He was fixing me with an intense stare. "I'm sorry," he added. "I know he just lost his daughter and that it is a lot right now. But it has to be done. My guess is he killed both Henderson and Cassandra. Your case is solved."

"Why would he kill his own daughter?" I asked.

He threw out his long arms. "Who knows? Maybe she saw something? Maybe she threatened to tell on him. Maybe it was the other way around. Maybe he was abusing his daughter and the doctor saw something and threatened to report him. Lots of possibilities here. That's what you need to ask him about."

I nodded reluctantly and turned to leave the office. I didn't feel good about this, but he was right. It had to be done. I just couldn't figure out how this related to Emma, or if this was evidence that it didn't at all. Maybe Pete could answer that if we could get him to talk. Taking a deep breath to steady myself, I replied resolutely, "Yes, sir, I understand. I'll do whatever it takes to bring him in."

With that, I stepped out of the office.

We got Pete Perez in the next day, early in the afternoon. Luckily, he came willingly, as we had a local patrol drive by his house and ask him to come to the station. Tom and I did the interrogating. We went at it for hours, asking him about the murder of Bryan Henderson. We had him dead to rights with a lock of his hair found at the crime scene that matched his DNA profile. However, he remained steadfast in his claims of innocence.

"I don't even know who the guy is," he claimed. "I have never seen him before in my life."

"I know that's not true," I said. "I spoke to Dr. Henderson's nurse, and she said you brought in Marissa and Emma Clemens. You knew him."

That shut him up. He stared at me, biting the inside of his cheek. "Okay, so I did know of him. I'm a son of undocumented immigrants myself. I knew not to ask questions when Marissa came to me. I knew she was going to need a pediatrician, one who wouldn't ask any questions either. So, I asked around and that's how his name came up. But that doesn't mean I killed anyone."

I knew the Chief wanted this guy to confess, so we could move on with booking him. I was trying my best, especially since I knew the Chief was watching us through the one-way mirror. I didn't want to let him down and knew my career depended on me solving this case.

I leaned forward and said, "Pete, you're not fooling anyone. Just tell us what happened."

Pete's eyes darted around the room as if searching for an escape route. Finally, he muttered, "I honestly don't know what you're talking about. I have nothing to do with this. I can't keep saying the same thing over and over again. You have to believe me."

Tom chimed in, "Don't lie to us, Pete. The evidence is right here. You can either confess now or make things harder for yourself down the line."

Pete shook his head vigorously and said, "I swear on my mother's grave that I didn't do it. Why won't you believe me?"

I took a deep breath. "Let's cut the crap, Pete. Stop playing games with us and give us the truth."

Silence hung thick in the air like a noose waiting to be tightened.

Finally, Pete spoke up. "I'm telling you everything I know! Honest to God, I'm innocent!"

I placed the bag of hair on the table in front of him.

"Pete, you're not telling us everything. What are you hiding?"

Pete shifted uncomfortably in his seat. "I swear to God, I don't know what you're talking about," he said, unconvincingly. He looked at the bag. "I don't even know what that is."

"That's your hair," I said, tapping the bag. "Found at the scene of crime. A whole lock of it. We ran it against the DNA sample you gave us, and it was a match."

He shook his head. "That can't be. Are you sure it's mine?"

"Yes, we're sure," I said. "It was a match."

He looked desperate and groaned. "But I didn't kill anyone, I swear."

"Come on!" Tom chimed in, slamming his hand on the table. "Just tell us the truth and we can work something out."

"I told you already, I didn't do it!" Pete yelled back, sweat beading on his forehead.

"Okay, then why were you at Bryan Henderson's apartment?" I asked calmly, trying to reason with him. Stirring him up didn't seem to help anything. "We have clear evidence that proves you were at the scene." I grabbed the bag and held it up. "This proves you were there."

"But I wasn't," he continued.

We were getting nowhere with this. "Okay, let's get back to that injury of yours. The side that you keep touching and wincing when you move. How did you get that?"

"I told you I fell off my bike."

"Well, the other day you said that it was while doing yard work. So, which is it?" I asked.

"I... I don't... I can't tell you."

"That's convenient," Tom exclaimed.

"And why can't you tell us?" I said. "Is it because it stems from your run-in with the woman, Ashley Wittman, who was in the apartment when you murdered Bryan Henderson? She stabbed you so she could get away from you, right? We have the piece of glass and blood in her apartment; all we have to do is run a match with your DNA, which is being done as we speak. Then we will know for sure. You might as well tell us now. Save us some time. Where is Ashley? Where is Emma?"

His eyes hit the table. "I was attacked."

"You were attacked?" I asked. "Now that's rich. By Ashley Wittman, who is half your size?"

He shook his head. "No, at the park. Walking the dog late at night. Someone came up from behind me and kicked me down.

I tried to fight back, and that's when they grabbed me and pulled a lock of hair out of my head. Right here."

He turned his head and removed some strands of hair, so we could see a small bald spot.

I frowned. "And why didn't you report this attack to the police?"

His gaze was still avoiding mine. It made it hard to tell if he was lying or not. "Because... because I owe someone money. I borrowed some money from some bad people and hadn't paid them back. I assumed it was them, punishing me." He shook his head with an exhale. "My wife doesn't know this. I have a debt, from gambling. I didn't know it was a problem till I was on the ground being beaten up. I have been trying to stay away from it, but it's hard. My wife doesn't know anything at all. I lost all of our savings just a few months ago and have been trying to win it back. If I don't then we'll have to sell the house Marissa is in."

The desperation in his voice was palpable, and I got the feeling that he was telling the truth. We kept asking deeper into the ordeal, and soon we realized we weren't getting anywhere. I decided to let him go. I needed more evidence.

As he walked away from us into the darkness outside, I couldn't help but feel that there was more to this story than met the eye. A lot more.

But what was it I was missing? And why did it feel like we were constantly three steps too late, that this person was outsmarting us?

"Wilde, we have news," Scott said as I returned to my desk, feeling defeated.

"What news?"

"It's Ashley Wittman," he said, while staring at his computer screen. He was shaking his head. He looked up at me.

"The girl who was with Henderson?" I asked.

"Yes. She's been admitted to the medical center at Sebastian." He looked up and met my eyes. I saw fear in his. "And get this. A guy came in with her, and he was found dead in her hospital room. Strangled."

I grabbed my car keys and forgot all about dinner and homework with the kids. Joe had to take care of that tonight. My killer was escalating, and I had to stop him before he killed again.

FIFTY-SEVEN

Then

Kitty held the newborn tight in her arms. She was mesmerized by the beauty of his tiny face and loved feeling the warmth of his body against hers. Even the smell of him was divine. She smiled, feeling happy for the first time in a long time, as the baby fed from her. It had only been a week, and her body was still in pain sometimes. It looked different, and she was tired, consumed by caring for her little angel.

She thought for a moment about her own mother, and tears filled her eyes instantly. She would have loved to have shown her the baby, her grandson. She could use her advice now on getting the baby to sleep, and if he was getting enough food. She missed being able to talk to her.

Kitty sniffled and touched the baby's soft black hair. He was so amazing, this little creature. So wonderful. She couldn't dwell in the past now and think about her own mother. There was no time for it. She needed to focus on her baby boy and the future they held together. As a family. Even if it was taking place in this hot small shed, it was her life now, and as long as she held him in her arms, she was happier than she ever was on the outside.

She did miss the fresh air though. Damian hadn't been coming to let her out like he did when she was pregnant. He had only been bringing her food and rarely spent any time with her and the baby. They never watched TV anymore either.

She kind of missed those days.

Maybe he is just busy with work. Saving the world from dangerous criminals.

Kitty still admired him for his heroism. He would often tell her stories of criminals he had chased down and locked up. She liked those stories. Of justice being served. Mostly because she could feel how it made him happy to tell them. He liked the way she looked at him, like a true hero.

In her mind that's what he was. And she loved him for it.

Suddenly, she heard the bolt being pushed aside, and soon the door to the shed opened. Kitty looked up expectantly. Damian and Linda stepped inside. At first, she was happy to see Damian, but less so as she saw his wife's face coming up behind him. There was something about the way she had looked at her lately, since the baby came, that made Kitty think she resented her. Maybe because Kitty could have a baby and she couldn't? Damian had told her about it, that they hadn't been able to make her pregnant. That's why he was so surprised at how fast Kitty had become pregnant. And happy. He had been so happy too. He had always dreamed of expanding the family, he told her. And she had helped him with that. She was proud to have done that. Proud to be his woman.

But today something was different in the way he looked at her. When Kitty saw Damian's expressions, she froze in place.

They both had an almost sinister look about them. It worried Kitty. Usually, Damian was so sweet and smiling when seeing her. He had no love in his eyes today. Had he stopped loving her? How did this happen? What had changed? Was she not good enough? Was he not happy with the baby?

Damian spoke first. He stepped closer.

"We need the child," he said.

Kitty's body tensed, and her grip on the baby tightened. She could not and would not let go.

What did he mean? Why did he ask for the baby?

"No," she said, her voice shaking. "This is my baby."

Damian's wife stepped forward and put her hand on Kitty's shoulder.

"It's all right," she said in a soothing voice. "You can trust us."

Kitty looked into the woman's eyes and saw compassion in them. It made her ease up. Slowly, she loosened her grip and handed over the baby, heart racing in her chest, fear rushing through every vein in her body. Damian took the child without a word, and his wife followed him out.

"Wait. Stop. When will he come back?"

But it was too late. The door slammed shut, and she heard the bolt close on the other side.

Kitty screamed, her heart aching with the sudden absence of the baby. She needed him back; she needed him close. She couldn't live without him. Didn't they know that? Crying, Kitty fell to her knees inside of the shed.

She had thought that this joy, this moment of bliss, was the start of a new life for her and her son. But instead, she was left in her prison, with only her memories of him for companionship.

FIFTY-EIGHT

BILLIE ANN

I hurried inside the old hospital building and went up to the front desk. I noticed a couple of police cars out front and wondered if they were there because of the guy. I feared they were already interviewing Ashley. I hoped I could get to talk to her right away.

"Ashley Wittman's room, please?" I said to the woman at the lobby.

She gave me the room number, and I rushed into the elevator. I got onto the floor, then walked out, seeing a lot of distressed faces on my way. The place was crawling with police, and that puzzled me. I stopped a nurse to ask for directions.

"I'm looking for Ashley Wittman."

She clasped her mouth and shook her head. "You're... you're too late."

"What do you mean I'm too late? Too late for what?"

She let out a small shriek. "She was... one of my colleagues walked into her room about an hour ago, and found her..."

"What do you mean, found her?" I asked, heart throbbing in my throat. "What happened?"

She shook her head, fear in her eyes. "She was dead."

My heart dropped. *Dead?* How was this possible? Was I too late? Was I too freaking late?

I spent most of the evening in Sebastian, at the medical center, talking to the investigators in charge. I got as many details as possible from the medical examiner, and only had to take a brief glance at both victims' necks to know that the bruises around their throats were a little too similar to those found on Cassandra Perez and Bryan Henderson. There was no doubt in my mind we were dealing with the same killer.

And possibly the same as Cole Durham, don't forget that.

I called Tom and got him to find out everything on this Alex guy who had come in with her, and it didn't take him long to find out that he lived in Sebastian, and we concluded that Ashley had to have been staying with him, probably hiding there, when the killer found them. The thought terrified me.

I requested that the casefiles be transferred to me and my department, so we could investigate further. What bothered me the most was the fact that Ashley had been alive when she got to the medical center, they told me, but died in her bed later. They couldn't tell yet if she had died from her initial injuries, and just taken a turn for the worse, or if she had met her killer again in the hospital room.

I feared the latter.

Unfortunately, there was no surveillance showing anyone entering her room since the police came to talk to her, they told me, which struck me as odd. There were no recordings of anyone else going in there. Could the killer be someone from the hospital?

It was past midnight before I made it home to Cocoa Beach and drove into my street. I was so exhausted as I parked in the

driveway and got out. The house was completely dark, and only
Zelda came running to greet me as I walked inside. I took her
out so she could pee, then went back inside and found Joe in the
kitchen getting a glass of water.

He nodded to greet me. "Hi," he said.

I took the leash off and the dog ran to her bed and lay down
with her favorite toy, a stuffed porcupine that she had been
gnawing on for so long she had pulled out all the stuffing and
now it was completely flat. But she still loved it more than any
other toy she had.

"Hey," I said. "Everything good here?"

He nodded. "Yeah, I just couldn't sleep."

"How did the evening go with the kids?"

"It went okay. The usual."

"Did Zack do his homework?" I asked.

He looked at me, annoyed. "Of course. As soon as he came
home from school. I even checked it, even if it is Friday and he
could wait till Sunday to do it. You don't think I can take care of
the kids alone for one night?"

I shrugged. "Just checking. Zack has a tendency to forget his
homework when we wait till Sunday. You know I'm grateful for
you taking care of them while I work. That's not what I meant."
He didn't say anything. I continued. "And what about dinner?
What did you have to eat?"

"I made chicken alfredo," he said. "There's some in the
fridge if you're hungry."

I realized I hadn't had dinner, but I really wasn't hungry. I
was too tired to eat. I grabbed a banana and ate it instead.

Joe glanced at his phone, scrolling through his Instagram
feed. Guess we were done talking.

"So, no problems?" I asked.

He shook his head, then walked to the stairs and went up. I
looked after him, feeling lonelier than ever. He didn't even ask
where I had been. I had texted him to tell him that I was

working late, but he had just answered with an OK. He used to hate it when I worked late and would always say he believed they were exploiting me, and that I deserved more free time with my family. He hated it when I wasn't home. But now he seemed almost like he no longer cared.

That happened fast.

"Good night," I said, but he was already in the bedroom and had closed the door. I looked at Zelda with a shrug. "Guess it's just the two of us then."

She had become my sleeping buddy and, even if she did make a lot of noise at night, I enjoyed her company more than anything.

"Let me just go check on the kids," I said. "Kiss them good night. Wait for me here. I'll be right back."

FIFTY-NINE
MARISSA

Marissa had been locked away in the shed for days, helplessly watching Emma slowly grow weaker with each passing hour, no one coming to their aid.

Emma was still burning up with a high fever that refused to break, and had become so disoriented that she wouldn't wake, only groan in her sleep. Marissa tried desperately to keep her daughter comfortable, and as cold as possible, but it was hard in the hot shed with the sun scorching outside of it during the day. She feared that, without help, it wouldn't be long before Emma would succumb to the illness and slip away.

"Please, someone help us," she screamed while hammering her fists on the door.

But it was no use.

She had been pounding on the door of the shed for hours at a time, till she had to rest because her hands were bleeding. Yet no one heard her cries for help. The silence was making her feel desperate. Tears streamed down her face as she pounded her fists against the metal over and over again, her last hope of finding help quickly fading away. She screamed out in despair, yet there was no sign of anyone coming to her rescue.

"My baby girl," she said and sat on the bed with her, holding her in her arms, while struggling to keep back the tears. They had given them water to drink, in bottles, but now they were slowly running out. Emma needed water to help fight this fever. "My poor, poor baby."

She sat with her in her arms rocking her back and forth, heart aching desperately for help.

What am I going to do?

She had nowhere to turn and was left with no other choice but to wait and hope that someone would hear her cries and come to help. Whether it be in the form of a miracle or a tragedy, Marissa didn't care anymore.

Anything would do. Anything but this darn silence!

"Please," she cried.

But as the hours passed, Marissa began to lose hope. She felt herself slipping into a fog of despair, her mind becoming disoriented and her thoughts a jumbled mess. She couldn't remember how long she had been locked away, or how long Emma had been ill. All she knew was that they were trapped in this shed, alone and helpless.

Her eyes felt heavy, but she refused to close them, afraid of what might happen if she did. Emma's breathing had become more and more labored, and Marissa knew that time was running out. She sank to the ground, her back against the shed door, and prayed for a way out of this nightmare.

Late at night on the third day, she had almost dozed off, even if she didn't dare to.

Suddenly, there was a creaking sound, and the door slowly began to open. Marissa blinked in surprise, her eyes adjusting to the sudden flood of light from a lamp outside. A figure stood in the doorway; their features obscured by the bright light behind them.

Startled, she scrambled to her feet, not daring to hope too

much. Her heart leapt with desperation as she tried to make out the features of this person.

Friend or foe. It didn't matter at this point.

"Please," she pleaded, her voice hoarse from hours of screaming. "Emma is sick. She needs help. You are the only one who can help her."

SIXTY

BILLIE ANN

I slowly climbed the stairs, my body feeling the exhaustion from a very long day as I passed by Zack's room. The door was slightly ajar, and I could see his small figure curled up in bed, blankets pulled up to his chin.

I snuck into the room, cautious to not make a sound and wake him up. I gently brushed his hair away from his forehead and pressed a featherlight kiss to his temple. He stirred slightly, and I froze, holding my breath. After a few moments he settled back down, and I exhaled with relief.

"Sleep tight, my love," I whispered and closed the door as I left.

I continued down the hall to William's room, expecting to find him passed out with his phone still in his hand. Sure enough, as I pushed the door open, I saw his phone lying on the floor next to the bed. William had gone to sleep without putting it away, a habit of his that I had been trying to break. I smiled fondly as I watched him sleeping, his chest rising and falling in a peaceful rhythm.

The next stop was Charlene's room. I pushed open the door

slowly, expecting to see her in her bed. But much to my surprise her room was empty.

My heart sank.

She wasn't there.

"Charlene?" I called.

I walked inside of the room. My heart beat wildly as I stared at the empty bed in my daughter's bedroom. Then I saw the curtain move and realized the window was open. I stuck my head out and looked down.

Yup, she had definitely crawled out the window, there was no doubt in my mind. There was a ladder leaning up against the side of the house. She wasn't even trying to hide it. But where had she gone? Could she be in some kind of trouble?

With a sudden urgency, and rising anger, I rushed to Joe's bedroom. He was fast asleep. I shook him awake. My mind was a flurry of panic and anger.

"Where is Charlene?" I asked, my voice trembling with emotion. "Joe."

He groggily stared at me, still not fully conscious of the situation. He blinked his eyes.

"W-what?"

"Charlene? She's not in her bed. Where is she?" I asked frantically.

Joe's eyes widened as the realization of what I was saying slowly sank in, and he shot up quickly, finally understanding the gravity of the situation. He looked up at me with a grim expression.

"She's not? But I thought she was. She was in it last time I saw her. I said good night to her at eleven."

"Well, she's not there now."

I felt a sharp pang of worry as I reached into my pocket and pulled out my phone. I felt my heart racing as I called her number, my thumb shaking slightly with the urgency of the moment. As I expected, she didn't answer, and so I left a voicemail, desperately pleading with her to call me back and tell me where she was.

I tried again, but still had no response. I tried to find her location on Find My Phone, but she had it turned off, even though I had specifically told her to turn it back on.

I couldn't help but feel a sense of dread wash over me. Where was she? And what had happened to her? I had no way to know for sure, but I knew that this wasn't good. I feared she was out drinking and driving again.

"Can you see where she is?" Joe asked, rubbing his eyes. "In that app?"

"No," I said, frustrated and worried. "She's turned it off again. Breaking the rules. She's grounded, Joe. She's not supposed to go anywhere."

"I know that," he argued. "Why do you always think that I'm some idiot that—"

I snapped my finger. It was Friday. Of course.

"Peyton's party," I said.

"What do you mean?"

I pointed at him. "She got mad at me for grounding her because that meant she would miss out on this birthday party that she had been looking forward to. I guess she decided to go after all."

Joe shook his head. "I see. She's being a teenager; well, big surprise there. She went to a party. So what? She'll be fine."

I stared at him, puzzled at his reaction. Why wasn't he angry? Why wasn't he jumping out of bed and into the car to go pick her up? What was wrong with him? I barely recognized him. It was like he'd given up.

"What do you mean?" I said almost spitting in frustration. "She lied to us, Joe. She broke the rules and you're not even mad about it?"

He exhaled and rubbed his chin. "Maybe we should cut her some slack."

My eyes grew wide. "Slack? What do you mean? She's lying and running away. Breaking every agreement we make. And you want to cut her some slack?"

He sighed. "She's going through stuff. We all are. She's acting out."

"You're darn right she's acting out—" I started, but he placed a hand on my arm to stop me.

"Because of you. Because of what is going on at home," he said, gazing into my eyes. "Because of what you're doing to us."

He was right, in a way. Of course, she was acting out because of what was going on. She had even told me so herself that she knew and that she found it... well, appalling, is the nicer word for it, I guess.

Charlene's and Joe's words hurt like nothing else in the world. But I had to remember what my therapist had told me: "Let go of the guilt." I can't save everyone all the time. I wasn't responsible for other people's actions and reactions, only my own. I knew what was happening at home was out of my control and yet, some part of me still wanted to take responsibility for it. To be the hero who saved the day. I had always been super mom. But now I had to realize that I wasn't. That I couldn't make everything perfect again, by blowing on scrapes and bruises and putting Band-Aids on, or cooking their favorite meals or taking them out for ice cream. Those days were over.

I wasn't perfect.

I wanted to do something, anything, to make things right, but I just didn't know how. All I could do was stand there, helpless and alone. I sighed and turned away, my eyes heavy with unshed tears.

"Geez, thanks, Joe. Guess it is all my fault. Way to make me feel better."

"I didn't know it was my job to make you feel better," he groaned. "You're certainly not doing your best to make me feel good, are you? These past weeks have been the worst in my life.

But I guess you don't care about that. Because that's just me, right? Your husband. A man. And you don't like men anymore."

I scoffed and shook my head, hands on my hips. Of course, he made this about him. "You're just... you're... this is too much. I can't do this right now. I need to go find my daughter."

With that I stormed out of the room, biting back my tears and replacing them with frustration and anger toward my daughter who—once again—had treated me with no respect.

This was going to get ugly. I was done being nice.

SIXTY-ONE

Then

"Come back with him. Bring my baby back to me."

Kitty couldn't stop crying. Her heart was in pain, every part of her body was aching, from missing her newborn baby. It was like a part of her was ripped from her. She couldn't believe that Damian and Linda would take her newborn son away from her.

Didn't she do a good enough job? Had she messed it up somehow?

Kitty wiped her tears away and sat on the bed, thinking maybe they were going to bring the boy back. It just took a while. Maybe they just took him to the doctor, to make sure he was healthy? Yes, that was probably it. He needed a checkup. She took in a deep breath to calm herself down and lay on the bed, staring at the metal roof above her. Then she finally fell asleep. Exhausted from crying and screaming, she passed out.

She didn't know how long had passed, but she woke up to the sound of the bolt being shot aside, and sat up straight, her pillow soaked from crying in her sleep. She gasped, blinking away the tears.

"W-who is there?"

It was Linda. She didn't look at Kitty, just stepped in carrying water and food. She placed it by the entrance, then turned to leave.

"How's my baby? How's Oliver?" she said, even if she knew they didn't know she had named him that. It was after her grandfather who died when she was a young child, but she had loved so much. "Is he okay?"

Linda paused but didn't look up. She stared at her feet, then began to leave.

"No, wait," Kitty said. "Please?"

Linda paused again.

"Can I see him? Please? I miss him."

Linda shook her head.

"Please?" Kitty said. She got off the bed and fell to her knees, hands clasped together. "Please?"

But Linda just shook her head again, then walked away and closed the door.

"NO!" Kitty screamed and ran to it. She clenched her fists and hammered on the inside of it, crying helplessly.

"Please, please. Just for a few seconds? Just let me hold him?"

But all she received in return was a deep silence.

As the days passed, Kitty became more and more desperate to see her son. When she was brought food, which by now was always done by Linda, she begged the woman to let her hold him, to let her feed him, but all her pleading was ignored. She felt like she was going crazy, trapped in this shed with no one to talk to except for the roaches scurrying around in the corners.

Days turned into weeks, and Kitty spent her time sobbing and wishing for her baby back. She even told herself that she could hear him crying sometimes, and it broke her heart.

She didn't understand why they would take him away from her. She began to lose hope, convinced she'd never see her child again. And she also wondered why Damian had stopped coming. Was he tired of her? Had he lost interest in her? Was she not good enough for him anymore?

Did he forget about me?

One night, as she was lying on the floor where it was the coldest in the hot shed, she heard a sound coming from the outside. It was faint at first, but then it grew louder and louder until she could make out the sound of footsteps approaching. Her heart raced with hope.

She knew it was probably just Linda bringing her food as usual, but the footsteps seemed heavier and more determined than usual. Could it be someone else?

Could it be... him?

The door creaked open, letting in a slight light from the now so mysterious outside world. The face greeting her in the doorway made her heart beat faster.

She smiled and rose to her feet.

"Damian!"

He walked in and closed the door behind him, then took her in his arms. She hugged him and clung to him as tightly as she could. He lifted her up and carried her back to the bed. She cried and enjoyed being held so much, she didn't want to let go of him again. She had felt so alone these past weeks. It had been like the whole world had forgotten about her. Like she was going to just rot away in that shed.

But now she felt a sliver of happiness again. Now that he was back. He loved her and always had. She knew it. He would never forget her.

"I have some good news for you, Kitty," he said with a handsome smile that made her stomach flutter.

"Good news?" she asked, thinking it had to be about her baby. Was she going to get to see him? To hold him? Would they let her into the house and be with him? She could promise to never try to do anything bad. She never would. She didn't want to upset them.

"You're going to be a mother again."

Kitty's heart stopped. "What do you mean? What happened to my baby? Where is Oliver?"

"Don't worry about him," he said. "He's fine."

"But... how?"

He smiled even wider, then removed a lock of hair from her face and put it behind her ear. Then he caressed her cheek.

"You know how. Just like last time."

"Just like last time?" she repeated, feeling confused. All she could think about was Oliver. Her baby. Why couldn't they just let her see him? And hold him? Why was he talking about another baby, about her becoming a mother again? She was already a mother.

"I don't understand?"

He shushed her, then leaned forward and placed a hand over her mouth to stop her from talking. Then he whispered.

"I think you do."

SIXTY-TWO

BILLIE ANN

I could feel my heart pounding in my chest as I drove to Peyton's house. She and Charlene had known each other for many years, and she lived only two streets down. Peyton's mom was one of those who had given up on her teenage daughter years ago, and often left her alone in the house, where anything could—and would—happen.

I wasn't going to let Charlene stay there for one minute longer. I knew I was about to humiliate her, but this was needed. She was grounded and supposed to be at home. She had put this on herself.

And I was angry. Not just because it was disrespectful, but also because Charlene knew how important my job was. How important my time was. Right now I should be out finding Emma or Marissa, and not looking for my own daughter.

When I arrived, I could feel the dread rising in my throat. There was a gathering of teenagers outside, some vaping or smoking, some laughing. Music blared from inside, the bass shaking the walls. I went up to the door and knocked, hard, but it wasn't locked and slid open as I put my fist against it.

At first glance, I spotted Charlene, slumped against the

wall. I hurried to her, and she barely noticed me. Then our eyes met, and my heart sank. She was glassy-eyed, and I felt a wave of anger and disappointment wash over me. I grabbed her arm and yanked her from the house.

"Mo-o-m! What are you doing?"

"You're high, Charlene. What do you think you're doing? You didn't think I would find out you were gone and come for you?"

"I don't care, Mom. You can't just come here and... and... look they're all laughing at me."

"I don't care, Charlene. This is not okay."

She pulled her arm out of my grip. "So what?"

"So, we're going home now."

"No, we're not."

"Oh, yes, we are."

I reached out my hand to grab her, but she pulled back. "If you touch me, I'll scream. I'll tell everyone that you're a kidnapper. Or even worse that you're... a lesbian."

Is she for real? Where is my little girl?

"Charlene, you need to come with me right now."

She shook her head. There were people everywhere, standing in groups and staring at us, and the last thing I wanted was for them to call the police. Technically I was the police, but I didn't want these kids to get in trouble. And they would be once the police came here. Including Charlene.

We stood out on the lawn, the smell of marijuana and sweat heavy in the air. We glared at each other, neither of us wanting to give in. I wanted to yell, to scold her for her recklessness, but I bit my tongue. At least I tried to. Yet I couldn't help myself and some of my rage escaped anyway.

"How could you be so careless?" I seethed, my hands trembling.

She dropped her gaze and sighed softly.

"Just let me go."

Her voice was quiet but determined. I shook my head vigorously. "No way. You're my daughter and we're going home now."

We silently stood on the lawn, our bodies almost touching. I opened my mouth to scream at her but quickly snapped it shut. She narrowed her eyes as if daring me to say something, but I refused to give in. Instead, all that escaped my throat was an exasperated groan.

We fiercely locked eyes, neither of us ready to back down. I wanted to shout, to chastise her for her thoughtless actions and disrespect, but she had hit me where it hurt. I knew deep down that this was all my fault. Joe was right, she was acting out because of me. How could I punish her for that?

"Let's get you home," I said, guiding her toward the car. Charlene stumbled as I pulled her arm, her body swaying with each step. I knew she was going to be a handful, but I was determined to get her home no matter what. As we made our way to the car, I could hear the snickers from the teenagers behind us. I ignored them, but secretly wondered if they heard her remark about me being a lesbian. I knew most parents around here and that rumor could spread faster than I felt comfortable with.

Once we were inside, I breathed a sigh of relief. Charlene slumped into the passenger seat, her head lolling to the side. I took a deep breath and turned on the ignition, making sure to keep my movements slow and steady.

As we pulled out of the driveway, I could feel Charlene's eyes on me. Her gaze was heavy, and I knew what she was thinking. She was angry, furious even, that I had ruined her fun. I didn't care. I was her mother, and it was my job to protect her.

We drove in silence for a few minutes until Charlene finally spoke up. "You're ruining my life, Mom," she slurred, her words barely coherent. "I hate you."

Ouch, that hurt.

I took a deep breath before responding. "You don't mean that, Charlene. I love you, and I'm just trying to keep you safe."

Charlene scoffed. "Safe from what? Having fun? You're so boring," she spat, her words sharp like knives. "But I guess all lesbians are like that. Boring."

I remained calm, refusing to let her words get to me. "Fun shouldn't involve breaking the rules and putting yourself in danger," I said firmly.

Charlene rolled her eyes, sinking deeper into her seat. "Whatever, Mom. You just don't understand."

As we pulled into our driveway, I turned off the car and let out a sigh. I faced Charlene and took her hand in mine. "Listen, sweetie. I know what's happening right now is a lot to take in, but I need you to not—"

"How could you not know?" she interrupted me, suddenly sounding almost sober. "How are you all of a sudden gay?"

I swallowed. I wanted to have this conversation, I really did, but was this the right time for it? The right place?

I decided the right time and place would probably never come.

"I have always been gay," I said.

"But how is that possible?" she asked. "What about Dad?"

"I fell in love with your father, and we wanted to have children. I wanted a life like everyone else, and where I come from, with how I was brought up, it simply wasn't an option to be gay."

"So, you don't love Dad. Is that it? Can't you just get a normal divorce like normal people?"

"I love your father, I still do. It's just different now. I can't live a lie any longer."

"So, it was all just a mistake? Me? William? Zack?"

I grabbed her arm and made her look into my eyes. "No! I don't regret a single thing. It was never a mistake, any part of it.

I just couldn't ignore who I was anymore. Someday you'll understand."

I hope.

She pulled away. "I don't think I will ever understand. I can't believe you would do this to us, and to Dad. Everyone will be talking about us because of you. Everyone."

Charlene got out of the car, before I could say anything, slamming the door behind her as she stormed into the house. I watched her go, feeling a mix of sadness and frustration. She was my daughter, and I loved her more than anything, but this really hurt.

I sat in the car for a few minutes, letting myself calm down before making my way inside. As I walked through the house, the sounds of Charlene slamming doors echoed through the halls. I sighed, knowing that we had a long road ahead of us. But I was determined to be there for her, to help her get through this. I had to. I knew it wouldn't be easy, but nothing worth doing ever was.

SIXTY-THREE

MARISSA

Marissa couldn't stand the wait. It was simply unbearable. She knew she had no other choice but to let them take her from her, again, yet it still terrified her. Marissa had been trapped in the sweltering shed for hours, her mind and body slowing as the intense heat weakened her. She had given Emma away to her kidnapper, freely, and asked that she be taken to a doctor, and since then a terrible silence had been her only companion, slowly filling her with a growing sense of desperation. Being without her beloved daughter again felt like the end of the world.

Where is she? Where's my baby girl? Is she okay?

Just as Marissa was about to succumb to despair, and fell crying to her knees, the door to the shed opened with a loud creak. Instinctively, she shrank away in fear, her heart thundering in her chest. Standing in the doorway was the man she had let take Emma, even if she didn't know if he would help her or not. He was a large, powerful figure, his face obscured in the shadows of the doorway.

He surveyed her with a dispassionate eye, a hint of amusement playing on his lips.

Did she even dare talk to him?

Marissa had nothing to say, no words to plead her case or plead for her daughter's safety. All she could do was stare at the figure, waiting for whatever fate he had in store for her. After what seemed like an eternity, the man finally spoke.

"It is done," he said, his voice deep and hollow like the rumble of distant thunder. "Your daughter has been taken to the doctor. Now, it's time for you to go."

"Where is she?" she managed to gasp out, trembling with dread.

He didn't answer, yet raised his belt and wrapped it around her neck in a swift movement.

In a flash Marissa felt the leather biting into her skin, and before she could even register what was happening the man tightened his grip around her throat and snarled through gritted teeth, "You'll never see your daughter again."

"Please!"

Tears stung Marissa's eyes as she shook her head frantically and tried to grab the belt and pull at it. Between gasps she pleaded for him to at least spare her daughter's life. Knowing it may cost her own, she begged desperately between sobs.

"Please! She's just a child! Please don't hurt her!"

But the man only tightened his grip further until Marissa felt faint from lack of air.

SIXTY-FOUR

BILLIE ANN

I arrived at the police station a little late the next morning. I needed some sleep, and I didn't get a lot of it the night before. I knew something was up when I saw Big Tom waiting for me by the door. His face was grim as he approached me and said, "They've arrested Pete Perez."

"What? Why?" I asked. "I let him go."

Tom shrugged. "Ask the Chief. He ordered it. He wants to see you in his office as soon as you get in."

I was shocked. What had happened? Why did they arrest Cassandra's dad? I knew we had the hair, but I just didn't think he was our guy. I had made that decision. As the head of homicide. I ran down the hall and into the Chief's office. He motioned for me to sit down as he looked at me gravely.

This was my case, I was the head of homicide, and a decision like that should belong to me. Why hadn't he at least told me this was happening? It wasn't right. My anger boiling, I looked at the Chief, and asked, "Why did you arrest Pete Perez?"

The Chief sighed heavily. "Because of the hair at the crime scene in Henderson's condo—it matched his DNA. That's enough for me. It should be for you too. It was a full lock of hair found on the floor, and some of it still clutched in the hands of the victim. He was pulling his hair to make him let go of the belt, he was fighting for his life. I should rather be asking you, why did you let him go? You certainly weren't following procedure. He should have been booked, and you know it. The hair is strong evidence. Enough for a conviction."

"But... I literally just got the report this morning from the medical examiner's office, and the blood on the piece of glass and the blood found in Ashley's apartment didn't match his DNA, even if they did match each other."

He narrowed his eyes. "I think the DNA found at the crime scene weighs a little heavier."

I shook my head in disbelief. "His hair at the scene doesn't mean he killed Bryan Henderson! And it's certainly not enough to prove he killed his own daughter," I exclaimed. "It could be circumstantial evidence! There must be more to this story."

The Chief nodded grimly. "Yes, there is more—a witness saw someone fitting his description entering Alex Johnson's house in Sebastian, where Ashley and he were, around the time of their murders. We believe these pieces of evidence are enough to prove that Pete Perez, Cassandra's father, is the killer."

He paused before continuing, his voice heavy with sadness. "People are scared, Billie Ann. All the parents in our town are terrified. We needed to get him off the streets. But that's not why I called you in here."

I stared at the Chief in disbelief. Something was very off in the way he looked at me. It made me feel uneasy. He folded his hands on his desk and that made me nervous. He wasn't his usual self.

"What is it?"

The Chief nodded solemnly and handed me a photograph of a truck. I looked at it, my heart beating faster.

"What's this?"

"You tell me," he said. "You recognize it?"

I felt my heart drop. "Yes, it's my daughter's truck. She got it for her sixteenth birthday."

"That may be, but it is also registered in your name."

"So?"

"This is the same truck that hit Travis Walker, your old partner," the Chief said gravely. "He was left paralyzed from the accident six months ago. There has been an investigation into it, and this is where it has been led to. To you."

He paused before continuing. I could barely think straight. What was this? What was going on here?

"You have a motive for wanting him dead, Wilde. You're being investigated for the attempted murder of your former partner," he said with a sigh, "meanwhile, you're suspended. I have no other choice."

I felt a wave of panic wash over me as I tried to gather my thoughts. All I wanted was for this nightmare to end—but it seemed like every time I turned around, something else was cropping up to make matters worse.

"Suspended? But... but—"

"I need your badge and gun."

I couldn't believe what was happening. I had been a good cop for years—no, an excellent cop and detective—and now, my reputation was on the line. More than that, I could end up in jail. I felt like I was in a bad dream, and I couldn't wake up from it.

"Chief, please. You don't understand. I didn't do anything wrong. I would never do anything like that. Someone must have framed me somehow, by using my truck. At least let me investigate this," I pleaded with him.

The Chief sighed and leaned back in his chair. "I understand why you'd want that, but I have to follow procedure. You're suspended until this investigation is over."

I felt tears welling up in my eyes as I took off my badge and gun, placing them on the Chief's desk. It felt like I was losing a part of myself, and I didn't know how to handle it.

As I walked out of the station, I couldn't help but feel like everyone was staring at me. I felt like a criminal, even though I knew I was innocent. I needed to clear my name, but I didn't know how.

I stepped outside, and the bright sunlight hit me like a wave. I felt like I couldn't breathe, like the whole world was closing in on me. I leaned against the wall, trying to catch my breath, and that's when I saw him.

He was in a wheelchair, pushed by Betty. At first, I thought it had to be a dream, an awful nightmare. But it was him. I could feel my heart racing as he came closer, and I felt like I was going to pass out.

"Detective Wilde," he said, his voice low and strained. "Or wait, I don't believe you're a detective anymore, am I right? I was hoping I'd see you today."

I couldn't find my words, couldn't even think. I just stared at him, frozen.

"I can't say I was surprised to find out that it was you," Travis said. "Felt good to tell your boss, though."

I still couldn't speak, couldn't move. I felt like I was underwater, everything moving in slow motion.

"I didn't... someone must have framed me."

That's when I paused and realized something. A huge piece fell into place. What if I hadn't been framed, as I first thought. What if?

What if it was Charlene?!

What if she had overheard me and Joe talk about the rape, like she had heard other stuff and then decided to hurt Travis? What if that was why she was acting out so much right now? Because she knew what she had done.

The thought was beyond terrifying and almost floored me.

I stepped forward.

Travis grinned.

"Please," I said. "Please don't press charges. I think—"

That made him laugh. "Will you look at that, Betty? Look who is crawling in front of me, finally. Look who is begging for my mercy. This is a sweet, sweet moment." He signaled for Betty to roll him closer to me. "Okay. We won't press charges, on one condition."

"I'll do anything."

"I want you to take away your statement about the rape."

"Excuse me?"

He leaned forward and narrowed his eyes. "Clear my name."

I shook my head and backed up. I had lied. I wouldn't do anything. I wouldn't do that. Never.

"No, no. I can't do that. We both know what happened, and what you did to me."

He shrugged. "It's up to you and your conscience."

With that he signaled for Betty to push him so they could leave. She sent me a look as she turned his chair around, one of disgust and contempt, which made the hairs rise on my neck. I watched them go, feeling like I had just been hit by a ton of bricks.

As I walked back to my car, I couldn't shake the feeling that I was being watched. I looked around but saw no one. I shrugged it off and got in my car, starting the engine and driving away from the station, not knowing when or if I would ever set foot there again.

SIXTY-FIVE

Then

Kitty slowly ran her hand over her stomach, feeling the small swell that seemed to get larger by the day. She had known for weeks that there was a life growing inside her. Now she felt it too, as the baby moved. It was like a thousand little fishes were living inside of her, swimming around. It felt so odd, yet strangely comforting at the same time.

"Calm down, little baby," she said when she felt a huge kick.

Kitty felt a surge of joy that was quickly followed by a wave of fear. The last time she had been pregnant, they had taken her baby away from her. She was scared it might happen again. But this time she was determined to be different. She knew she had done something wrong, that's why they had taken Oliver. She just wasn't sure what it was. But this time, she vowed, would be different. This time, she would do everything right. Was it the way she had breastfed? Was it the birth and how much she had screamed? Maybe she had done it wrong? It had been hard for the baby to latch on properly; maybe they took him away because he wasn't being fed properly?

Or maybe there was something wrong with him. What if he was sick? Maybe they were protecting her and didn't want her to know. No, Damian had said he was fine. Right? He didn't really want to talk about him, and he would change the subject every time she asked how he was doing. Would he tell her if he was sick or if something terrible had happened?

No, she couldn't believe it. She felt it. He was alive.

It had to have been her. She had to have been the one doing something wrong. And it wasn't going to happen again. She would do better this time around. She was older now, more mature. She had tried it before. She could do it differently. If only she knew what she had done wrong the first time around. She had tried to ask Damian but received no answer. She would have to figure it out by herself. Somehow.

"I won't fail you this time," she whispered, months later, on the night when the contractions started. She recognized them from the last time and let them happen. Let her body take control. She screamed in pain and gave birth all alone. The night became long and strenuous, but finally, it happened. Kitty held her tiny baby in her arms, cradling its fragile body, feeling a profound love more powerful and deeper than anything she had ever experienced before. She looked into the little eyes of the newborn and promised to protect and nurture her.

"I won't let them take you as well, little baby," she whispered, stroking her daughter's face gently.

Kitty had never felt so connected to someone before. Except for Oliver, of course. Even though she was exhausted, she stayed up all night with the baby, not wanting to let go of the moment. She shed tears of joy and relief that she had made it.

The sun slowly rose in the sky outside, quickly warming up the shed, and when Damian walked in the next morning, he found Kitty and the baby in the same position. His eyes widened with surprise and wonder as he looked at her. As Damian approached her, he noticed the bloodstains on the bed. He looked up at her, his gaze meeting hers, as he saw the newborn baby in her arms.

"Is everything okay?" he asked with a hint of worry in his voice.

She nodded, tears streaming down her face. He walked over to her slowly, his eyes never leaving the baby, and knelt down beside her.

"You did it," he said softly, his voice filled with admiration.

She looked up at him, a small smile spreading across her lips.

"We did it," she replied, her eyes never leaving the tiny bundle in her arms.

Damian's eyes widened with shock and happiness. He reached out and took the baby, and even if it filled her with fear, Kitty didn't fight him. She was simply too tired. He held the baby in his arms, looking down at her tiny features.

"She's beautiful," he said with a smile.

She watched as Damian held their little girl, scared he wouldn't give her back, but too tired to fight it. The exhaustion soon caught up with her and she felt herself drifting off to sleep, trying hard to stay awake. The last thing she remembered was Damian placing the baby back in her arms and kissing her on the forehead. Then she could finally let go and fall asleep.

When she woke up, she found herself alone in the shed. Panic set in fast. It was rushing through her body as she sat up and looked around. Where was Damian? And more important, where was the baby? She got out of bed and stumbled toward the door, her legs feeling weak and unsteady.

"Damian? Damian?"

No, no, no! This can't be happening. It can't be happening again!

She hammered on the bolted door, fists clenched tightly, as fear twisted in her gut. After a few minutes of fruitless pounding, she stopped, realizing that no one could hear her. She had been in there long enough to know that.

Fear consumed her and she collapsed onto the concrete floor. As she sat there, sobbing, she tried to piece together what had happened. Had Damian taken their baby away from her? Was she ever going to see her child again?

What had she done to deserve this?

What had she done wrong?

SIXTY-SIX

BILLIE ANN

As I stepped through the doorway of my home, dread slowly crept upon me. My feet carried me to the kitchen for a glass of wine, and one soon led to another, while trying to forget, to drown out all the noise. Yet with each glass I moved closer and closer toward an agonizing decision. One I wasn't willing to make. Through the window, I saw the serene waters of the canal, boats peacefully drifting by, their lanterns guiding them like fireflies in the night. But despite its tranquility, turmoil was brewing inside of me—should I recant my rape statement against Travis? A million thoughts flooded my mind at once. What would be the consequences if I changed my story? Would he do it to someone else? Even while wheelchair-bound, his sadistic nature made him more than capable of harming another innocent soul. Speaking out for justice had been a major struggle; could I bear to go back on my words now? They had been like family to me. Travis, Betty, both of them. Telling what happened had been the hardest thing I had ever done. No, I couldn't go back on it, I refused to.

But what would happen to Charlene if I didn't? Her life

could risk getting ruined. Her future. How could I live with myself?

I began to weep. Hiding my face in my hands, I let the tears roll.

Joe was already in bed, but he came downstairs when he heard me cry.

"Is that you, Billie Ann?" he asked, his voice thick with sleep. He walked down the stairs, staring at me, scrutinizing me. "Have you been drinking?"

I sobbed in response, my legs giving out beneath me, and I slumped onto the couch. Joe scrambled over to me and sat down next to me, his pale blue eyes wide with concern, but also angry.

"What's going on with you?" he said. "I can barely recognize you anymore."

"I had wine, I needed it."

"Oh, I see," he said, leaning back in the couch and facing away from me. He crossed his arms in front of his chest.

"What's that supposed to mean?"

He shook his head with a sigh. "Nothing. I'm just... well, I don't want to start anything now. It's late and I'm exhausted so—"

"Something happened, Joe," I said. "Something awful."

He looked at me, head tilted slightly, eyes narrow. "What happened?"

"Travis," I said, sobbing slightly.

A frown grew between his eyes. "Your ex-partner? What did he do now?"

"I got suspended today."

He shook his head, startled. "What? Why?"

"Because of Travis. They think I hit him with my truck, that I put him in a wheelchair. They're investigating it. They think I have a vendetta against him."

"I'm confused. You don't have a truck," he said.

"I know. That's what worries me."

"I'm not following you."

"Charlene has a truck. It's registered in my name. For insurance, you know?"

He stared at me, biting his lip. "No, no, that's—"

I placed a hand on his arm. "It's true. I think she did it. But I can make a deal with him, he said."

"Really? What kind of deal?"

I looked down at my fingers. The buzz from the wine was quickly wearing off now, and reality hit me again like a brick wall. "If I take back my statement. About the rape."

He sat up straight. "What?"

"He wants me to say that I lied. He wants me to clear his name."

Joe stared at me, his nostrils flaring. "But... you can't do that."

"That's what I said, but there is no other solution, the way I see it. Charlene is more important. They think it's me, but it wasn't, and if it was her... I have to protect her. She's just a child."

Joe rose to his feet, and he started to pace back and forth. "I can't believe this. I can't believe it."

"I'm gonna do it," I said. "I have to. For my daughter's sake. It will ruin her life if she is convicted."

He kept shaking his head and rubbing his neck. "No, no. There has to be another way. The guy raped you. We can't let him get away with it. We simply can't."

"But there is no other way, Joe."

He paused, then hid his face between his hands. I couldn't tell if he was crying or raging in anger.

"Joe?"

He lifted his gaze and looked at me. That's when I realized it. I could see it in his eyes. I stood up, suddenly feeling completely sober.

"It was you, wasn't it? You did it? You hit Travis with Charlene's truck?"

He exhaled deeply but didn't say anything. He didn't have to. I already knew.

"You're kidding me!" I almost screamed. "Why would you do that? Why, Joe?"

His nostrils were flaring, tears streaming down his cheeks. "I... I was so angry. Years of bottled-up anger just... made me lose it. I kept imagining him hurting you again and again and couldn't sleep at night. So, one day I took Charlene's truck and drove to Ridge Manor. I waited for him to leave his house, then followed him downtown. It wasn't planned, I promise you, it wasn't. It just happened. I saw him walk across the street and that's when I lost it. I couldn't believe he had hurt you and was still allowed to walk around a free man. I hit him with the truck. I didn't plan it, I promise. I just... I couldn't control it."

I stared at Joe in shock, unable to comprehend what he had just confessed to me. He had hit Travis with Charlene's truck, risking everything just to seek revenge for what he had done to me. I reached out and took his hand in mine.

"Joe, why didn't you tell me?" I asked, my voice barely above a whisper.

"I was scared," he replied, tears still streaming down his face. "Scared of what would happen to us, to our family, if anyone found out. I didn't want to lose you, Billie Ann. I love you so much. And now I am losing you anyway, how's that for irony, huh?"

I felt tears prick at the corner of my eyes as I looked at Joe, the man I had been with for eighteen years, the man who I thought I knew everything about. But at that moment, he seemed like a stranger to me.

"We have to tell the police," I said firmly, my hand still clasping his.

"No, Billie Ann, we can't," Joe replied, shaking his head. He pulled away from me. "They'll arrest me, and our family will be ruined. I'll lose my job, and we'll lose everything."

"But Joe, you committed a crime," I said, my voice firm. "You have to take responsibility for your actions. And they already know—they think I did it, and they might think Charlene did it."

Joe sighed heavily, rubbing his face with his hands. "I know. I'm not sure what to do. I just couldn't let him get away with it, Billie Ann. I couldn't."

"I understand that, Joe," I said softly. "But we have to do the right thing. We have to tell the truth."

His voice was shaking now. "I'll go to jail. And what about our children? They need us."

"But Joe, we can't just keep this hidden."

"I know, I know," he said, his head hanging low. "But please, just give me some time to think."

I nodded slowly, still in shock from what had just transpired. I couldn't believe this was happening to us. "Okay, but it's only a matter of time until they charge me or blame Charlene."

"I know," he said, his hand still clasping mine tightly. "I'll figure something out. I promise. Let's just go to bed for now."

I watched him walk up the stairs to our bedroom, and suddenly I couldn't shake the feeling that things were about to get much worse before they got better. I didn't feel good about it, and there was no way I could just go to sleep, knowing this. It tormented me for an hour, and that's when I made the decision. It was the right thing to do, even if it felt awful. It was my duty. I had sworn to uphold the law. I was suspended, with a killer out there—I was the only one who was still looking for Emma and Marissa. And I needed to protect my daughter.

I grabbed my phone and called the station.

Moments later they arrived.

SIXTY-SEVEN

BILLIE ANN

"Are you sure you want to do this?" Officer Steele was on call this evening, and as he came to my door, he looked at me with sadness in his eyes. I explained the situation to him, and to the Chief, and we all agreed that Joe needed to be taken in.

Even if it broke my heart to do so.

I nodded and let him and Officer Craig inside.

"He's in the bedroom. Up the stairs and to your right."

"Will he be hostile?" Steele asked.

I sighed. "It's possible."

Officer Craig placed a hand on my shoulder and bobbed his head. "We will take it from here, Wilde. I'm sorry that it has come to this."

"Me too," I said. "Me too."

I watched as they marched up the stairs and into my bedroom, then closed my eyes and braced myself for the reaction. It came promptly.

"What is going on here?" my husband yelled.

I couldn't hear what they were saying but knew they were telling him to go with them quietly. I had done this many times myself as a younger officer, but never to a colleague's spouse.

Someone they used to see at our yearly Memorial Day picnic, or who would come in and pick me up regularly with flowers and stealing me away from work on our anniversary or my birthday. They knew Joe, and that had to be tough. I know it was for me.

I saw his face as they escorted him out and down the stairs. He was fully dressed; they had let him do that. His face was red with anger, his eyes ready to kill. When he saw me, he started to yell and scream at me, his voice suddenly booming through the house.

"Why? Billie Ann? I thought we agreed on this. Why have you done this? Why would you do this to me?"

I wanted to explain, to tell him that I had been left with no choice, but the words wouldn't come. Tears welled in my eyes and streamed down my cheeks. I couldn't stop them no matter how hard I fought. Seeing the man I loved like this, in hand-cuffs, being taken away, screaming and cursing at me, made me lose it completely. I tried to avoid his eyes, but he put his face close to mine, and hissed, "This is not the end of it. This is not the end."

"That's it, we're leaving, come on," Steele said and pushed Joe away from me.

He growled at me, then did as he was told. I watched him be guided into the back of the cruiser, before they took off.

Then I closed the door and slid to the floor, sobbing.

"Mom?"

I looked up and saw Charlene at the top of the stairs. Behind her stood Zack and William.

"What's going on?" she asked, her voice shaking. "Why is Dad yelling?"

I shook my head, unable to deal with this now. "Go back to bed."

"But Mom? Why was Dad taken away by the police like that? Why was he screaming at you? What did you do to him?"

I stared at her, then exhaled, exhausted, drained. "Just go to bed all three of you, please."

"But Mo-om—"

"NOW!"

The moment I yelled it, I immediately regretted it. But it was too late. The kids rushed to their rooms, the sound of their sobs following them.

SIXTY-EIGHT

Then

Kitty's pregnancy was nearly over by the time the idea of escape first began to take shape in her mind. She had been pregnant three times and three children had been taken away from her almost immediately after birth. Years had passed since she was kidnapped and kept in the shed. She was tired and her body was broken but she had grown older and wiser. She had sunk into a deep depression after the third time, refusing to eat or even leave her bed. And Damian had left her alone for a while, not touching her, at least not very often. But soon he started doing it again, not caring that she didn't want to be with him. And she let him. She didn't even fight him. She simply didn't care anymore. But when she discovered that she was pregnant for the fourth time, something changed in Kitty. She knew she wouldn't be able to survive losing another child. This one she was determined to keep.

I can't do this anymore.

Against all odds she began to find a glimmer of hope. She started to plan her escape in earnest, seeing a way out of her situation. As her stomach grew larger and larger with the baby, so did her ideas. But she still lacked the courage to actually fulfill any of them.

Will they kill me if I try and fail? Will they harm any of the children?

She knew now that all of her children lived in the house. Every time they played in the garden, she put her ear to the door to listen for their yells and laughter and sometimes cries. She knew instinctively it was them. She recognized her children anywhere. And that gave her strength to go on.

Kitty knew she had to move quickly if she wanted to make a successful escape. She knew the door to the shed only opened once a day, when they brought her food and changed her bucket. That was her only chance if she was to get out of there, with her baby, and alive.

As the days crawled by, Kitty grew more and more anxious. She knew the baby would come soon. That's when she remembered the tiny rusty nail she had found under the bed. She had found it a few months ago all the way in the back against the wall. It had been lodged in the wood, but slowly made its way out and loose enough for her to wiggle it free. Yet she didn't know what to do with it. But now she saw its potential.

Kitty waited patiently until she felt she was close to giving birth. She lay in bed, pretending to sleep, while listening intently for any movement outside. She knew no one would be worried about her—she was so big, no one would think she was capable of much. She heard the bolt slide back on the door and the creak of the hinges as it was opened. The soft footsteps of Damian were barely audible, but she could hear them, nonetheless. She peeked through her half-closed eyes and saw him, then closed them again fast.

Thinking she was asleep, he put the tray of food down, then exchanged the bucket and put another one down. As he went about his routine, Kitty reached under the bed and retrieved the nail. She held it tightly in her hand, waiting for the perfect moment to strike. And then, it came. Damian approached her, then bent down to change her bucket, just as Kitty lunged forward, the nail held tightly in her hand.

With a swift motion, she plunged the nail deep into Damian's neck. He gasped, his hands reaching up to grasp at the wound, but it was too late. Kitty was on her feet, stomping out the open door, out into the fresh air and freedom she had only been dreaming about for years and years. As she ran, she felt the weight of her unborn child bearing down on her, making her wince with pain. But she didn't stop. She couldn't afford to. This was it.

She was free.

SIXTY-NINE

BILLIE ANN

I didn't sleep at all that night, and the next morning the kids barely spoke to me. I made them pancakes because it was Sunday and their dad wasn't there to do it, and they ate, but barely said a word. At least not to me. They kept their eyes down on their food, or their phones, and for once I let them have them at the table. Because it made it easier on me. Fewer questions that way.

As I cleaned up the kitchen, I tried to think of how I could make it up to my children. How I could explain to them what had happened and how it was for the best. But their father had been their rock, their protector. He had always been there to pick them up when they fell, and now he was gone. And it was all my fault.

But as the day went on, their silence became more and more deafening. It was like a constant reminder that I had destroyed our family. I wanted to talk to them, to explain why I had done what I had done, but every time I opened my mouth, nothing came out. I just couldn't bring myself to say the words. I couldn't admit that I was the one who had called the police on their dad.

I decided to take a walk to clear my head. I needed to refocus. I had a child to find, a killer to stop. I ended up at the beach, the one place that had always brought me peace. I sat on the sand and watched the waves crash against the shore. It was a peaceful sight, but my mind was anything but peaceful.

I still couldn't stop thinking about Emma, the child who didn't exist anywhere. Why would anyone keep their child hidden? Out of fear, of course. Out of fear of losing her, of someone finding them. It could be an abusive ex-husband or father or both. But what if it was more than that?

The fact was, I needed to know who Marissa Clemens was running from and why.

I got up, then went back to my car and drove to her address. I knocked on her door, but no one answered. I knocked again. Still no answer. I tried the handle, and, to my surprise, the door was unlocked. I peered inside. The house was dimly lit, and the air inside was thick with a musty smell. I called out Marissa's name, but there was no answer.

"Hello? Marissa? Emma?"

Nothing. I could tell that no one had been in the house for a very long time. The bread on the counter was moldy, the fruit left out was rotten and the milk in the fridge smelled awful when I opened it.

Where had she gone? I walked to her room and saw her clothes in the closet. She had left a pair of earrings on the dresser and not taken her toothbrush. If she had left, it had been in a hurry. She hadn't taken anything, it seemed.

It was odd. I called Tom when I got home.

"That is very strange indeed," he said. "What do you make of it?"

"I'm not sure," I replied. "We know she was running from something or someone. She definitely hasn't been home for a while. I know Perez is looking like our killer, but that doesn't mean there's not something else going on here. Even if you don't think her child is real, this woman is in danger."

There was a moment of silence before Tom spoke again. "All right, we will have to look into it. But be careful, we don't know what we're dealing with here."

"I know."

I ended the call and sat back in my chair, overwhelmed by the mystery that was unfolding before me. I couldn't shake the feeling that I was getting in over my head. I stared at the white walls in front of me that definitely needed painting soon, while drinking my coffee, when it hit me.

Emma.

I knew that name rang a bell. Why hadn't I thought about it before?

Oh dear God!

My heart throbbing in my throat, I rose to my feet, almost tipped my coffee cup over, then grabbed my car keys and ran out the door.

SEVENTY

BILLIE ANN

The sun was burning high above me from a clear blue sky, and it was getting hot outside as I pulled into Ridge Manor's only mobile home park. I killed the engine and looked at the home in front of me, its white facade a stark contrast against the deep blue sky. Suddenly I felt sick, and my stomach tightened into a knot. I hated being back here, I hated it so much. I hated being reminded of that time in my life.

Yet it was hard not to think of it now, while standing there again. Just like I had the first time we went there together to talk to the mother. Travis had brought me in on the case, and he had wanted me to shadow him. Train me if you will. He had deliberately asked for me, for the Chief to put me on the case with him. I had been so excited. Beyond ecstatic. This was it. The beginning of my career. My first big case. This was one that made national headlines. The disappearance of a young girl on her way to school. It meant the world to me that he asked me to join the investigation. That he believed in me. Me. A young girl with no experience. I remember feeling so proud. I felt like I owed him everything for giving me the chance.

And apparently, he felt the same way.

I got out of the car and took a deep breath, hoping it would calm my nerves. The air was humid and heavy and smelled faintly of newly cut grass, but it did nothing to soothe me. I could almost feel the memories rising up, overwhelming me.

My mouth went dry, and my heart raced as I climbed the stairs that led to the front door. I heard the distinct echo of my footsteps against the steps, an unwelcome reminder of the frustration I had felt the last time I went up them.

I took in a deep breath, then opened the screen and knocked on the door behind it. It was so hot standing on the porch waiting for the answer. I almost wanted to run away, to get back into my car and drive away, but I didn't. The exterior of the mobile home was faded and worn, and its paint had been chipped away by time, leaving only dull shades of blues and grays. The windows were hazy and cracked, and it was obvious that no one had taken care of anything for years.

In back of the home was a child's wooden swing, hung from a tree that had grown wild and overgrown, unused for many years.

The door creaked open, and a small face appeared. She looked worn out. Like she was tired of life. Her cheeks sunken, deep furrowed lines in them and around the eyes. Seeing her again made my heart sink. I remembered those eyes. I remembered them so well as they begged me to help her find her daughter.

She didn't recognize me at first.

"Yes?"

As our eyes met, she realized who I was, and her shoulders slumped. "Oh, it's you. What do you want? I thought you left town."

I swallowed, trying to get rid of the knot growing in my throat. I had seen this woman's face so many times in my nightmares. Her eyes haunted me, her deep-set crying eyes.

"Please find my daughter. Please help me find Kitty."

"Can I come in?" I asked, barely able to speak. I had let this woman down. I hadn't found her daughter when I promised to. I had run away instead. Because of what happened. I had done what I needed to do to survive but left my responsibilities behind. I had been her only chance of finding Kitty. I knew that. And yet I had gone away. Left. And since then, no one had been able to find Kitty. I didn't even know if they tried anymore after what happened. The last I heard they closed the case and filed it under *unsolved*. They had told her Kitty had just run away. Lots of kids did that. It wasn't unusual. And it wasn't a crime.

"Sure," she said and stepped aside to let me in.

I smiled and walked past her.

As I entered the mobile home, memories flooded back, creating a suffocating feeling in my chest. The cramped living room was filled with cheap furniture, the kind that people buy when they have nothing else. I could see that nothing had changed since the last time I had been here. The same old couch, the same old curtains, and the same old smell of stale cigarettes and despair.

She led me to the kitchen, where she offered me a seat at the small table. I sat down and looked around, taking in the emptiness of the room. The walls were bare, and the only decoration came from the dirty dishes piled in the sink. It was clear that this was a place where nothing thrived, where nothing good happened. It was a place where hope went to die.

"How have you been?" I asked, trying to make small talk to ease the tension in the room.

She scoffed, "How do you think I've been? You left, and my daughter is still missing. Fourteen years this year."

I winced at her words, feeling the guilt wash over me. "I'm sorry," I said quietly, "I shouldn't have left. I should have helped you find Kitty."

She looked at me with a mix of anger and pain. "You

think?" she spat out. "You promised me you'd find her, and then you just left. You didn't even say goodbye. You just disappeared. And now, fourteen years later, you come back here? Why? To rub it in my face that you failed?"

I shook my head, feeling tears in the corners of my eyes. "No, I came back because I want to help. I've been working on another case, and I think it might be connected to what happened to Kitty. I think I have a lead."

Her eyes hardened as she listened to me. "And what makes you think I'll help you? After what you did?"

"I don't expect you to forgive me," I said, my voice failing me. "But I need your help. And if this new case is connected to what happened to Kitty, then maybe I can finally give you the answers you deserve."

She stared at me for a long moment, her eyes searching mine. Then she sighed heavily and leaned back in her chair.

"Okay, what do you want to know?"

"I need to know what happened to Cole, Kitty's stepdad?" I asked.

She shook her head with a sniffle, then lit a cigarette. Her hands shook as she lifted it to her lips.

"What's there to say? He killed himself. Hung himself with a belt in the back room. I found him one day when coming home. I rarely ever go in there anymore. I hate it so much. He was devastated when Kitty disappeared. He felt so guilty and helped search for her everywhere. He and his friends did. One of them was a cop, and he helped us so much. I think Cole couldn't live with himself," she said and blew out smoke. Then she shrugged. "At least that's what I was told after it happened."

I wrote it down on my notepad, then looked up at her again. "Were they that close?"

She shrugged again. "I don't really remember much from back then. I drank a lot. I'm sober now. Three years."

I smiled as she showed me her coin from AA.

"I know it hurts to talk about," I continued, "but I would like us to go over all the people in your life once again. Everyone who came in contact with Kitty."

She nodded. "I can do that. I guess."

"I remember you talked about a family friend, someone who came here a lot, but he was never a suspect."

She nodded. "I told your partner about him, and how much he cared for Kitty, but—what was his name again?"

"Travis."

"Yes, Travis said he wasn't a suspect."

"Really? Hmm, that is odd," I said. "He was the one who gave her those dolls, right? I remember you told us how much she loved those dolls, so much she gave them names. What were their names again?"

She thought about it for a minute, then said, "Oliver was the boy, and Emma was the girl."

SEVENTY-ONE

BILLIE ANN

I pulled away from Ridge Manor with a sense of unease and dread. I had learned pieces of the puzzle, and it was all starting to make sense. The old winding road curved and dipped through the darkness as I navigated my way back to Cocoa Beach. Streetlights flickered on as I turned onto the final stretch, feeling relief that I was almost home. But I wasn't going back to my house. I had one more stop to make first. One important one.

I turned onto the familiar street, slowing as I came to the house that had been my destination. I stopped my car in the driveway and looked at it uneasily. It was a pale blue two-story house with a wraparound porch and a wide bay window.

Nerves surged through my veins as I got out of the car. I took a deep breath and made my way slowly to the porch, feeling as though I was walking into the unknown. I hesitated in front of the door, finding the courage.

Then I knocked.

The door opened, and I found myself face-to-face with the Chief. His face was weathered and creased, but his eyes held a twinkle of wisdom and kindness. He regarded me with curiosity, which made me feel even more nervous. He was very tall, and I had always found him quite intimidating, probably because of his seniority, but it was what I was here to say that was making me anxious. I was suspended after all, and I knew I had been pushing my luck on the case even when I was on it.

I had been to his house before, doing cookouts with the crew at his pool area. He would usually invite us over for Labor Day and sometimes Easter. I always found his house warm and embracing. It looked much larger than I remembered. The house seemed to be watching me, waiting for me to make a move. It was sitting on a big lot, ten acres, and reached farther than the eye could see. It was surrounded by tall trees and wild bushes. My favorite tree was the big magnolia in the middle of the backyard. It was more than a hundred years old, he would tell us, and covered in Spanish moss that dangled from its long winding branches. It was gorgeous. He had horses on the property as well, and his children loved riding and taking care of them, he often told us. His daughter had been in many equestrian competitions and won a state championship once, some years ago, before my time at his department.

"Can I come in?" I asked hesitantly. "Or is this a bad time?"

"Of course," he said with a nod, opening the door wider and motioning for me to enter. He led me to his study, a small room lined with bookshelves. He sat down in a comfortable chair and gestured for me to do the same.

The Chief regarded me with an even gaze, and I could feel his eyes probing me for some sign of my intentions. I cleared my throat and began to speak.

"Sir, I was wondering if I could have a few minutes of your time. I need to talk to you about something important. About the case."

"Which case?" he said.

I stared at him, surprised at his reaction. "Look, I know I'm suspended but now that Joe... well, you know, I was thinking I could get back on it."

He cleared his throat and shook his head. "No can do, I'm afraid."

"Why not?"

"It's a delicate matter, Wilde, but the thing is, he is your husband. As long as the investigation is undergoing, I can't give you your badge back."

"But why not?"

"As I said, he's your husband."

"So, you think I made him hit Travis with the car? Is that what you're saying?" I asked, baffled.

"As I said, there's an investigation into your part in this incident as well, yes."

I leaned back. I hadn't thought about that. "Oh."

The Chief nodded in understanding.

"I will, of course, help you however I can."

"Yes, of course, and I appreciate that. I really do," I said.

"Just understand that my hands are tied," he said.

"Naturally. That makes good sense," I said.

He smiled. "All right then."

I could tell he was eager to get me to leave, but I wasn't going to give in. I got up and walked closer to him. His eyes were watching me when I stopped in front of him.

"I really think I'm on to something, though. Don't you want to hear what it is?"

He took in a deep annoyed breath then threw out his arms. "You just won't quit, will you?"

"No. Not till you hear me out."

He rolled his eyes. "Okay, then. What is so important you absolutely have to come here to my house and tell me?"

I paused, then took a step closer again. "I think Marissa Clemens is Kitty Durham."

"Remind me again, who is Kitty Durham?" he said.

"She was the girl who went missing when I worked at Ridge Manor PD, when I was in training to become a detective, fourteen years ago. Under Travis Walker."

"Ah, that's right," he said, snapping his fingers. "I remember that one. She disappeared on her way to the school bus and was never found, right?"

"Right. I was on the case, but... well, I had to leave—"

"Because of that story with your partner, yes. I have recently been reminded of that."

Story. It wasn't a story. His words made me feel embarrassed, like I had caused him trouble for making something up. He had never made a comment like that before. It made me uncomfortable. Yet I continued unabated.

"I know it might be farfetched, but hear me out," I said.

"I have a feeling I don't have a choice in the matter," he said and squirmed in the leather chair.

I sat across from him and started to explain. "Here's my theory. What if the kidnapper, the one who took Kitty Durham, what if he was from our town or nearby area? What if he lives here in Cocoa Beach?"

"And what makes you come to that conclusion?" he asked, scrutinizing me like I had gone mad.

"I think she escaped her kidnappers somehow. But she didn't run very far."

SEVENTY-TWO

Then

Kitty knew she had to act quickly. Her desperation gave her an energy she hadn't felt for months, and she scrambled out of the shed, running as best she could despite her swollen belly, her feet slipping on the wet grass as she tore across the yard. Her heart was pounding in her chest as she ran up the steps of the main house, her eyes searching for her three children.

When she finally saw them, asleep in their beds, she burst into tears. She wanted to take them with her, but there was no time. She had to make a decision and she had to make it now.

Just then, a figure emerged from the shadows. She advanced on Kitty, her voice filled with scorn.

"You're not taking these children anywhere," she spat. "They're my children."

Kitty's chest constricted with fear, but she refused to be intimidated. She backed up. And that's when she saw it. The gun in Linda's hand. She gasped and stared at it. Then she decided something. She bent forward, then ran headfirst into Linda's stomach, clutching and protecting her belly, causing the gun to fall to the floor. And then they fought. Punches fell and Kitty received one on her chin that sent spasms of pain through her entire body, and several more on her cheeks and nose. She grunted in restraint, then grabbed the woman by the throat and used her weight to press her down.

"They're *my* children," she hissed, while tightening the grip on her throat and pressing. This was for all the years she had lost in that shed; this was for all the times Damian had raped her in there. And finally, this was for all the children they had taken from her, leaving her with only grief and sadness.

"This is for all you ever did to hurt me," she whispered. "And for you letting it happen when you could have stopped it."

Then she reached over, grabbed the gun from the floor, lifted it and fired. She shot her right in the forehead and, panting, Kitty stared at the hole in her head. She was fascinated by how easy it had been, and how small it was. Linda's eyes stared empty at her, and her body became limp underneath her.

"What have I done?" she exclaimed, then rose to her feet. "What have I done?"

In desperation she opened the window and threw out the gun. The children had woken up with the sound of the gun going off, and they were staring at her, shaking in one another's arms. She looked at them, and they looked at her.

"No, don't cry," she said. "I'm... I'm..."

But it was futile. The children had no idea who she was. They cried and shook, and then one of them screamed. Seconds later she heard the front door slam open, and she could hear someone enter, groaning loudly.

"Where are you?"

It was Damian.

Kitty knew she had to run, but she didn't know where to go, and she couldn't leave the children. She didn't want to. Yet there was no other way. At least not for now. She would have to come back for them later.

The last thing she saw before dashing out the door were the children clinging to one another in fear. She stormed out the back door, hearing Damian growl as he hurried up the stairs. Then she ran. Against all odds, against the heaviness of her stomach and the pain stemming from the beginning of her contractions, she ran, and ran, and ran, through the dark of the night, the rain falling on her like little stars from the sky, and she didn't stop until the wetness of her clothes had seeped into her skin.

Kitty looked around and realized she was surrounded by trees. She sat down on a log and looked at the night sky, her hand supporting her stomach, while the pain came and went. She sat there and listened to the sound of the tree frogs and cicadas. The sky seemed endless, even if it was covered in clouds, and the rain pouring nonstop on her face. It was a feeling and a sight she had only dreamed of for years.

"What have I done?" she gasped, and then closed her eyes, and wept. "I killed someone."

Kitty took a deep breath and rose to her feet, regaining her strength. She let out a cry and ran like the wind, away from the madness and the fuss, she ran right out of her past.

She didn't stop till she reached a small neighborhood, where she spotted a house, but more important, she noticed it had a small shed in the backyard. Feeling overwhelmed with weariness, she opened the gate and went inside the yard, then ran toward the shed and got inside. She collapsed on the floor, worn out by exhaustion.

Minutes later, she heard a noise by the door and lifted her head with a gasp.

A man. He was small and dark and looked at her with terror in his eyes.

"W-who are you?"

SEVENTY-THREE

The Chief sat in his study, his head bowed, as I paced back and forth before him, my words spilling out of me like a stream. He nodded occasionally, his expression attentive as I revealed my theory.

"Pete Perez told us that Marissa—or Kitty—as I believe her real name is, came to him, pregnant and in labor. He found her in the shed, and he helped her give birth to the baby, to Emma."

I paused to see if he was still listening. He was. He nodded and said, "Interesting."

I continued. "She ran away from her kidnappers, but couldn't make it far, because she was, well, about to give birth. That's why I think our killer and kidnapper is somewhere nearby, in our area."

"That makes sense," he said, leaning back in his chair.

"Pete then decides to help her out and lets her stay in the house that he owns that is currently vacant. She stays there and never gets farther away from where she was being kept. Now this is where it gets a little uncertain but hear me out. Maybe she stayed here, close to her kidnapper, because she had other children. I'm not sure about this one but think about it. Kitty was kidnapped fourteen years ago. She could have had more than one child in that time. Maybe she stays close in order to keep an eye on them, see them once in a while. I think... but I'm not sure, this will be another guess, but what if she became a prostitute? We heard there was a man coming to the house often. A neighbor told us so. Maybe he came to pick her up. Perhaps there was more than one. Maybe that's how she made a living. You know, because she couldn't get any other job. And she had been raped so many times that it was the only thing she knew how to do, sad as it is. We know for sure that she didn't work at the hospital like she said. And she did work often at night. She definitely didn't have any social security number, and no ID or even a bank account. It's hard to find work without any of those things these days. She lived completely off the radar, and so did her child. Until the kidnapper found her. Whoever took Kitty back then on her way to school, he is the one we're looking for. He killed the stepdad, Cole; he killed Cassandra Perez, who was Emma's babysitter; he killed Bryan Henderson, Emma's pediatrician. He killed Ashley because she was in the room with him when he killed Henderson, and she saw his face, or at least might be able to recognize him. He killed Alex Johnson because he was with Ashley, and he too probably saw who he was. He attacked Pete Perez and took a lock of his hair and planted it in the condo, so he would be a suspect, as he was connected to Cassandra, Emma, and Henderson now. And that brings me to the most important part that I realized just a few hours ago."

Chief Doyle lifted his eyes and met mine. He looked tired. I didn't care. I was on a roll here.

"And that being?"

I paused and collected my thoughts, then said, "He is one of ours."

A frown grew between his eyes. "What do you mean?"

"Think about it. The planting of the hair, the disappearance of Ashley's belongings from the condo. And get this. You told me that someone matching Pete Perez's description was seen outside of Alex Johnson's house, but as I went back into the files, I couldn't see any statement saying that. I believe it was a lie."

Doyle was biting his lip while looking at me. "I don't believe that. This is a little far out there for my taste."

"I thought so at first, but then I went to talk to Kitty's mom, and guess what?"

He sighed. "What?"

"The stepdad, Cole, had a good friend who came to the house often and who helped them start search parties for Kitty, and he took the lead in the search for her. And he was a police officer. Officer Damian was his name. She said he also knew Travis Walker, my old partner, and that's why no one ever looked into him. Because he was police. Because he knew the head investigator."

The Chief waited a few moments after I finished speaking, his eyes thoughtful as he seemed to contemplate my words in silence. I felt a thrill of anticipation shoot through me as he slowly lifted his gaze to meet mine.

"Very interesting," he said, his voice heavy with the weight of his years. "You have a keen mind, and I must say I am very impressed."

"That's all I've got so far," I said. I was hopeful, he seemed to believe me. "Now will you put me back on the case?"

He contemplated for a few seconds, then rose to his feet. "Let's walk."

He walked to the door. He held it for me, and I walked out into the foyer, still awaiting his response. I really felt like I was on to something here.

We walked to the front door and stopped. He placed a fatherly hand on my shoulder. "Listen," he said. "I can tell that you have worked really hard on this theory and I'm not saying I don't believe you, I really do. I think you're definitely on to something there. You make some valid points."

"Why do I feel like there's a *but* coming?"

"Because there is. Wilde, you're under investigation for your involvement in the attempted murder of your ex-partner. Now if it comes out in your favor then by all means we will let you get back on the case, if it hasn't been solved by then."

"But... that could take months," I said. "I'm worried about Marissa."

He shook his head. "I have had enough of this now."

A little girl showed her face in the doorway behind him. I smiled at her. "Hi there, little girl."

Doyle turned with a gasp. "How did you get in here?"

He rushed toward her, grabbed the girl in his arms, then put her in the study and closed the door. I stared at him, puzzled. He seemed agitated, frantic even.

"She's been sick," he said. "High fever. Strep throat. Luckily, it's coming down now after I got her some antibiotics."

"Hmm," I said, puzzled. I was about to leave, when I stopped. "I didn't know you had a little one. I thought your wife died years ago."

"She did," he said. "She had our baby right before she died. Now if you'll excuse me, I have more important things to do."

He had almost pushed me toward the door, when I spotted a framed diploma on his wall. I paused again.

I read his name. Jake Damian Doyle.

I turned to look at him with a gasp. That's when I saw the gun in his hand. It was pointed at me. Without thinking, I lunged forward and grabbed his arm, with a loud scream, but he was too quick. He pushed me back and lifted his gun, but instead of firing, he hit me in the face with the grip. Everything went black and I tumbled to the ground. I could hear him panting, agitated, and felt a sharp pain in my head, before I drifted into oblivion.

SEVENTY-FOUR

MARISSA

Marissa opened her eyes slowly, squinting against the inky darkness. What was that? What had woken her up? Was someone screaming? Or had that been a dream? Was it Emma?

Emma!

She felt the rug beneath her, rough and scratchy against her skin, and sensed her arms were bound tightly. Every muscle in her body quivered as fear coursed through her veins like an electric current.

Where am I? Why can't I move?

She heard an engine turn on and, seconds later, she felt movement. She realized she was inside some kind of vehicle. There was the faint smell of motor oil and the rumble of an engine. She blinked and soon her vision adjusted to the gloom. She tried to remember what had happened.

She remembered him. He was there, in the shed.

Damian.

Her kidnapper. The man who had taken everything from her. The father of her four children. He had tried to strangle her with a belt, but somehow—by luck or miraculous intervention—she had managed to trick him. She had let her body go numb and he had let go of her. She had passed out.

He must have thought I was dead, she thought, dread washing over her again. *I need to get out of here.*

Desperately, Marissa tried to push away the rug and move her limbs but found herself tied up too tightly. Her breath came out in shallow gasps as panic welled up inside her chest.

Where is he taking me? she wondered frantically, while her heart pounded in her chest.

She thrashed in the darkness, searching in vain for a glimmer of light. As the vehicle rumbled on, Marissa tried to calm herself down, to think rationally. She closed her eyes and took a deep breath, trying to focus on her surroundings. She could hear the sound of other cars passing by, and the occasional honk of a horn. They must be in the city, she realized. Maybe she would get lucky, and a cop car would find reason to pull them over.

But as the vehicle continued to weave its way through the streets, Marissa began to lose hope. Soon she heard barely any cars pass them, and everything seemed to go quiet around her, except for the engine of the car she was in. She didn't know where she was or where they were going. It was as though she was moving through a dark, never-ending tunnel, with no idea of what lay ahead.

She was alone, bound and helpless, with no one to turn to. She had to remain calm and think clearly if she was going to survive.

As she struggled to free herself, she felt a glimmer of hope. Her captor had underestimated her. He had thought she was dead and had let his guard down. She had to take advantage of that.

Marissa closed her eyes and focused on her breathing, willing herself to remain calm. She had to find a way out of this situation. She couldn't let Damian win.

Finally, Marissa heard the vehicle come to a halt and the engine was turned off. She heard footsteps approaching and held her breath.

SEVENTY-FIVE

BILLIE ANN

I woke up to a burning sensation. A pain that traveled up my body as I was dragged across the ground. I squinted, feeling the dried mud and muck on my face, and when I opened my eyes, I saw the sun peeking out from behind the clouds.

My head was spinning, pain radiating from a sharp ache at the temple where I had been hit with the grip of the gun.

I know this place, I thought as I managed to look at my surroundings. The air felt damp on my skin, and the lush bushes surrounding me reminded me of a place I knew very well.

Damian had taken me into the swamp, and I knew what he was planning to do. It was the perfect plan. He had brought me here to kill me. No one would ever find me, and my body would be eaten by gators and vultures before they even realized I was gone.

The ground was soggy beneath me, and the smell of the nearby marsh was overpowering. I felt my strength waning with each passing minute, and I knew I had to draw on some inner reserve if I was to survive this. I tried to scream but could only muster a low groan. I was scared. Like crazy afraid. I realized that I had to fight him, I had to resist, had to fight my way out of this. I had to make it back to my children.

My children need me!

Damian stopped and put my body down, and I knew I had to act fast. I chose my moment carefully and then got on my knees. He was tired from dragging me, and that gave me an advantage. I lunged forward, pushing him away with all my weight. He fell backward, and I scrambled away from him, the mud and vegetation tearing at my feet as I ran. I could hear his curses behind me, his threats to finish me off.

"I will find you, Wilde. You can't escape."

But I didn't look back. I just kept running as fast as I could. And that's when I heard the gun go off. I felt a sharp pain in my right shoulder and fell to the muddy ground, my face landing in muddy water. I gasped for air, feeling the water seep into my nose and mouth, filling it with the taste of dirt. My vision blurred, and I saw the world through a hazy filter. The pain in my shoulder was immense, but I knew I couldn't stop. I had to keep going. I tried to push myself up, but had no strength left.

I couldn't breathe, couldn't move. The pain was excruciating, and I knew I had to fight through it. I had to keep going. My survival instinct kicked in and I started to crawl, dragging my wounded body through the muck.

The swamp seemed to stretch on forever, the murky water up to my waist. I stumbled and fell, the pain in my shoulder sending shockwaves through my body. I gritted my teeth and pushed myself back up, the adrenaline pumping through my veins. I made it back on dry ground and crawled forward.

The sound of Damian's footsteps grew closer, and I knew that I was running out of time. I had to come up with a plan, and fast. I looked around for anything that could help me, and my eyes landed on a thick branch nearby. I reached out, grabbed it, and hoisted myself up, using it as a crutch.

"That's it," he said behind me, pointing the gun at me. "This is as far as you'll go. It's over. There's no way out."

As Damian approached, I took a deep breath and swung the branch at him with all my might. It slammed into the side of his head, and he fell to the ground. He was still conscious, but barely. I knew I had to act fast before he regained his strength.

I stumbled over to him, and with shaking hands, picked up the gun that he had dropped. Hands shaking heavily, I pointed it at him.

"No, *this* is it, Doyle." I stuttered, through the pain, teeth gritted. "This is as far as you'll go."

He laughed. "You'll never find your way out of this swamp. The sun is about to set. We're in too deep. You'll die here before you find your way out. We both will."

That made me smile. "That's where you're wrong," I said, kneeling in front of him. "I grew up here exploring every inch of this swamp. I know every tree trunk and every lake. I know exactly where we are."

It was the truth. This place was like home to me. I knew which way to turn and which route to go, and I was counting on that knowledge to save my life.

SEVENTY-SIX

MARISSA

Marissa was exhausted. Her muscles ached from the hours of confinement in the back of the van; her skin had become coated in dirt as she'd wriggled around trying to break free of her restraints; and her eyes felt heavy and swollen from crying. She had done her best to stay quiet, and maybe she had succeeded because the footsteps had come and gone. She had heard commotion next to her, and something hitting the ground with a thud. She had remained completely still, and barely taken a breath, not wanting Damian to realize how close she was to breaking out of the rug she was bound in. She had wiggled it carefully, and started to roll from side to side, once she realized the footsteps were gone, when at last she had managed to free herself. Breathing agitated, she had scrambled to untangle her legs from the rug and opened the door of the van. As she looked outside, she heard a gun go off, and she fell backward into the van, startled. It took her a long time before she finally dared to peek out again.

That's when she realized she was by the entrance of the Green Swamp. She immediately realized this was where Damian wanted to dump her body. That had to be why he had taken her there. Here, the body would never be found, and it would be unrecognizable before dawn even came. The animals would tear her to pieces. She swallowed hard and felt so fearful that it almost had become her fate. Then she hurried outside, and she ran. As soon as her feet hit asphalt, she knew civilization was there somewhere at the end of the road.

But the road was dark, not a sign of any streetlights anywhere. Marissa frantically ran, following the road to wherever it might lead her. She looked around for any signs of life, a house, or a car, but was met with nothing but darkness. Until suddenly, she saw a set of headlights moving toward her. It was a car. It was driving down the road and she made a split-second decision. She stopped in the middle of the road, waving her arms and screaming for help.

The driver of the car, a woman, immediately stopped and spotted Marissa standing in the middle of the road, her face streaked with tears. The woman lowered the window.

"What's wrong? What are you doing out here all alone?"

She approached the car. "I need help," she said. "Someone is trying to kill me. I escaped but... can you take me to Cocoa Beach? To the police station?"

"Y-yes of course, get in," the woman said and nodded in understanding. She didn't ask any questions. She simply unlocked the doors and motioned for Marissa to get in. With a feeling of immense relief, Marissa quickly climbed into the car, and the woman drove off.

"My name is Clara, what's your name?" she asked as they rushed down the road, and Marissa could finally see lights from a town on the horizon.

"I'm... Mar—" she paused, then looked at the woman, before continuing. Crying heavily, she said with pride.

"My name is Kitty. Kitty Durham."

SEVENTY-SEVEN

BILLIE ANN

Maybe I have overestimated myself, I thought. It had after all been years since I was last in this dense swamp. It was harder to find my way than I thought. The ground was soggy beneath my feet, and I could feel the thick humidity in the air. The trees were shrouded in shadows, and the eerie stillness of the swamp made my heart race. We had been walking for hours, but the sun was setting quickly and soon it would be too dark to find our way out.

Come on, Billie Ann, I can do better than that.

"I told you. You'll never make it out." I gripped the gun tightly in my hand while Doyle taunted me, and he became louder with each step we took. His words echoed off the trees like a warning bell, but I kept my focus on finding the trail I knew so well. With every stride I felt a growing sense of urgency, knowing that if we didn't make it out before darkness fell, things could turn very dangerous indeed.

"We're both going to die in here," he said. "You will probably die first, with how much you're bleeding from that wound in your shoulder. I give you about an hour, and then you'll lose consciousness. I will then take the gun from you and leave you here to die."

I chose to ignore him. The best I could. But he was right. What if I didn't make it out? What if I had lost too much blood? Who would find Emma, alone in that house, where Doyle would return? And what had happened to Kitty? I was feeling the weakness already and dizziness was taking over. I could hear rustling in the bushes next to us. It could be anything at this hour. Deer, wild turkeys, maybe hogs, but also alligators or even black bears lived in these areas.

The mosquitoes were out in full force, humming an incessant chorus of angry buzzing around us. My shoulder ached from my injury and exhaustion was settling into my bones, making every movement heavy and stiff. Despite all this, I kept walking, eyes ahead and focused solely on finding some sign of safety.

The darkness began to deepen with each passing minute, and fear of the unknown grew larger with it. Doyle's breath came out in labored rasps, matching my own rising tension as we desperately searched for an escape. We continued onward—shouldering our way through raw nature—until finally a glimmer of hope appeared on the horizon.

It looked like a small house. It was hard to tell in the dimness. I used every ounce of energy I had left to push forward toward it. As we got closer, my heart lifted with the hopes of safety and rescue, even as Doyle's taunts grew louder.

"I told you, Billie Ann. You'll never make it out alive."

But I refused to listen to his words, letting the adrenaline and determination fuel my body.

As we burst through the trees and into a clearing, I saw a small hunting cabin nestled among the trees. Relief flooded through me as I realized that we might just make it out alive after all. Doyle's breathing was ragged and uneven. I slowed down, and that was my mistake. He turned around and lunged at me.

"I'm not leaving this swamp with you still alive!"

Panic gripped me as I realized the true extent of his intentions. I had to act fast. Without hesitation, I aimed my gun at him. There was a split second when we both froze, locked in a deadly stare. Then he lunged at me again, grasping for the gun in my hand, and I pulled the trigger.

The sound of the gunshot echoed through the swamp, and for a moment, everything was silent except for the ringing in my ears and birds taking off from treetops. Doyle stumbled backward, blood staining his shirt. He fell to the ground, gasping for air. I stood frozen, staring at him in shock. It was an intense feeling, a mixture of relief and horror. But I had no idea if he would manage to get up.

I turned around and stumbled to the abandoned cabin. It was very small, more like a shed and, as I entered it, I fell to the wooden floor, tired and weary, unable to still stand on my feet. I felt like the earth was spinning, and I closed my eyes for just a few seconds.

When I opened them again, the cabin was shrouded in complete darkness. The adrenaline had left my body, and the exhaustion had finally caught up with me. I was lying on the dirty floor of the cabin, my breathing ragged and uneven. My shoulder throbbed with pain, and I could feel the sticky blood seeping through my shirt. But most of all, I worried for Emma and for Kitty.

The darkness was all-encompassing. Not a lamp or light in sight, and I couldn't see anything. I didn't know if Doyle was still out there or not. Would he soon be coming for me? I had one bullet left in the magazine. One chance to save myself from him.

SEVENTY-EIGHT

BILLIE ANN

My eyes shot open, and I gasped for air. A bright light hit me and blinded me for a few seconds. It was moving. No that wasn't it. *I* was moving.

Where am I?

I realized I was on a stretcher, my body still and quiet, as if my spirit had escaped my flesh. I felt an overwhelming sensation of relief, as if I were returning home after a long journey. My vision was blurry at first, until I could make out a face. It was Big Tom, his expression a mix of worry and determination. He held my arm lightly, as if to ensure that I remained still.

"You're safe now," he said gently, his voice barely audible over the commotion of the hospital. "We're here to help you. Just stay with me, okay?"

Startled, I tried to remember how I had gotten there, but I couldn't. It was all a blur. But Tom was there, and that made me happy. And at that moment, I knew that I was safe. I knew that no matter what happened, Big Tom would be there, and that no matter how scared I was, I could hold on and make it through. He was my friend and right now my rock.

I thought about Emma and felt my heart start to race again.

I felt myself drifting off. In the distance I could hear voices as they were yelling.

"We're losing her. Get a move on!"

And then I didn't hear anything else. I just felt myself getting weightless and drifting off into a black vast space. I felt nothing but happiness, and relief, and didn't have a care in the world.

As I drifted off into the black void, I felt a sudden jolt that woke me up. My eyes fluttered open, and I was back in the hospital room, surrounded by beeping monitors and the smell of antiseptic. My head was pounding, and my throat was dry. I searched for Big Tom, but he was nowhere to be found. Panic set in, and I tried to get up, but my body was too weak. It succumbed once again, and I lost consciousness.

The third time I woke up, Big Tom was the first person I saw. He was sitting in a chair next to my bed. As I opened my eyes, he breathed a sigh of relief.

"There you are. Dang it, I thought we lost you."

I shook my head. My mouth felt dry, my voice hoarse as I spoke.

"Nah, you ain't getting rid of me that easily."

I let out a breath I didn't know I was holding and sank back into the pillows. The memories of what happened started to flood back and my heart rate picked up. I remembered the attack, the fear, and the pain. My body shuddered at the thought. "What happened?"

He cleared his throat. "Marissa Clemens, or Kitty, came to the station late at night. The sergeant couldn't get a hold of the Chief, so they called me in, knowing I was still on the case. I spoke to her, and she told me her entire story. She told me the man who took her was from the police, and as she saw Doyle's picture in the hallway, she began to shiver. I knew then how it was all connected. I asked her if that was the guy and she said yes. He had tried to take her to the swamp and dump her dead body. She knew he was in there when she escaped. She didn't know about you. But I drove her to his house, and we got Emma. Kitty showed me the shed she had lived in for fourteen years before she escaped. It was nasty, I tell you. He had the thing soundproofed. Think of all the times people went to his house. She was there, in that shed at the end of his property, and nobody could hear her."

I shivered.

"Imagine that. It's a big property and you couldn't see the shed from the house. It was hidden by the tall trees. I then had DCF come take the three other children, and they're in their custody so far till we figure out what will happen to them. Then I realized your car was in the driveway, and I became suspicious. I had Kitty take me back to where she escaped from. I called in a search-and-rescue team and had them out there all night till we finally found you inside of the small cabin. You had passed out, with the gun on top of you. You were in a pool of blood and at first, I feared that you were dead."

He exhaled to steady himself, tears welling up in his eyes.

I squeezed his hand, then whispered, "You saved my life. Thank you."

He sniffled and wiped his cheeks.

"You saved that little girl. Doyle focused on you, and it gave Kitty the chance to run—to get help and save her daughter."

I began to well up.

He continued. "We found Doyle's body on the ground outside. It had been half-eaten by animals, and he looked awful. I figured you shot him in self-defense."

He shook his head again and hid his face in his hands. "What he did... I can't believe it. It's... so awful. I have been talking to Kitty, interviewing her for these past two days and I can't... I can't even imagine. How will she be able to move on after this?"

I smiled, even though it took all of my last strength. "At least now she has a chance of getting a normal life again."

"That's true." He smiled faintly. "She told me she didn't dare to go to the police when she escaped, because the man who held her prisoner was a police officer, and she didn't trust us. Also, because she had killed Doyle's wife. She was afraid of going to jail for it. She took the name Marissa Clemens from a tombstone she passed at the cemetery on her way to the Perezes' house. She thought she could live under the radar and not be found, while still staying close to her other children. She didn't want to leave them. But when Emma disappeared, she panicked. She got so desperate to find her, she didn't know what else to do, and finally went to the police, but later regretted it because she found out that Doyle was the Chief, and she got scared away. Oh, and there's another thing. I don't want to over-whelm you, but I think you need to know."

"What's that?"

"Travis Walker is gone. He left."

My eyes grew wide. "He's gone?"

"Yes. He was friends with Doyle. I guess maybe he knew too much and got scared once he heard what happened."

"Huh. I wonder if he knew it was Doyle who took Kitty all along."

"You think he covered for him?"

I exhaled. "I don't know. And now I guess we will never know. What happened to Betty? She might know."

"His wife has disappeared too. Vanished from their house. Took clothes, personal items, passports, and stuff."

I exhaled. I didn't like the fact that Travis had gotten away. I had a feeling he knew a lot more than what he had said.

"We will search for him, of course," Tom said. "Oh, and Doyle was wearing a belt like the one we assume is the murder weapon when we found him, and we have secured it as evidence and sent it to the lab, where they are checking if that is the murder weapon."

"That sick bastard," I said. "I can't believe he was right here under our noses this entire time."

"I know. And as soon as you got too close for comfort, he made sure you got suspended. But good news is that Joe will be released later today, because Travis never pressed charges and, now that he is gone, the DA has decided to let Joe go. There're no longer any grounds to keep him."

I nodded, thinking about my husband. I wondered where he would go after this. Would he come back to the house? I would have to tell him to find his own place. We needed to separate. It was time.

"That is good news, thanks."

I heard voices in the hallway, and seconds later my kids stormed inside of the room. Big Tom snuck out to give us privacy, while they jumped on my bed, and I winced in pain, but it was worth it. Even Charlene was there, but she stayed a few steps behind, her eyes avoiding mine. I hugged Zack and William as tight as I could without screaming in pain, then looked at her. I reached out my hand toward her.

"You're not gonna say hello?" I asked, my voice strained and hoarse. "Your momma almost died and you're not gonna hug her?"

She gave me a reluctant look. I could tell she had been crying.

"Come here, you," I said.

She came closer, and I grabbed her hand, then pulled her the last bit of the way.

"Is it true you almost died?" she asked.

"Ah, don't believe everything you hear," I said. "I'm tougher than that."

"That was pretty cool how you saved that child and her

mother who had been kidnapped for years. It's all over the news."

I smiled. "You think that was cool, huh?"

"Yeah. Everyone is talking about it."

"So, they're not all talking about me being a lesbian anymore?"

She shrugged.

My mom came in through the door. She looked awkward.

"I was just... I brought them here, to see you, and I thought I'd just—"

"I'm glad you did, Mom," I said, interrupting her. I knew we had our differences, and she had a hard time accepting me for who I am. But right now, I was just happy to see her. Sometimes a person just needs their mom.

"Your dad is here too," she said. "Waiting outside. The kids have been staying with us while you were getting better."

"Yeah," Zack exclaimed. "And I got to help Grandpa fix the old car. He is teaching me everything I need to know."

"That's wonderful," I said and kissed my son as he slid down from my bed. William sat on the edge, and I grabbed his hand. "Hey there, buddy. You okay?"

He nodded with an exhale. "You know I don't care, right?"

"About what?"

"About you being a lesbian and all that."

That made me laugh. "That's good, buddy, I'm glad, because it isn't going to change."

He shrugged. "So what?"

My eyes met my mom's and I realized he was right. *So what?* was the answer. For both of us. So what if we didn't see eye-to-eye? We were family.

She came closer.

"William is right," she said, like she had read my mind. "What business is it of mine or of anyone else's? As long as you're happy, my girl."

She tapped the top of my hand with her palm, and I could tell she was fighting her tears.

"Thanks, Mom. I really appreciate it."

She sniffled and corrected a lock of my hair. "Are they going to let you go home soon?"

I nodded. "I hope so. I'm already tired of this bed."

"That's good," she said and cleared her throat. "I'll go tell your dad you're awake. He's been waiting for hours. He'll be happy to know you're better. He was really worried."

She turned and left. I knew she wasn't only talking about my father. I understood now that I was her daughter and she loved me. And I knew that she had been here all the time. I was sure of it.

And there was another thing I was sure of at this moment. We were all going to be okay.

Because we had one another. And that was all we needed.

A LETTER FROM WILLOW

Dear Reader,

I want to say a huge thank you for choosing to read *Don't Let Her Go*. If you enjoyed it and want to keep up to date with all my latest releases, just sign up at the following link. Your email address will never be shared, and you can unsubscribe at any time.

www.bookouture.com/willow-rose

I hope you loved *Don't Let Her Go* and if you did, I would be very grateful if you could write a review. I'd love to hear what you think, and it makes such a difference helping new readers to discover one of my books for the first time. This book felt very personal to write. I recently went through a divorce due to the fact that I realized I am gay. It has taken me many years to be able to speak about it openly and admit it to myself and my surroundings. But now I am. So, in many ways, Billie Ann's story is also my story. Realizing that I was hiding an important part of myself, the journey into finding out what this means and then telling the world my truth, has been one of the toughest yet most rewarding things I have ever done in my life. Everything just makes sense to me now. And for the first time I can recognize myself when I look in the mirror. It feels right and it feels good. I am me now. Fully me. And I have been met with nothing but support from my family and friends, luckily.

The story of Kitty Durham was actually inspired by a real story that I came upon. And I knew I had to write about the kidnapping of Jaycee Dugard, who was taken by her kidnappers while walking to the school bus one morning. She wasn't found till eighteen years later, after having two children with her kidnapper and living in a shed in their backyard. The kidnapper's wife also played a big role in the abduction, and she was later convicted for her part in it, along with him. It's an ugly story, but deeply fascinating. You can read more about it here.

As always, I want to thank you for all your support and for reading my books. I love hearing from my readers—you can get in touch on my Facebook page, through Twitter, Instagram, Goodreads, my website, or email me at madamewillowrose@gmail.com. You can also follow me on BookBub or Amazon.

Finally, I want to shout out a huge thank you to my wonderful editor, Jennifer Hunt, for believing in me and helping me to develop this series.

Take care,

Willow

www.willow-rose.net

facebook.com/willowredrose

x.com/madamwillowrose

instagram.com/willowroseauthor

bookbub.com/authors/willow-rose

Made in the USA
Monee, IL
08 April 2024

56527246R00177